Rogue Shift

by

AJ Skelly

Rogue Shift

Cover Art by *Jennifer Greeff*

The Wild Rose Press, Inc.
PO Box 708
Adams Basin, NY 14410-0708
Visit us at www.thewildrosepress.com

Publishing History
First Edition, 2021
Trade Paperback ISBN 978-1-5092-3752-4
Digital ISBN 978-1-5092-3753-1

Published in the United States of America

Something clattered at the entrance to the shed. My body froze as a board scraped against the threshold. I willed myself not to whimper, to face my future with quiet dignity and as few hysterics as I could manage.

The door creaked on its hinges, driving my blood pressure up to dangerous new heights. Light flared at the corners of my vision. My teeth clenched as I squared my jaw and I faced the door as my heart careened inside my chest, banging my ribs and making my breath painfully stuttered.

Dedication

Because the first needed a second.

And for Sarah. Because Megan and Rachel wouldn't have their friendship without ours.

Acknowledgments

Mihi Pater, gratias ago tibi quoniam donum verba.

My wonderful husband—thank you for the time to write.

Mom, Dad, Landon, and Grandma—thanks for all the support, ideas, help, and general encouragement. Landon, I can't wait for that song.

To my eternal cheering section. Ya'll are the best! Tami, Lacey, Sarah, Jessica, Portia, Jo, Lindsey, Karen, and Brittany, writing would be so much harder (and less enjoyable!) without you guys.

Those of you who have come alongside, contributed to this journey, and become friends, I'm so thankful! Teri, Jessica, Meghan, and Jordan.

To the folks back home who have showered me with their unwavering support. I've never been prouder to come from a tiny, tight-knit community. I've been overwhelmed and astounded at the outpouring of love. Both for me and my characters in Rock Falls.

The Wild Rose Press, thank you for making *Rogue Shift* a reality!

And for my readers. If you read the book, purchased the book, told someone about the book, shared the book, left a review of the book, thank you. You've upped the stakes and made this writing journey so incredibly *more* than it was before. I'm grateful for and appreciate each of you.

Chapter 1

Rock Falls, Delaware
November
Friday Night

Rachel

I clicked the phone off, my fingers clenching around it so hard that pins and needles stabbed up to my wrist. I blinked. Once. Twice. Inhaled. Refused to feel. Refused to think. Would not, could not, accept the information the call had delivered. When my hand started shaking, I forced my fingers to release their grip and watched as my phone seemed to tumble in slow motion onto the fluffy purple comforter of my bed.

Slowly my lungs drew in a shaky breath. My brain raced. My heart hammered. I shivered and watched my hands continue their shaking as if they were attached to someone else's arms.

The coo-coo clock downstairs chimed and my heart about leapt out of my chest as my body jerked at the sudden noise. Six o'clock. I glanced at my window. It was already full dark. There was a party tonight, and I knew *he* would be there. He would pay for what he'd done. I would make sure of it.

****

Two hours later

I was dressed to kill. I'd forced myself to raid my sister's closet, knowing she would have things in there I needed tonight that I'd never have in my own wardrobe. I'd nearly lost it when I went into Joanie's room, but held it together, focusing on tonight's mission.

Shutting the car door, I resisted the urge to tug down the black leatherette mini skirt and refused to scratch at the massive itch the fishnet stockings were causing on my inner thighs. Inhaling shallowly against the tight black crop top, I sucked in my belly. I wasn't as small as my sister, but the skirt was high waisted and didn't leave room for my softer curves to spill out. They were all tightly contained in my warrior dress. While I felt completely insecure and out of my element on the inside, the thick black eyeliner and red lipstick provided a sort of mask. I was simply playing a part. I was co-president of the drama club and excelled at all things dramatic. I could do this.

Tonight, I was a dark temptress, a Fury, a Valkyrie, a woman who wanted to ensnare and bring pain to the one who had shattered my heart.

My three-inch black heels clicked against the cement of the walkway, though the noise was drowned out by the blasting music and drunken laughter that spilled out of the house and into the front yard.

Gratifying as it was when high schoolers and college students alike stopped what they were doing and stared as I walked past, I was terrified. I'd never played this role. This was not who I was. For a moment, my resolve weakened. What was I doing?

Then I remembered Mom's broken voice on the phone. The pain stabbed my heart all over again.

Another breath and a toss of my straightened hair—I'd decided to forgo my natural riot of dark red curls in lieu of sleekness—and I sashayed up the front steps. Tonight I was using my curves to what I hoped would be my advantage.

I was bumped and jostled as my fellow seniors, and quite a few older students I didn't know, danced and swayed in drunken stupors, oblivious to the carnage inside my chest where my heart should have been. A shudder rippled down my shoulders as the stench of beer, sweat, and sex hit me in the face like a brick wall. I loathed everything about this. But tonight, I would not be deterred. Not by the couples scattered around the room in various stages of foreplay. Not by the cat calls when I moved into the living room of the huge house. Not by the keg in the kitchen and the tables of food and other drinks. No, I moved with the litheness of a panther through the chaos.

Until I saw my prey. I stumbled in my heels, gripping the doorframe to the room where he had set himself up like a king. He sat enthroned in a decorative blue and white striped silk chair. He wasn't a big guy, but the smallness of the chair made him look imposing. His arms were casually draped over the sides, his eyes admiring the backside of one of the girls clustered around him. His groupies. His junkies. I swallowed down the bile that rose in my throat. The base drumming through the speakers downstairs reverberated in my chest. Wiping my sweaty palms on my fake leather skirt and randomly hoping it didn't show wet streaks, I dropped my eyelids so they were half-hooded. I relaxed my lips so the bottom one hung open just enough to hopefully appear sultry like in the magazine ads, not like I was trying to catch flies. Elongating my neck and pushing out my hip, I stepped into the role of dark temptress and strutted slowly into the room.

The moment he saw me coming toward him, his attention was riveted. He looked me up and down, devouring me with his eyes. I refused to give way to the squirming dirty feeling it gave me and sauntered to stand right in front of his striped chair. His perusal finally made it to my face and confusion lit his eyes. His eyebrows drew together then his eyes went wide in disbelief.

He belted out a horsey laugh and slapped his knee.

"Rachel?" He snorted in a way that made my blood boil. "What are you doing playing dress-up?"

"Hi, Lenny," I ground out. I had to swallow down the bitterness that rose again, and he spoke before I could get anything else out.

"Slut run in the family?" he asked as his eyes assessed my dress. His gaze was hard, cold, and disturbingly interested.

"Excuse me?" was the only thing that escaped the tightening in my throat.

"I'll make an exception for you. First-time buyer and all. I'll give you the same deal I gave Joanie last time she couldn't pay." He winked lasciviously at me. At his mention of my sister's name, I lost all rational thought. This dirtbag was the cause of my sister's torment, of my family's pain, of my shattered heart.

Blood raged through my veins and a wild, foreign rush took over me. Without another thought, I shoved my face into his space.

"Don't you ever say my sister's name again."

"Yeah? Or what?" His voice was playful, but his eyes were slits. "You're as worthless as she is." He sneered.

"My sister isn't worthless! And thanks to you, she may die!" I shouted drawing my fist back. I slammed it into his nose, and pain rocketed up my arm as I registered that I had punched Lenny DiVen, drug dealer extraordinaire, in the nose.

His head whipped back, and he touched his nose gingerly, bringing his fingers away red. His face turned to stone and my heart along with it. What had I done?

Lenny jumped to his feet. The room hushed in shock. "*You are dead.*"

Fortunately, my flight response was quick to kick in and I turned in time to see Lenny jerk his head at two guys standing at the glass door behind the striped chair. I didn't wait around to find out if they chased me or not. I knew they were right on my tail. A cluster of kids played beer pong to the right of the door I'd come in. There was a loud cheer and then gasping when a ping pong paddle crashed to the floor. I glanced back just enough to watch the taller of the two men chasing me run into the kid who bent over to pick up the paddle. It was all the opening I was going to get. I kicked my heels off and stumbled down the stairs amidst shouts of annoyance as I carelessly bumped into people, sloshing drinks and stepping on toes.

"Stop her!" one of the men chasing me shouted as I careened down the last step. A solid chest hit me like a wall of concrete, and *wet* poured over my head.

I didn't stop. My heart pounded against my ribs and fear was a metallic tang in the back of my mouth. Adrenaline surged through my limbs, making me equally fast and clumsy in the sea of gyrating bodies on the main floor.

"Move!" Tall One shouted. I was short, and I ducked down even smaller, weaving in between the packed room. The backdoor was right off the kitchen. I hit the room and skidded on something slick. My arms flailed like a windmill and terror seized every part of me as a hand clamped down on my wrist.

"I got her! No one does Lenny that way." Short One's breath hit me like rotting garbage. Panic clawed my gut. In an adrenaline-fueled spike of desperation, I brought the heel of my bare foot down as hard as I could on the instep of his. He howled and I yanked my arm as hard as I could. His watch caught my skin and ripped a chunk off.

The door! I wrenched it open and tore through the bodies on the back patio. The yard was completely dark past a row of tiki-torches. I ran through their glowing border, not caring about anything save getting into the darkness and away from my would-be captors.

Darkness engulfed me and it took my eyes a minute to adjust as I ran blindly into the night, stepping on stones and bashing my shins against unseen undergrowth. Forest butted up against the back of the property and once I was past the first few trees, I leaned against the back of a tree to try and catch my breath and figure out the next step before I got lost in the woods.

Would I never learn to think before I acted? My car was parked in front of the house. In the middle of the crowd of vehicles and drunks. I silently cursed my impulsiveness then choked back a sob. If only I could morph into a giant wolf and melt seamlessly into the forest to make my escape the way my best friend

Megan would have. Werewolf though she was, Megan was much too sensible. She wouldn't be here in the first place. I bit back a whimper and listened. I listened hard. Nothing but the din of the party filtered to my ears, but that could be masking other noises. Noises that people trying to catch me might make.

Peeking around the trunk of the old tree, I could just make out the shape of Tall One by the tiki torches. And was that—yes! It was Short One loping up next to him. They were checking the crowd of bodies on the back patio. Tall One waved an arm toward the front of the house and my heart plummeted. I was safe for the moment, but there was no way I was going to be able to get to my car.

I shivered, realizing that I was drenched in beer and it was freezing out. My teeth chattered as if in response to my thoughts. Relieved that I'd worn a tiny little cross-body purse only large enough for my phone and my keys, and that it was still swinging by my hip, I dug out my phone and ducked back around the tree, certain no one would see the light as it came on.

I punched the number for the person I trusted more than anyone else in the world.

"Rachel?" She picked up on the second ring and my best friend's voice brought tears to my eyes.

"Megan, I'm in trouble." I gasped the words.

"Where are you?" she demanded.

"I did something really stupid. I'm hiding in the woods behind Darnell Thompson's house. I need you to come get me."

"We're at least twenty minutes away from there," Sam, Megan's mate, answered.

"Please hurry," I whispered.

AJ Skelly

"Rachel, are you safe right now?" Sam asked, taking charge.

"I think so?"

"Okay. Kyp is only five minutes or so away from there. He'll come get you and bring you here," Sam said. A perk of pack life. Always someone around to help.

"Rach?" Meg's voice was all concerned. "What else can I do?"

"I don't know." I bit back the sob that threatened.

"Kyp is on his way. I'll stay on the phone with you until he gets there," Meg said, apparently having gotten confirmation from Sam who was probably on his phone with Kyp right then.

"Better not. I'm hidden in the woods at the back—in the dark. Phone might be seen."

"Rachel," she started.

"See you in a few," I rasped.

"To the ends of the earth," Megan whispered our childhood mantra.

"To the ends of the earth," I echoed.

I hugged the phone to my chest and screwed my eyes shut, willing the tears to stay at bay. I wished I was a werewolf like Megan—like Sam, even Kyp, who was only half werewolf. I wouldn't feel so helpless right now. And Kyp. I cringed as the red heat of shame crawled up my neck and pooled in my cheeks. How would I ever look at him again after he saw me like this?

I'd only known Kyp a few weeks, but I really liked him. He was sweet and thoughtful, and after being thrown together several times among our group of human and werewolf friends, we'd become good friends.

Dressed like a hooker with my hair frizzing back into curls from a beer bath, near hysteria, and heartbroken like I'd never been before wasn't exactly the impression I wanted to leave with Kyp. But my safety outweighed the coming humiliation.

Minutes passed in the darkness. Raised voices sent my heart racing several times. I stayed put behind my tree, shivering as the biting wind blew through the pine trees, making them creak and groan.

"Rachel," a voice whispered.

I yelped and my feet left the ground.

"Shh! Sorry, it's me." Kyp materialized out of the darkness right in front of me. He tentatively took my hand, like he would touch a spooked animal. I couldn't help it. A sob escaped.

"It's okay. I couldn't get my truck back here without drawing more attention, so we're going to need to sneak back to it. I'm parked two houses down. We're going to go through the woods and cut through a couple of neighbors' yards."

A sigh gusted through my teeth. It was such a relief to have a friend—an ally. Someone else to make the decisions for me right now. My brain was soaked in panic, despair, pain, and confusion. He squeezed my hand lightly and I squeezed back.

"I'll lead. My eyes are better in the dark," he explained unnecessarily. Although it merely confirmed another thing that would have been helpful tonight if I was a werewolf.

I hissed as a nasty, sharp stick poked into the soft hollow of my foot.

"Rachel?"

"Sorry, I kicked my shoes off when I ran."

"You're barefoot?"

"Yes," I whispered back, angry at the offending branch and on the edge of terror.

"Come here. I'll carry you. You'll break your leg trying to go through these woods at night."

My heart did a little flip.

"I…"

"Come on." Kyp turned his back to me and crouched down so I could climb up on his back. I was a little self-conscious about Kyp carrying me two or more blocks back to his truck. I wasn't skinny by any stretch of the word. I wasn't fat, but the curves were present. And no guy had ever offered to carry me before. It was a strange feeling to throw into the mix of churning emotions already stomping through me.

A twig snapped to our left and I climbed on without another thought. I heard Kyp's quick intake of breath as his hands closed over my fishnet clad calves and I cringed, my eyes shutting as I felt the heat of mortification sliding up my face again. To his credit, he said nothing, only took off at a brisk pace in the direction we had been going.

We kept to the trees, and a few minutes later, we were poised to cut across the neighbor's yard. Kyp's truck was parked on the curb in front of the house. I hoped we were far enough away and shadowed enough in the dark that nobody would notice us.

"Do you want me to walk? It's probably only grass here," I murmured as Kyp glanced over a few backyards to the party still going full strength.

"Are you okay to walk? We might be able to move a bit more stealthily if we're both on foot."

"Okay," I whispered, breathless. He crouched down, and I slid off, the feeling of his hands on my legs burning little fires of embarrassment right through the fishnets.

On Kyp's mark we moved. We were silent in the grass, still manicured though it was the beginning of November and had been below freezing at night for weeks. My teeth started chattering again as my bare feet moved over the cold grass. The beer that had been dumped over my head had mostly dried, leaving me smelling and feeling as dirty as the bathroom floor of the boy's locker room.

Mercifully, no one sober enough to care saw us moving across the yard. I didn't know if they'd given up the chase for me, or if they were still out there, but I was profoundly grateful for Kyp and his truck as he ushered me in the seat and quietly closed the door behind me.

Chapter 2

Kyp

I shut the passenger door with Rachel tucked inside my truck and scanned the area once more. Whatever Rachel had done, she was totally spooked. I'd seen a few guys milling around, watching, hunting around the party, and assumed they were searching for her. I didn't see them now, so my focus moved back to the truck.

Pulling open the driver's side door, I glanced up at Rachel, just enough light from the streetlamp across the road spilling over her so that my wolf's enhanced vision saw her clearly.

"Oh, wow." The words tumbled gracelessly from my lips without my permission. I could have swallowed my tongue as Rachel's eyes clinched in embarrassment and she turned her face away from me.

The sweet, outgoing girl who had become my first friend in Rock Falls, my first real friend in a *long* time, sat in my truck in a black leather skirt that barely hit her thighs—thighs covered in ripped fishnet stockings. Her boobs had been shoved into a tiny, tight black top and I was momentarily distracted by the line of white skin showing above her skirt where the teeny top didn't meet. The little jacket she wore only covered her arms but wouldn't be doing anything against the cold November air.

I shrugged out of my own coat even as I took in the globs of black running from her eyes down her cheeks, her mass of hair matted and wavy, and smelling like a brewery. Handing her my coat without a word, I cranked the heat and aimed the vents at her.

Quickly clicking my seat belt with fumbling fingers, I scanned one more time in the rearview mirror. No one followed. Pulling the truck into the street, no one seemed to notice our departure. I sighed in relief.

Rachel hiccupped. Her eyes were still shut, and her head was bowed, the rest of her curled up under my coat.

"Rachel?" She was in pain. I could tell that much—the why I didn't know. People reading had been a skill I'd been forced to perfect early in my life with the Kentucky pack where getting an accurate read on someone had been the difference between praise or fierce punishment. I couldn't reconcile this broken-looking creature with the vibrant, vivacious redhead who was my friend.

A sob echoed in the cabin of my truck. Rachel swiped at her eyes, smearing the black stuff more.

"Thank you for coming," she whispered.

"Of course."

"My mom called this afternoon." She paused, and I said nothing, not wanting to pressure her, although I wanted the back story. "Joanie's into bad stuff." The words strangled themselves from her throat.

"Joanie—your sister?"

She nodded before her face crumpled into a mass of wrinkles and tears. Completely perplexed and out of my element, I reached over and took hold of one of her hands that gripped my coat like a lifeline.

"She overdosed. Nearly killed herself. Might still have done." Rachel sniffled and dragged a hand over her face again. My heart beat heavily in my chest. I knew Joanie was a few years older than Rachel and that the two of them had at least once been close.

"Rachel, I'm so sorry."

"She's at the hospital now. I was going to go, but I couldn't make myself. So instead, I went to face off with the guy I knew sold her stuff." She took a shuddering breath. "I saw her once, totally by accident last year on her spring break, buying something off Lenny DiVen. Wretch. She said it was only some pot. I told Mom and Dad, and they talked to her—but that was the day she stopped trusting me. She went back off to college, and things seemed great. She was making good grades, having fun, hanging with her friends. We only saw her once a month or so. And then she started coming home even more infrequently. We haven't seen her all semester. She was coming home this weekend." More tears tracked down her face. "And this came totally out of the blue. We had no idea. We, we thought she was growing up more and finding her own interests or was busy with classes." Rachel stopped, her breathing stuttered. She gripped my hand harder and covered her mouth with her other. I had no idea what to do, so I just held on, letting her know I was here. Silently I navigated into town. Sam's cabin was on the other side, away from the prying eyes of townspeople and close to the rest of his pack.

"What happened at the party?" I asked quietly as I turned the corner past Huckleberry's Family Restaurant.

"He said horrible things," she whispered and

swallowed hard. "I punched him. Punched him hard enough his nose bled. And then he sent his minions after me."

My mouth dropped open in a silent O. I was still fairly new in town, but punching out the face of a known drug dealer in front of his posse didn't seem like the popular thing to do.

"It was stupid. I was stupid for even going in the first place. I had this great idea that I would get him alone, get him to offer me drugs, and that I'd record the whole thing. Turn him in. Get him sent to jail where he belongs."

Her pain was talking. I could practically feel it bleeding off her.

"Stupid, stupid," she muttered.

"No. *You're* not stupid. You're hurting. You want justice. Revenge. You want your sister back."

She glanced at me. I nodded solemnly. I got it. Grief made you do strange things. I'd spent half my life grieving a father I never knew, grieving for a place I belonged, grieving the lack of acceptance I'd found in my former pack. Rachel tipped her head back against the seat and closed her eyes with a shuddering breath. She still gripped my hand, and that was fine with me. More than fine. I wished there was something I could say, something I could do that would make her feel better—make the whole situation go away. But of course, I couldn't, so I did the only thing I could. I offered her my presence.

****

The rest of the ride to Sam and Megan's cabin was quiet. A few more tears slid down Rachel's cheeks, but aside from the silent plea for comfort that her hand made against mine, we didn't say anything. The silence wasn't uncomfortable. It wasn't deafening. It wasn't happy with all the grief surrounding it, but I think it offered Rachel a momentary reprieve.

Shining cheerfully against the darkness, the porch light next to the front door welcomed us. The nearly finished addition going onto the side stuck up like a giant whale skeleton picked clean by scavengers. Moving like an old woman, Rachel shrugged off my jacket and crawled out of the truck. I would have gotten the door for her, but she climbed out the same time I did. I waited for her by the front of the truck and let my hand drift near hers in case she wanted to hold it again. She didn't, and we made it up the few steps. Before we could knock, Sam jerked the door open, Megan right behind him, concern and worry written on both their faces.

Sam ushered us both into the warm light of their kitchen, and Megan took one look at her friend.

"Rachel Everley Crumb!" Her voice incredulous, she didn't say another word, only wrapped Rachel up in a giant hug. Sobs erupted from somewhere deep in Rachel's throat and my skin crawled.

I felt like an intruder into such a private moment, even though I'd just spent the last half hour with Rachel and her grief. I glanced uncomfortably at Sam and he nodded his head to the front door. He met Megan's eyes over Rachel's head. Snagging his coat, he followed me out into the cold night air.

"Thank you for going after her, Kyp." I heard his wolf's deep rumble in his voice.

"I'm happy I was able to help," I replied honestly. Rachel was my friend. I was flattered and honored that

Sam, the Beta of the pack I desperately hoped to join, trusted me enough to go after his mate's best friend. That was a pretty big deal in the werewolf community, and I wasn't even an official member of Sam's pack.

"Tell me what you know," he said quietly.

I gave him all the information I had about Rachel and what happened, which wasn't much.

Sam groaned. "Not good," he muttered. "But not as bad as it could be. I don't know of any ties Lenny DiVen has with any werewolves." He sighed and ran a hand through his hair. "I'll talk to Dad about how he wants to handle it."

"Even though it's not actually pack business?" I questioned, feeling free to do so with Sam—something I wouldn't have dared to do in the Kentucky pack.

"Rachel is practically pack by proxy. Kind of like your mom will be," he transitioned, and I felt my heart hit my ribs. Probably hearing the quickening beat of my heart, Sam continued. "I spoke with Dad yesterday," referencing Dominic Wolfe, the Alpha of the Wolfe pack, "and we'd like to set up your pack joining two weeks from now. Does that work for you?"

I couldn't stop the grin that split my face. "Yes. Yes, that works for me." Bubbles of joy threatened to lift me off the ground. My head buzzed. A home. A family. A pack. One that didn't care that half of my genes were straight human and not all wolf. A place to *belong*. "Is it okay if my mom comes?" I still wasn't sure how much involvement they allowed humans inside pack business. The number of humans that even knew of werewolves' existence was next to none. My mom, Rachel, and Megan's grandpa were the only regular humans I'd ever met that knew about shifters.

And Rachel only found out a few weeks ago when Sam turned Megan.

Sam laughed. "Your mom is definitely welcome. She might as well be an honorary pack member. She's put more stitches in me than I can count. Having an EMT around who knows all about us is pretty helpful."

"She enjoyed working as an RN in Kentucky—that was the one good thing that came out of being in that pack. They put her through nursing school in order to make her work for them." I gave a sad sigh. Life had been hard in Kentucky. "She's liking the change being on an emergency response crew, although I think she'd take another nursing position if one opened up."

"I'm glad. I think you both are going to make excellent additions."

I felt the heat of his words down to my bones while Wolf chuffed in satisfaction inside me.

"You guys can come in now. She's in the shower," Meg called softly from the door. Sam nodded and we went back in. I resisted the urge to shiver when goose bumps broke out over my forearms under my flannel shirt as I entered the cheery heat of the cabin. My coat was still in my truck where Rachel left it before she slithered out.

"Is she okay?" Sam asked as Meg gave him a sad stare then set to getting bowls out of the cupboard. "Not okay then." Meg baked when she was stressed. Rachel said it was something they had in common.

"Joanie is mixed up in drugs. She's at the hospital now. The doctors are doing everything they can for her, but they're not sure she's going to pull through." A crease appeared between Megan's eyebrows as she measured out flour into a bowl. She set it aside and grabbed measuring cups and the bag of sugar.

"I'm so sorry, Meg," Sam said quietly, going over and wrapping his arms around her shoulders. I turned my head, uncomfortable with such overt affection. It wasn't that I was opposed to it—quite the opposite—I just didn't know how to behave around it. It wasn't something the Kentucky pack had embraced. Literally or figuratively. I wasn't sure if I was supposed to leave now that I'd dropped Rachel off, or if I should stay.

I wanted to stay and make sure Rachel was all right. I didn't want her to think I bailed on her, but I didn't want to hang around if my being there would make her uncomfortable. I had become the awkward third wheel. Wolf nudged me uneasily.

"Kyp, what did she say about Lenny DiVen?" Megan glanced at me as she cracked eggs into the other bowl on the counter.

Jerked out of my awkwardness, I stuttered and felt my cheeks heat. "Sh, she said she punched him in the nose, and he sent some of his guys after her. She was hiding in the woods when I got there. I had to sniff her out to find her," I admitted.

Megan bit her lip. "You think Lenny will retaliate further?" Meg shot her question to Sam.

"If I were Lenny, I absolutely would. She made him lose face in front of a room full of people he needs to impress and keep under control." Sam ran a hand through his shaggy hair.

Megan sighed heavily as she threw in an extra dash of vanilla.

"Kyp, you might as well take a seat. I'll send some cookies home with you. Rachel will probably want to thank you again once she's looking more like her normal self." She shook her head as she packed brown sugar into a measuring cup. Her caramel-colored hair swished against her back. I sat and waited, my heart beating faster than normal, unsure what to expect next.

Chapter 3

Rachel

Stupid. It was the stupidest thing I'd ever done. I'd always been impulsive, but my impulsivity had never before put me in danger like this. An icy chill swept over my shoulders and down my back despite the hot water beating down from the shower. I shook my head and wiped the water out of my eyes before snagging Meg's bottle of pink body wash. I scrubbed and scrubbed, wishing I could scrub off the fear and despair that still clung to me.

Lenny wouldn't just let this go. I knew that. I didn't think he'd go out of his way to make my life miserable, but if I ever crossed paths with him again, it would be a different story.

Cursing my impulsivity again, I shut off the water and wrung out my auburn hair. Meg had set out a towel for me and I snatched it up and wrapped it tightly around my body, warding off the steam-filled air. Red crept into my cheeks again as I glanced at the foggy mirror and realized that the oversized towel covered far more than the skimpy outfit I'd had on earlier. My eyes slid shut in mortification. What Kyp must have thought—what he must think—of me?

I swallowed my shame as best I could and threw on the sweats and t-shirt Meg let me borrow. I rolled the

21

pant legs twice. Megan was all leg where I was all curve. Fortunately, we could still share clothes if there was stretch or elastic involved. With a fortifying breath, I opened the door and exited with a waft of steam.

The smell of warm cookie dough met me, and I inhaled deeply, the smell relaxing my shoulders a fraction. Megan had made walnut chocolate chunk cookies. My absolute favorite.

"They've got about three more minutes in the oven. Here." Meg handed me a steaming mug of tea.

"Thanks," I replied as I took in the two boys sitting at the table at the other end of the tiny kitchen. I cleared my throat. "Thanks for coming after me tonight, Kyp. Sam, thanks for your part, too." I meant it to my toes. I wasn't entirely sure I wouldn't still be freezing in the woods right now if they hadn't put things in motion and gotten me out of there.

"Anytime," Kyp said, his dark brown eyes serious. His reddish-brown hair was longer on top and had just enough wave that a few pieces stuck up, giving him a rakish appeal.

Sam nodded, concern evident in the way his dark blonde brows drew together.

"What do you need right now?" Megan came away from the counter and put an arm around my shoulders. I put my tea down on the table as I felt my chin wobble. I took a deep breath, determined not to sob all over everyone again. The shock of things was wearing off and it was leaving me spent and completely drained.

"I don't even know. Let me call Mom and Dad and see what Joanie's status is and go from there." I glanced around for my phone.

"In your purse?" Kyp asked as he handed me the

tiny black bag. I flushed again for no good reason.

"Thanks," I mumbled as I got the phone out and saw a text from Mom. "Mom says Joanie is stable for the moment." A collective breath left the group. "But she's still pretty fragile and things could still go either way." I bit my lip and screwed my eyes shut. The timer beeped on the oven and Meg got the tray of cookies out. I stared at the phone like I'd never seen it before, too numb to do anything more.

"Do you want some privacy to make your call?" Sam offered. I glanced up at him. These three werewolves had already witnessed me at my worst; I didn't think there was much else that would shock them tonight.

"No, it's fine." I gulped and punched Dad's number.

"Rachel, Sweetheart?" Dad's voice was tired and old. Brittle.

"Hey, Dad. How's Joanie? I saw Mom's text."

His voice wobbled. "She's not good. She's stable, still hanging in there, but whatever she took did a number. She's—" he cleared his throat, "she's on a ventilator. Some of her organs are trying to shut down, but the machines are doing their job." His voice faltered again. "Do you want me to come get you tonight so you can come up? They won't let you sit in there, but you could see her for a few minutes."

I glanced up, tears standing in my eyes.

"We'll come with you," Megan whispered. Those four words were like a balm to my frazzled nerves. I was not alone. I nodded and grabbed her hand.

"Dad, I'm actually with Megan. She's going to bring me up to the hospital. Can you text me the floor and room number?"

"Of course, Sweetheart. I love you. Be careful coming up, all right?"

"Always. Love you, too, Daddy." Emotion clogged my throat as I stared at the screen, trying to process. I glanced up. It was obvious the wolves in the room had overheard everything. Perk of super-sonic wolf ears. I sighed. Sam was grabbing his coat and Megan was putting on her shoes. Kyp stood awkwardly by the door, watching me, unsure what to do.

"Do you want to come, too?" I asked quietly, inviting him into my crazy even though he'd already been thrust into the middle of it. His features softened and his eyes gentled.

"Yeah. I do." His soft-spoken words sent little tendrils of heat pinging through my middle.

My phone dinged with Dad's text of floor and room number.

"Here." Megan handed me a hoodie and a pair of flip-flops. Our feet were as different as our body types. Megan was a solid eight-and-a-half or nine. I was a petite seven. "Sorry I don't have anything warmer for your feet." Meg grimaced. I cracked a grin. It felt strange on my face.

"Really, it's the least of my concerns. They can't be any colder than the fishnets," I quipped.

Kyp gave a startled snort of a laugh. "Sorry," he mumbled around a grin.

I felt my equilibrium leveling, surrounded by my friends, one of them my oldest and best. Laughter and support had a way of doing that. With a final sigh, I shrugged into the hoodie, and we marched out to Sam's car.

Chapter 4

Kyp

Megan sat in the back with Rachel, holding her hand, huddled up next to her in silent support. Rachel clung to her like a lifeline. I was both surprised and honored that Rachel had invited me. It hadn't been the flippant invite of obligation, either. Her offer had been genuine and that sent warmth all the way through me. I shrugged my shoulders into my jacket I'd grabbed on the way out and Rachel's smell of something floral, bright, and tangy wafted up. My nose was nearly as good as a full-blood werewolf's, but not quite. I couldn't distinguish between smells and sounds quite as well. It was frustrating that I couldn't pinpoint Rachel's smell any more than that, but it was uniquely *her*. I'd never smelled anything else like it. She smelled like kindness and laughter.

Tonight had provided a side of her I'd never seen—I wasn't sure she'd ever seen that side of herself either. It was clear that her heart had never been broken like this. Her pain was raw and bleeding, her grief suffocating.

****

The hospital's brightly lit letters glared off the mirror as we pulled into a parking spot. I was not new to hospitals. Mom had worked in hospitals and been on

25

call for the Kentucky pack most of my teenage years. Still, it looked sterile and unwelcoming with the light from the blue letters announcing *Rock Falls Emergency* showering the ground in an unhealthy pallor.

I glanced back at Rachel as she climbed out of Sam's car. We all met on the side closest to the entrance and gathered around Rachel, insulating her within the ring of our support.

"Okay, Joanie's on the third floor," Rachel needlessly reminded us. We went to the bank of elevators, and I quickly punched the number three when I saw Rachel's hands were shaking. Her face was calm enough. The exhaustion was setting in and she had shadows blooming under her normally animated green eyes. They were dull and resigned now. Megan had her arm around Rachel's shoulders and Rachel leaned into her friend.

I felt like a third wheel again. I was the outsider, the newcomer, and while I was Rachel's friend, Megan and she had been friends since the dawn of time, and Sam had always been in the periphery of their social circle. I wanted to be included in Rachel's inner group. I was happy to be with her—not happy that her sister was sick—but I wanted to show her she could count on me. But I didn't know how to do that. Where girls were concerned, I was fairly inept. I could read people, and read them well, but I didn't always know how to respond. It made me a little socially awkward. The awkward feeling was rising in my gut, and I wasn't sure what to do. Wolf wriggled uncomfortably inside. I glanced at Sam as the elevator dinged. His face was still drawn in concern, and his body language was protective. He ushered the girls out and I fell in beside him.

The nursing desk was a hive of activity; Rachel looked bewildered at all the commotion.

"I'll go find out where Joanie is," I said quietly. I knew how to navigate hospitals and had spoken with many hospital staff over the past few years. This was something I could do. Rachel nodded gratefully. Sam gave me a nod of thanks as I made my way to the desk situated in the middle of five or six hallways like spokes coming off a wheel.

"Excuse me," I said politely to a harried woman in wrinkled scrubs. She must have had a rough shift. She spared me the briefest of glances.

"I'm sorry, Honey, but visiting hours are long past."

"I know, and I'm sorry to bother you. I know you're busy, but my friend's sister was brought here tonight. She's trying to find her parents and check on her sister." I nodded my head toward Rachel still standing by the elevators.

"Poor girl." The nurse's face softened. "What's the name?"

"Joanie Crumb."

The nurse's face contorted, wrinkles forming in her dark skin. She knew the name. "Right down hallway number five. She's still in the ICU, but you'll find the waiting room at the end of the hall to the left."

"Thank you so much...Tabitha." I read her nametag. Her eyes brightened under her tired features.

"You're welcome."

"She's still in the ICU, and your parents are probably in the waiting room beside it." I told them as I rejoined them then started leading them toward hallway five.

"Rach?" Megan glanced back when Rachel didn't move.

"I'm okay. Just dreading going in there. Ignorance is bliss, you know?" Rachel rambled.

"Ignorance is bliss, but knowledge is better. You can help your parents better if you know what's going on," Sam offered. Rachel's spine straightened.

"That's true. Okay. Let's do this." She marched forward.

We walked down the hallway and Rachel hesitated again before entering the waiting room. With a swallow and quick intake of breath, she rounded the corner and saw her parents. "Mom, Dad!"

The haggard couple rose from their seats and Rachel ran to them, leaping into their outstretched arms, all three of them sobbing together. I gulped at the display of affection and grief. Glancing at Sam and Meg, I followed suit and we slid into seats on the other side of the room, giving the family space and as much privacy as the small waiting area allowed.

No one said anything for long minutes. Sam held Megan's hand and mine fidgeted in my lap. I knew my way around hospitals, but I'd never been in this position. I didn't know what the protocol was or quite how to behave. Wolf squirmed inside, my anxiety making him nervous as well.

Rachel and her parents finally broke apart, each of them wiping their eyes and running noses.

"Tell me everything." Rachel hiccupped.

"Thank you for bringing her." Rachel's dad looked up and acknowledged us before turning back to his daughter.

"They're still running some tests." His voice cracked and he cleared his throat while Mrs. Crumb dabbed her swollen eyes with a tissue. "They aren't sure what chemicals were mixed in with what she took. Whatever it was wasn't pure." A shudder rippled through his wide frame.

"Do they know the main drug at least?" Rachel's voice was quiet, and Wolf whined at the anguish in her voice.

"Cocaine," Mr. Crumb said and wiped his right eye again.

Beside me, Megan gasped and I glanced at her fallen expression. Sam rubbed his thumb over her hand and leaned over and kissed the side of her head.

"How did, why would she, how long?" Rachel stammered.

"We don't know, Honey." Mrs. Crumb spoke brokenly. "It's possible this was her first time using cocaine. They didn't find any initial needle marks, so there's not a history of her using that way—at least not that they've told us. They're still doing tests to check out her brain." Her face dissolved into a wrinkled mass of grief.

The pain in the room was raw and it pricked at my insides. Wolf hung his head.

A noise in the hall had us all glancing at the door. I startled when I recognized the person that walked through the white door frame.

"Kyp?"

"Hi, Mom," I answered and nudged my head in Rachel's direction. Mom quickly put two and two together and with a quick nod to me, Sam, and Megan, went to Rachel's parents.

"Jennifer!" Mrs. Crumb gushed. She glanced at me as if seeing me for the first time. "Oh, is, is that your son?"

Mom glanced back and smiled at me. "Yes. This is my son, Alexander, but everyone calls him Kyp."

Wolf preened at the unmistakable pride in her voice.

"Oh! You're Kyp! I'm so sorry. We've been so rude! Megan, Sam…" Mrs. Crumb's words fell all over themselves as she gripped Mom's hand and looked over and really saw the three of us sitting against the far wall.

"It's fine." Megan smiled kindly as she went over to them and joined the group. Sam and I followed so that we were all clustered around Rachel and her parents.

"I wanted to come check on you all again and see if there was anything else I could do for you," Mom said.

"Oh, Jennifer, you are so sweet. We can't thank you enough." Mrs. Crumb's chin trembled again, and she released Mom's hand and covered her mouth. "So sorry," Mrs. Crumb mumbled.

"No, no. You cry. It's all right," Mom soothed as Mr. Crumb put an arm around his wife and Mom patted her back. Rachel's face was torn between pain and confusion as she watched her parents. I took a step nearer to her, wanting to comfort her, but unsure what to do.

"Jennifer was the EMT that got the call out to, to your sister," Mr. Crumb began to explain. "Jennifer is the reason Joanie is still alive," he finished, voice husky.

Rachel's mouth dropped open as her eyes welled

up again. Mom gave Rachel a soft smile as she patted Mrs. Crumb's back.

"Do you guys want anything to eat? Can I get you anything right now?" Mom asked again. A quick check of the clock on the wall let me know Mom's shift had recently ended, so she'd be ready to head home—or help the Crumbs now. "There's a good little coffee shop across the street. Can I bring you something back?"

"Oh, I um," Mrs. Crumb started.

"It's all right. Mom, I'll go. Do you guys just want coffee, or snacks, too?" Rachel volunteered.

"We left the cookies in the car," Megan said. She glanced at Sam, "Let's go grab those and bring them up. Do you want us to bring coffee on the way back up?" she asked Rachel's parents.

"I actually wouldn't mind a quick walk," Rachel confessed. Her dad nodded at her, understanding Rachel's need to be active.

"Here." Mr. Crumb dug out his wallet and handed Rachel a credit card. Rachel took it and seemed to shrink in on herself, unsure what to do next.

"I'll go with you," I broke in quietly as Meg was about to offer. I wanted to be useful, to let Rachel know I was her friend. Meg peeked at Rachel who nodded.

"I'll stay here with you two," Mom said and took the seat that Rachel had just vacated.

Meg, Sam, Rachel, and I walked to the bank of elevators together in silence.

"Rachel?" Megan whispered once the metal doors swooshed shut.

"I'm all cried out," she said hollowly. The doors opened and we exited into the main lobby, the long sterile hallway to the left led to the parking garage and

Sam's car. I knew the coffee shop Mom mentioned and it was out the main exit and to the right, down the street a little way.

"Want me to come with you?" Megan asked.

Rachel shook her head and sniffed. "No. Go get the cookies. We'll get coffee and meet you back in the waiting room."

"If you're sure?" Megan's eyebrows drew together. Rachel gave her a firm nod.

"Unless there's more bad news, I think I'm over the worst of things tonight."

Sam caught my eye and nodded solemnly. I knew he was reminding me about the threat of Victor Atwood—a werewolf who had recently come to the area and had kidnapped Sam and Dominic Wolfe barely a week ago. We still weren't sure what he wanted, or even where he was. But we knew that we needed to be on high alert, especially after dark. Victor had enhanced control abilities. He could force his entire pack to do things against their own will—all at the same time. It was terrifying. I nodded back. I had not forgotten.

We shuffled toward the front door. I left my hand where Rachel could take it if she wanted to. Still unsure how to give her what she needed, I tried to watch her and read any cues she gave off.

"The coffee shop is down the block there." I pointed outside the glass double doors as we approached.

"I need a giant latte. With extra milk froth. And probably a double pump of pumpkin spice flavoring."

"You going to stay here tonight?" I asked, thinking about all that caffeine.

"Probably. Although I'm not sure if my parents

would prefer me to stay, or for me to go home so they can pretend at least one of their children is getting a good night of rest." She sighed. "I imagine Clary will be flying in sometime tomorrow, so she probably isn't sleeping either."

"Clary is your other sister?"

Rachel nodded and then shivered as we exited the double doors, our breath frosting ahead of us as the cold night air hit. "Clarice. She lives across the country in Washington now. She's working her way up the advertising agency ladder. She's doing a great job of it, too." A small smile toyed with her lips.

I scanned the surrounding area and let Wolf stretch out with all my senses to check for any threats.

"Do you have a favorite coffee drink?" Rachel surprised me by asking. She'd seen me drink coffee a few times in the weeks we'd known each other.

"Just black. But I haven't tried too many other types. It's kind of unmanly to walk up to a counter and order a tall, non-fat, skinny, mocha, gelato, whatever with fluff on top."

Rachel giggled and the sound brought a smile to my lips. Wolf's hair suddenly stood on end as the breeze blew a scent in my direction. It was werewolf, but with my part-human nose, I wasn't sure if it was one from Sam's pack or not. I hadn't met his whole pack yet and had only scented the ones I'd fought with to save Sam and Dominic from Victor.

"Rachel, we need to move a little quicker," I said quietly. My hand found the small of her back, ushering her down the sidewalk, her too-big flip-flops slapping noisily against the concrete.

"What is it?" Wariness tinged her tone.

"I smell wolf."

Her heartbeat accelerated. Half a block to go to get into the coffee shop. The neon *OPEN* sign blinked brightly in the window and represented a haven of light and at least one other person.

The breeze blew again, and the scent came but softer, fainter. I strained my ears for any sounds out of place, for footfalls, but heard nothing beyond the hum of the hospital and the distant traffic. Rachel stepped closer to my side.

"Do you think it's one of *them*?" Her whisper quavered.

"I hope not. It's fainter now, so they must be walking away from us."

Rachel pressed herself against me the remaining yards to the coffee shop, my arm never leaving her back.

We both issued quick sighs as we came into the puddle of light from the flashing neon sign. A few other patrons stood in line at the counter of the shop.

I held the door open for her and immediately the dark, rich, earthy fragrance of roasted coffee beans covered every other smell. Rachel ducked through the door, tugging my hand behind her, surprising me yet again. Her hand shook and I squeezed it lightly.

"I'll be right with you," a cheerful barista called from the espresso machine as it whirred to life. I did a quick scan of the room. Three people waited in line behind the cash register and two more sat at a table in the far corner. Rachel's hand was still shaking in mine and when I saw a short, mostly secluded hallway leading toward the bathrooms, I led her there, rather than getting into line.

"Can't...stop...shaking." Her teeth chattered as she leaned against the wall.

"It's all right. You're safe now," I whispered, leaning toward her, assuming her tremors were a result of the stress of the hospital and then the unknown wolf.

Her green eyes glanced up at me through her lashes and then she leaned her head against my shoulder. My eyes widened, not expecting that, but let my arms pull her into a hug. Her body twitched as her hands fisted the front of my jacket. I wrapped my arms tighter, Wolf and I both curiously warming at her trust and the way she felt snuggled up against me.

"I'm here," I whispered to her, unsure what else to say, or if she needed me to say anything at all.

Her shaking eased and then a loud rumble gurgled up from her stomach. Rachel gasped.

"Guess I'm hungry after all."

"Did you eat before..." I trailed off, realizing talk of the party might be taboo. Her cheeks stained pink.

"No, I didn't. I was too upset." She didn't duck her head away in embarrassment this time, though her cheeks still blushed.

"Mom says they have a great turkey sandwich here."

She smiled. "I think I'll try one."

I scanned the room again and as far out into the darkness as I could beyond the windows and reflections at the front of the shop. Nothing seemed out of the ordinary, aside from more customers than I expected at nearly midnight.

"What can I get for you?" the barista chirped when it was our turn.

"Two large coffees, one black, one with three

creams and two sugars. One large pumpkin spice latte with extra pumpkin spice and extra froth on top. One regular pumpkin spice latte." She turned to me. "Can I get your mom anything?"

I was touched that she thought of my mom at all under the circumstances. I shook my head. "She'll have a cup of tea when she gets home. But thanks." Rachel nodded.

"One hazelnut latte—make that one a medium and decaf, and one more medium black coffee." She stopped to peruse the menu as the barista rang up drinks. "What is the turkey sandwich your mom gets?" Rachel asked me.

"Uh, that I don't know. Sorry."

Rachel pursed her lips. "I'll go with the turkey and artichoke panini. Kettle chips and an extra pickle, please. Actually, throw in four extra bags of chips. And go ahead and add the ham on rye with extra mayo, and the chicken with smoked gouda panini, please."

I wondered if Rachel was planning on feeding a small army or if she was that hungry.

"Pickle fan?" I asked as the barista handed Rachel back her card and the receipt.

"Mmm. I love pickles. Megan hates them. I always eat hers." The thought brought a smile to one side of her mouth.

Soon there was a growing collection of coffees on the counter. Rachel picked up a cup and handed it to me.

"Try this," she said with a grin. I looked at her then the coffee cup, puzzled.

"What is it?"

"I got you a fancy coffee to try so you didn't have

to unman yourself trying to order one."

I laughed—a genuine laugh that made the barista glance over her shoulder from where she was snapping the lid on another coffee.

Bringing the coffee cup to my nose, I sniffed. The rich coffee tones were offset with pumpkin and several dark spices that made me think of Christmas.

"You're sure about this?" I teased her.

"Definitely." She grinned back, her eyes appearing pleased, though still cry-swollen.

I took a tentative sip and felt the hot, sweet liquid melt all the way down my throat, leaving behind the taste of fall, bonfires, and chilly nights all wrapped up in a mouthful. I blinked at the cup then looked at Rachel.

"You can't tell anyone, but this is delicious," I whispered, half-serious. If anyone in the Kentucky pack had found out I liked a frilly coffee drink, it would have resulted in insults, name calling, and probably a skirmish or two. I didn't think anyone from Sam's pack would care, but I didn't want to take any chances. Not with my impending acceptance into the pack. Rachel smiled back and then her face lit up all over when the barista put Rachel's coffee on the counter. She cradled it and closed her eyes, hands seeping up the heat from the paper cup. She inhaled like some food critic gone rapturous and then sipped ever so gingerly.

"Heaven in a cup," she said. "It's a shame pumpkin spice is only around a few months a year."

"Well, it does taste like fall."

"It does." She smiled back and watched me take another sip.

With a large two-handled bag and two drink

carriers full of coffee, we were ready to go back to the hospital.

Rachel's face shuttered as we reached the cafe door.

"Let me slip out first and scent," I whispered. She nodded, her face drawing up.

I slid out the door, letting it fall shut behind me to block out the aroma of the coffee. My senses sharp and on high alert, I checked the surroundings and let Wolf up to the fore. I smelled nothing unusual. No wolf.

Reaching back, I kept my eyes on the darkness where the lights didn't reach and opened the door for Rachel. I took the bag and one of the drink carriers from her once she was on the sidewalk.

Neither of us said anything until we'd quickly made our way back into the hospital. Rachel's steps faltered as we exited the elevator onto the third floor, and she was practically dragging by the time we reached the waiting room door. I gently nudged her in camaraderie, and she gave me a weak smile.

"There you are." Megan rose from her chair to take the drink carriers from us.

"Large black for Daddy, cream and sugar for you, Mom," Rachel offered. "Meg, I got you a decaf latte. I know you don't like caffeine this late. Sam, black coffee for you, too."

"Thanks, Rach." Meg's eyes were kind and sympathetic as she bumped Rachel's shoulder with hers since Rachel's hands were full of drinks. Meg took over handing out the beverages while Rachel wilted into a chair.

"Nothing new." Mr. Crumb rubbed a hand over his jaw. Rachel nodded and took a long pull from her coffee.

I stared at Sam and he was quick to pick up that something wasn't right and gave me a nod, letting me know he'd be sure to speak with me.

Megan twitched. I figured Sam had spoken into her mind. I was a little envious of this ability. All Alphas and Betas could communicate mentally with their packs. True mates, like Sam and Meg, were rare but also often developed the ability. But I was left out of this perk of pack life. It was one of my greatest failings as a werewolf that I had never been able to fully link with my Alpha or Beta back in the Kentucky pack. It was always a sore spot and something that had driven my Alpha up the wall. Just another obstacle in being only half werewolf.

"Rachel, do you want to come back with me and stay the night?" Megan asked as she sank beside her friend.

"Oh, Honey, why don't you?" Mrs. Crumb encouraged. "At least one of us will get some sleep. I'd feel better if you did."

Rachel glanced slyly at me and I barely kept my grin under wraps. Mrs. Crumb had fulfilled Rachel's earlier prediction nearly word for word.

"I don't mind staying." She held up her large coffee. "I'm properly caffeinated."

"I know, Baby. But this way you'll be fresh tomorrow when we need to nap. Clary is coming in and you'll want to catch up with her, too."

Rachel's shoulders slumped slightly. "All right. Are you sure?"

"Go home and rest, Sweetheart," her dad chimed.

****

In the end, Rachel decided to go back with Sam and Megan to their cabin. I rode home with Mom. I finished texting Sam about the wolf I'd smelled when Rachel and I went on our coffee run. Mom was driving and she covered a yawn with the back of her hand as she drove us to pick up my truck.

"Rough one tonight?" I asked as I put my phone up.

"You saw Rachel's parents," she said sadly. "I wasn't sure we'd made it in time when we first saw Joanie." She shook her head.

"You think she'll make it?"

"I hope so. How was Rachel? Actually, how did you end up at the hospital?"

"It's an interesting story," I hedged. My mom and I talked. About pretty much everything. But somehow, sharing Rachel's pain made me feel like I was outing her.

"And?" Mom nudged.

"Well, let's say I intervened in a difficult situation that Rachel would probably find embarrassing if I told you. But she wasn't in a good place when I got to her. I think she's pretty messed up about her sister."

Mom sighed sadly. "She has good reason to be."

We were quiet for a few minutes. My phone pinged. Sam got the info.

"So, anything more cheerful happen to you today? Let's find something less depressing to discuss," Mom said.

I couldn't help the way my mouth stretched wide, even though I felt guilty being so happy on the tails of Rachel's pain.

"Sam mentioned my joining the pack tonight.

Permanently. They want to set it up for the week after next."

My mom squealed like a teenager.

"Alexander! I am *so* pleased to hear this. I think this is what we've always been searching for. This pack seems to be the real deal."

"And they aren't making any stipulations about my mixed blood. It's like it doesn't even matter to them."

"And it shouldn't. It *doesn't* matter. You are important, valuable, and deserve to be treated with respect." Mom had been giving me variations of this speech most of my life, but it still made me smile grimly, thinking about why she had to give me such a speech. The Kentucky pack had made my life difficult and wasted no opportunity to put me firmly in my place—the Omega. The very last wolf in the pack hierarchy.

"I know, Mom," I whispered, sudden emotion rising. My mom and I had only ever had each other. Maybe now we'd both find a place we fit.

We pulled into the drive at the cabin, the porch light twinkling in the deep black of the late night.

"See you at home?" Mom asked as I opened the car door.

"Yep. I'll follow you out. Let me leave a quick note."

I yanked a piece of paper out of a notebook from my backpack, still in the tiny seat behind the driver's side of my truck. I scribbled my message then folded it. I glanced at the paper in my hands. It felt inadequate for what I was trying to convey, but it was all I had for the moment.

I scurried up the steps and put the paper right

inside the glass door, so they'd be sure to find it. The truck roared to life as I turned it over, testy from being out in the cold. Soon I was following Mom's taillights down the road and back to the rental we currently called home.

Chapter 5

Rachel

Riding back to the cabin, I found I missed Kyp's presence. He had been caring for me in ways I hadn't even realized until he was gone. A light touch to steer me, his silent support, talking to the nurses, just being next to me. Meg sat in the backseat with me again on the way back to the cabin, and her company was a familiar comfort, but I was surprised to find that I still missed Kyp. The caffeine had taken hold and my toes were freezing and twitching in the borrowed flip-flops.

Kyp's truck was already gone by the time we pulled into the driveway. My body tensed when we realized there was a slip of paper tucked in the door.

"I think we can all breathe again. It's a message to Rachel," Sam said after he checked it out. After Sam and his dad had been kidnapped and then the resulting skirmish with Victor Atwood's pack, we were all on edge.

Rachel, call me if you need anything. -Kyp. And he left his number. It warmed me all the way down to my jittery toes.

****

I showered again—I couldn't stand the smell of the hospital on me. When I exited the bathroom again, a jolt shot through me.

Sam and Meg had secretly married in this very room only a few weeks ago. I knew this. I was there. However, I was unprepared to see them in bed together. They were both sleeping; there was nothing weird going on, but it sent a rush of emotion to my throat.

I felt alone, out of place, like an intruder. Megan had been my best friend since first grade. No one on this planet knew me better than she did, and no one knew her as well as I did. But maybe someone else was starting to know her in a different, more intimate way than I ever would.

Tears pricked my eyes again as I stumbled as quietly as I could to the empty bed on the opposite side of the room. The cabin had been a meeting-gathering place for Sam's pack until he and Megan had moved in permanently, but there were still extra beds and couches around. It was nice for times like this, but I wished I was anywhere but in the cabin at that moment.

"Rachel? Are you okay?" Meg whispered across the room.

"Fine," I whispered back, keeping the tears out of my voice.

I was jealous. On top of all the other violent, wild emotions I'd felt over the past hours, I realized I was jealous of my best friend. Jealous that she had Sam, and jealous that she now had her wolf and a new family to which she belonged, and I didn't. Silent tears dripped down my cheeks into the pillow.

****

I woke early, groggy and achy. I glanced at my phone on the table next to the bed. Ugh. Six thirty-three. I rolled onto my back and let my mind drift over the events of the past twenty-four hours. Emotion swirled around inside me, my thoughts jumbled, but working themselves out. I needed to be quiet and still to let my thoughts out sometimes. Other times I liked to bake. Baking bread was my favorite. I wouldn't mind sticking my hands into a nice bowl of risen yeast dough and pounding it down a few thousand times right now.

A deep inhale sounded from the bed across the room, and last night's jealousy came flooding back. I swallowed thickly. I did not want to be jealous of my best friend. I told myself that I was only feeling jealous because she had recently found a new family and mine was coming apart. Megan had been my family almost as long as my sisters had been. I liked Sam. He was good for her, and she was good for him. I was ecstatic for both of them. I really was. I just…felt left out. I had no fur. No fangs. No mate. No pack. It felt like it was me against the world. The rational part of my brain knew that I had friends. That Megan hadn't gone anywhere. But I didn't have her full attention anymore. And it made me feel like a sucky friend that I felt that way.

My phone blared beside me and I yelped, jerking up and snatching the phone.

"Sorry!" I muttered as Sam and Meg sat up across the room. Stupid silencer—that I obviously forgot to turn on last night. I glanced at the caller ID and swiped my finger over the screen.

"Clary?"

"Rachel! How is Joanie! Is she okay? I didn't want to wake Mom or Dad if they were asleep. I'm here at the airport; can you come get me? Honeydew, be quiet. Stop yapping!" My sister's words tumbled out with no room for breath.

45

"I don't know how Joanie is. I was asleep. She was holding on last night. Honeydew?" My brain felt fuzzy.

"My dog. I couldn't get a sitter and the groomer wasn't open before I wanted to fly out, so I had to bring her. *Shush*, you little chatterbox!" I could hear high-pitched yelping through the other end of the line.

"I can get to the airport, but it'll probably be a little over an hour. Sorry. I didn't know what time your flight was getting in."

"Try to hurry." Her tone was exasperated. I swallowed again, unsure how to respond to her snippy voice.

"I'll get there as quick as I can. I'll call you when I'm close. Okay?"

"All right. I'm going to go find coffee."

"Bye." But she'd already hung up. I stared stupidly at the phone in my hand. My sister was never that short with me. She must be out of her mind with worry over Joanie. I knew I was. Anxiety rumbled in my belly.

"Clary's already in?" Megan sat up straighter against the headboard. I nodded, swinging my legs over the edge of my bed.

"Yeah. I need to go pick her up. Crap. My car is still parked in front of Darnell Thompson's house." I let my head fall into my hands and raked them through my tangled hair. It had dried in a wild riot of curls, knots, and snarls.

"We'll take my car," Megan quickly interjected. Somebody's phone vibrated softly, and Sam reached over Megan, her cheeks flushing as his arm grazed her chest and sent a knot into mine.

"You might not need to," Sam said as he checked his phone. He gave a surprised chuckle. "Kyp is on the way over with your car as we speak."

My eyebrows drew together in confusion. "But he doesn't have my keys. How can he be driving my car over?"

"I have no idea, but that's what he said." Sam shrugged.

Thirty minutes and a few rotations of the bathroom later, there was a knock at the door. Sam answered it and then let Kyp in.

"Hi, guys. I hope it was okay that I brought your car over, Rachel. I thought it might be less hassle and fewer questions if you didn't have to go back there."

Heat unfurled tiny petals in my stomach at his thoughtfulness and relief that I didn't need to go back to the scene of my greatest disaster was palpable.

"No, that's fine! I appreciate it. But how did you get it here? My keys are still in my purse."

Kyp's cheeks reddened and he cleared his throat. "I um, acquired an unusual set of skills living with the Kentucky pack."

Sam chuckled. "You hotwired it?"

Kyp looked abashed. "I did."

"Seriously? I thought that was something that only happened in movies." Meg grinned as she filled the coffee pot and flipped the switch on.

"Real life, too, on occasion," Kyp mumbled.

The atmosphere in the cabin lifted and I didn't want to bring it crashing back down again, but I needed to know how Joanie was doing.

"I'm going to call Dad real quick." I punched his number.

"Hey, Sweetheart." Dad's voice was gravelly over the phone.

"Hi. How's Joanie? Are you and Mom okay?"

"We're hanging in there. No change yet for Joanie. She's holding steady, but she's not doing great. About the same," he answered tiredly. I sighed. At least there was no negative change. I could deal with this.

"Okay. Clary's plane is in. I'm going to go get her and probably bring her straight to the hospital unless she needs to crash first."

"Are you all right to drive? Let me send someone," Dad started.

"No, Daddy. I'm fine. I need to feel useful. I'm not good at sitting in the hospital anyway. I'll bring a friend with me. Don't worry." I reassured him, knowing Megan would go with me.

"All right. If you're sure."

"I'm sure. Love you, Daddy."

"Love you, too, Sweetheart."

"How soon do you want to leave?" Megan asked, not questioning whether or not she'd be going with me.

"Probably as soon as we can get out the door."

Sam muttered under his breath, a faraway look on his suddenly flushed face.

"What's wrong?" Megan's whole body tensed in a way that sent concern tripping up my spine. Sam glanced at her, his eyes intense.

"Dad just used the link," he explained, probably mostly for my benefit, since I was the only non-wolf in the room. "There are fresh scent trails around the edges of our territory. And there's blood."

I whipped my head from Sam to Megan. While Sam's face was flushed with anger, Megan's drained of color.

"What exactly does that mean?" I was suddenly

aware that the scope of the problems at hand just got a lot larger, and that Joanie wasn't the only one in possible danger. Until Joanie overdosed, last month had been the craziest, most intense month of my life. Shelby Atwood, Victor's deranged daughter, had tried to kill Megan twice in as many weeks. We didn't know if she had accomplices, and she had completely dropped off the grid after Megan and Sam officially became a mated pair.

Sam took a calming breath and turned to Megan. "I don't know yet, but it's definitely Victor, and he's making a move. I've got to go help Dad." He stared at Megan and I knew they were using their mental link to have a discussion without Kyp or me overhearing. I hated being excluded this way. I glanced at Kyp to see if he felt irritated, too but was surprised to find him watching the other two carefully.

"Rachel, would it be okay if I went with you to pick up your sister?" Kyp asked, turning to me before Sam or Meg had finished their conversation. My eyebrows lifted, surprised at his offer.

"Sure." I was pleased he'd be coming, but still feeling like I'd missed a giant discussion and feeling peeved about it.

"I'm so sorry, Rachel." Megan blinked and took a breath. "If this is another threat, it's possible they may be after Sam or me again. I could put you in more danger if I went with you." Her eyes were sad, and my heart dropped as I realized what Sam and Megan's mental conversation had been about. Victor might still be after Megan. Or Sam.

"No, no. You have to be safe. Kyp can come with me to get Clary."

****

Ten minutes later, Kyp and I were on the road. We were in my car, although I was happy to let Kyp drive when he offered. I was still worn out, and the lack of sleep and jumble of emotions wasn't going to help my driving abilities.

We were quiet the first few miles while I turned over the morning's events.

"Kyp, were you in on the conversation between Megan and Sam? When they were using their link? Could you hear, too?"

"No. I can barely link with my Alpha, let alone overhear private conversations." He smiled ruefully. "And right now, I'm still Rogue. I don't belong to any pack."

"Oh. I thought all werewolves could link with their Alpha or Beta?"

"They can. I'm not one hundred percent werewolf," he reminded me wistfully. I cringed. Way to stick my foot in my mouth.

"Sorry. I didn't mean it that way."

"I know. I'm different. An anomaly. For all I know, I'm the only mixed-blood werewolf alive."

That seemed so sad to me. I could relate to feeling utterly alone.

"Sorry. I didn't mean to say the wrong thing. You looked like you understood what was going on."

"I can't use the mental link well, mostly not at all, but I have become good at people reading. I could tell something was up the way Sam was looking at Megan. His body language read over-protective and I just put two and two together."

"It was sweet of you to come with me to the

airport. I hope I'm not messing up all your Saturday plans." I changed the subject.

He smiled at me. "I'm happy to come. I didn't have anything planned at all."

The miles flew by as we tore down the highway toward the airport chatting amiably. I texted Clary as soon as we were close. She was waiting, her hair askew, her clothes rumpled, and an irate ball of fur yipping from inside her large purse when we pulled into the curb.

I jumped out and ran to hug her.

She hugged me quickly then thrust her barking purse toward me.

"Ugh, please give me a break from the dog!"

Startled, I glanced down at what appeared to be a scrawny, furry rat.

"Oh," was all I could manage. The dog glared at me. Kyp opened his door and gallantly grabbed Clary's suitcases and popped the trunk.

"Who is this?" Clary asked.

"Sorry! Clary, this is Kyp. Kyp, this is my sister, Clary."

"Nice to meet you, although sorry it's under these circumstances," he said as he shut the trunk. The dog howled and I nearly dropped the purse.

"Rachel!" Clary hissed as she jerked the bag away from me. "Don't you worry, little Honeydew. It's all right." My sister glared at me and I noticed the inflamed rims around her eyes. She hadn't slept, hadn't seen Joanie, and the barking dog must have taken its toll on a red-eye flight. I bet the other passengers weren't happy either.

"What's your dog's name?" Kyp asked as he sidled

up to the bag.

"Honeydew," Clary said, her exasperation evident. I watched as Kyp glanced at the dog then turned so that Clary couldn't see his face. He eyed the dog down, and I bit back a grin as I realized he was letting his wolf show his dominance over the little tuft of fur. Honeydew backed down and sat politely, gazing up at Kyp like he was the ruler of the world.

"Wow." Clary was clearly impressed.

Kyp smiled. "I'm usually good with dogs."

Chapter 6

Kyp

The ride from the airport to the hospital was tenser than I'd expected it to be. Rachel had always talked animatedly and happily about both her sisters until Joanie's overdose yesterday. Clary was stiffer than I anticipated, and Rachel seemed out of her element. I learned about Clary's job and some of the highlights of her life in Seattle. And how Seattle coffee is much, much better than the coffee at the airport this morning. I wasn't required to join in the conversation much as Clary's sleep-deprived talk rambled more than it probably would have normally. Mercifully, Honeydew curled up in a ball and slept. There were perks to being half-wolf.

I drove them all the way to the hospital and parked.

"Thanks for the ride," Clary mumbled as she exited the car. She snatched some dog treats out of her purse and put them on the seat next to the still-sleeping Honeydew.

"Leave the windows cracked," she ordered, then turned toward the hospital.

Rachel turned to me with wide eyes.

"Kyp, I'm so sorry! I only now realized that you're here without a way back. Ugh, I'm so scattered today."

"It's no problem," I assured her.

"No, it's rude of me. I don't mind if you want to take my car back. We'll ride back in Mom and Dad's."

"I'll at least walk you in first." I wondered if she would prefer I leave, or if she'd actually like a friend with her. Even if I wasn't Megan. I needed to check in with Sam to see if they needed me for anything. Sam's pack gave me a purpose I hadn't had in Kentucky, and I wanted them to know that their faith in me wasn't misplaced.

"Thanks," she said gratefully.

I clicked her door locks and handed her back her keys. She put them in her purse. I didn't know if it was out of habit, or because she wanted me to stay.

We walked through the doors and the smell of antiseptic, blood, and fear hit me in the face. Rachel stiffened beside me.

"Elevators?" Clary motioned.

"Yeah, third floor," I answered when Rachel bit her lip, her eyes lost. Holding my breath, I tugged her hand. "You okay?" I whispered as Clary punched the *UP* button with more force than was necessary.

Rachel shook her head. "Sorry. Just trying to hold it together."

I squeezed her hand and her fingers tightened around mine. "Need a frilly latte?"

A surprised chuckle tumbled from her throat.

"Yes. Yes, I think I do. Do you want one, or is it still too unmanly?" Some of her usual spark filled her eyes as she peeked up at me. I felt the side of my mouth tip up.

"Maybe. But you're still sworn to secrecy."

"Cross my heart."

"What are you two talking about?" Clary asked,

amused annoyance sounding in her voice.

"Coffee. All about the coffee," Rachel said.

"You have to try Seattle's coffee. You should fly out this summer." Clary gazed down at Rachel with real emotion, like she was seeing her sister for the first time since she flew in. Clary reached out and brushed Rachel's shoulder as the elevator dinged and the doors slid open.

Rachel squeezed my hand again and let go. "Thanks," she whispered. I nodded but was surprised to find that I missed her hand in mine. I didn't have a lot of experience with girls—basically none at all—and the emotion felt strange.

One hall down and we were in the cold, sterile waiting room again. Clary fell into her parents' arms as soon as we hit the door, and then there was loud sobbing and back patting and talking all at once. Rachel hung back, letting Clary have all of their parents for a few minutes. Her lip trembled. I scooted over and propped myself against the wall, my arm brushing hers. Whether or not she meant to, she leaned into me, and I was glad I had come upstairs with them.

We waited a few more minutes for her parents and Clary to disengage and then Rachel moved forward. I stayed where I was, now unsure what I should do or where I should be.

Rachel hugged both her parents.

"Still no change," Mrs. Crumb said.

"At least it's not negative change," Rachel said optimistically.

"You're right." Mr. Crumb patted Rachel's back. "Oh, Kyp! Did you come with the girls?"

"Yes, sir. I drove up with Rachel to the airport."

"Did Megan come, too?" Mrs. Crumb's eyes tracked to Rachel, obviously assuming as we had at the cabin, that Megan would go with Rachel.

Rachel's cheeks flushed.

"No, um…"

"She got sick right as they were getting ready to head out the door. I was in the neighborhood and offered to come with Rachel instead," I supplied quickly, hoping I'd given enough details without giving too many. Rachel glanced at me gratefully.

"Oh, that's too bad. I hope she didn't pick something up here last night." Mrs. Crumb worried her lip just like Rachel did when she was concerned.

"I'll call her in a few minutes to check on her," Rachel assured her mom.

"Good idea."

"I guess if there are no new updates and nothing happening, I'll go call her now, if that's okay?" Rachel asked.

"Of course, Sweetheart," her dad said.

"I'll come with you." I cut in and I noticed her dad's shoulders relax a fraction of an inch. I took that as a good sign.

We left the waiting room and Rachel shivered.

"Cold?"

"Not really. I don't like that room. It reminds me too much of why we're here, and how much we might still lose."

I nodded, understanding but not knowing what to say to that. Wolf nudged me encouragingly.

"You want to walk around until we find a quiet place? I want to check in with Megan, but don't need anyone else overhearing, you know?"

"Sure. There's usually a deserted consultation room or two. I would like to call Sam, too."

We found an empty consultation room not far from the chapel. The whole hallway was silent without a soul in view. I let Wolf up to the front to listen for anyone who might be out of sight. We heard nothing, so I figured we were safe enough to speak freely.

"Megan? Any news? What's up? Are you okay?" Rachel babbled into her phone. She glanced up at me. "Hang on. I'm putting you on speaker. Kyp's here, too."

I was warmed at her gesture of inclusion and leaned in to hear.

"Hey, guys. Sam is still running patrols with Dominic. I'm at the big house with Mary." Mary was Sam's mom. "Sam's been sending me updates every so often. They've found a blood trail. It's light, only a drop or two every little bit, but it's outlining the entire southern Wolfe border."

I clenched my jaws together. It was a warning. Victor Atwood was out for blood. Literally. Apparently, he'd already found some.

"Is the blood itself important?" I asked.

"Yes," Megan whispered. Rachel's eyes grew so round the whites showed around the green centers. I held my breath, waiting for Megan to continue. "It's Shelby's blood."

We stood in stunned silence for a moment.

"Shelby Atwood? Victor's daughter?" Rachel expelled a breath.

"Yes. Sam's certain. He knows her scent, and this is her blood. I don't know if it's enough blood to kill her or not, but she's missing a decent amount."

"Monster," Rachel whispered.

"We're assuming Victor is behind the blood trail, not Shelby. But we do still think Shelby is the one behind the two attempts a few weeks ago. At that point, Victor had no reason to come after me, but Shelby did. She wanted Sam. And if she did have the surgery to remove her werewolf glands, it's possible she could be deranged and crazy enough to do something this weird. Right?" Megan's voice sounded hopeful. It would be nicer to believe that this was the work of a lone crazed werewolf girl with a fixation on Sam, than it was to believe that Victor Atwood was sadistic enough to bleed his own daughter to send a message to a rival Alpha.

"I'll ask my mom if she knows anything else about how the disease progressed in the case she caught wind of in Kentucky," I said. My mom had been the one to recall the case where a werewolf girl had been diagnosed with a rare disease in her second set of glands. In a risky move to eradicate the disease, she'd had her werewolf glands removed. She was still all wolf, could shift at will, she just didn't smell like a wolf and couldn't secrete some of the chemicals werewolves used for communication. But it had resulted in her madness. She'd completely gone off the deep end and, in the end, she'd died anyway—though from the disease or the surgery, we didn't know. Shelby had had the same surgery. She'd had her glands removed. It was the only explanation for her intermingling with Dominic's pack for two years without being detected as a werewolf. That kind of dedication passed the line of *sane* and sent a shiver down my back.

"Are you okay?" Rachel asked Megan.

"I'm fine. I'm safe. How are *you* doing? How's Joanie?"

"Well, I don't think there's much change…Oh! Hang on. I got a text." Rachel held the phone away from us so she could read the message. "Oh, thank God! It's from Dad. Joanie's vitals are better! The doctor said there's been improvement in the past hour. I think we're going to head back up there now, but please call or text if you find out anything else!"

"I will. I'm so glad to hear there's improvement! Keep me posted," Meg replied.

I fired off a quick text to Sam on my phone while Megan and Rachel said their goodbyes.

At the hospital with Rachel. Heard about the perimeter. Let me know if you need me back. Otherwise, I'll stay with Rachel.

I didn't expect a quick reply since I assumed Sam was still in fur.

Rachel and I made our way back to the waiting room where Mr. and Mrs. Crumb and Clary all appeared better, though still haggard.

****

By early evening, Sam had messaged me back and told me to stay with Rachel and keep my eyes open. Joanie had shown slow but steady improvement throughout the afternoon. Enough so that the Crumbs decided to head home and get some much-needed rest before coming back tomorrow.

"Kyp, thank you so much for coming today. And for staying," Rachel told me as we were gathering our things to head out.

"You're welcome."

"Do you want me to take you back to your house?

Or is your truck somewhere else?" Rachel hedged.

I smiled. "No worries. Just let me out a few blocks from your house. I'll run home. I ran to your car this morning, so my truck is still in my own driveway."

Rachel stared at me, her eyes round.

I lifted my eyebrow. "What?"

"That's really kind of awesome." Her cheeks flushed slightly. It gave me a curious giddy sensation in my belly. I smiled back and held the door open for her.

Chapter 7

Rachel

Joanie held steady Sunday, and it was decided that I should go ahead and go to school on Monday, since there wasn't anything I could do at the hospital, and I wasn't good at sitting still.

I was both dreading and craving the normalcy of school. I needed the routine, the common, the boring. But I didn't know if my escapade with Lenny or if news of my sister had reached the gossip mill. If it had, it was going to be an excruciatingly long week.

When I got to school, the halls were abuzz with news—thankfully not about me. Although once I caught the rumors going around, my stomach churned, and it only added a new layer of anxiety.

"Did you hear?" Luke, a member of the drama club and a friend of mine, and also the son of one of our local deputies, asked as he saw me coming down the hall to my locker.

"What?" I asked, fearful of what he might say next.

"They found a body. Like, *right outside the police station*. It's insane. I don't even think they know who it is. The whole face was *ripped off*."

"Ripped off?" The words tumbled out of my mouth like a ghost, quiet and airy. I felt lightheaded.

"Yeah. They think some animal got ahold of the

61

body. There are stab marks, but also claw marks. And then there's the missing face."

"I think I'm going to be sick."

"I know! Totally sick, right?"

"Luke, did your mom say what kind of animal?" Whitney from drama club popped around the bank of lockers as Luke was dishing the details.

Glancing around, everyone was riveted on Luke's story, and he was loving being the center of attention. I quietly slipped down the hallway to my locker where Megan soon appeared, Sam on her heels.

"Rachel, I'm so glad Joanie's doing better!" I'd texted her first thing this morning. Joanie's vitals had continued slowly improving overnight.

"Me, too. I'm guessing you guys heard the news?" Anxiety spread from my belly to my spine.

Megan's expression fell and she glanced at Sam. He nodded at me, meeting my eyes. "Definitely wolf," he said so softly I almost missed it. The anxiety turned to dread and froze my insides up like a block of ice. It wasn't only Joanie I had to worry about. What if Victor Atwood made a grab for Megan? Was this his twisted idea of a power play? I could *not* lose my best friend. I suppressed a shudder and suddenly wished Kyp was here with his solid, quiet presence. I hadn't realized until that moment how much I had come to rely on him during my harrowing weekend.

****

The days felt like a blur of school, hospital visits— during which Sam, Megan, or Kyp always came with me—and homework I couldn't focus on. The gossip mill continued to thrive regarding the latest salacious news about the brutal killing of the man who turned out to be Harry Steinbach. He owned a little grocery store down on 7th Street. He wasn't someone who had enemies. He was a well-respected community man and a member of several service organizations.

Dominic Wolfe's take on it was clear. Mr. Steinbach had been a perfectly innocent person. Chosen specifically for his innocence. The thought of such evil sent shivers skittering over my skin. Dominic had already issued a cautionary recommendation for his wolves to go in pairs everywhere after Victor's abduction of Sam and Dominic. By Tuesday, he issued it as an order. I wasn't a part of the pack, but I knew what was going on, and I suddenly found Kyp around a lot more. He became a constant in the periphery of my life, and instead of feeling suffocated, I found it made me feel cared for and strangely enough, included. With my family so preoccupied with Joanie—and rightly so—I was more or less left to my own devices. Kyp became a fixture and quickly fit into a gap that had been left when Megan married Sam and when Joanie had disrupted our family.

Tuesday night, Joanie finally woke up and the relief was so strong it nearly sent me to my knees in the waiting room.

Wednesday morning Kyp met me at the doors of the school.

"Morning," he started. "How's Joanie?"

I rubbed my eyes, dark circles cupping them from the lack of sleep. "Kyp, I don't think I've ever been so grateful to see anything as I was to see my sister's eyeballs last night." I'd only gotten to be with her for about three minutes, but they had been the best three minutes of the last five days. He smiled as the skin around his eyes crinkled and my stomach fluttered for no reason.

"I'm glad. Really glad. Thanks for texting to let me know last night. I told my mom, and she was about as relieved and happy as you are."

I smiled at that.

"Tell your mom I said thanks, again. Seriously. I'd bet my college fund that Joanie wouldn't still be here if it weren't for your mom." I refused to let my chin tremble.

"I'll tell her. That will mean a lot to her. So, I was wondering." We paused as I opened my locker and frowned at the mountain of books. My teachers were being pretty lenient with me getting my work in this week with all the family upset, but that time was going to come to an end soon.

"Wondering what?" I pulled my mind back to the present and glanced up at Kyp. His eyebrows were drawn together, his forehead wrinkled.

"Would it be all right if I started bringing you to and from school?" I felt my eyebrows lift, unsure where that came from.

"I guess so?" I didn't mean for it to come out sounding like a question, but it did.

"I...it makes me nervous. There's a lot of uncovered area between your house and school." He turned to me, his eyes full of concern, and I realized with a modicum of disappointment that he was only thinking about my safety.

"Oh. Of course," I amended quickly. "But I have play practice and stuff after school. And crazy hospital visiting hours."

"That's all right. I can either pick you up or follow

you, whichever you'd prefer. I'm not trying to infringe on your entire life."

"I know," I said, a part of me wishing he wanted to take me to and from school for reasons other than that there was a madman on the loose. "I don't want my schedule to totally rule your life, either."

He grinned and shrugged his shoulders. "I don't have much of a social life." He winked as we rounded the corner for class.

Chapter 8

Kyp

Dominic let me know that I was running late patrols with Jonathan Stone and Steve and Cade Rivers Wednesday night.

"Mom, this is more than I expected. I'm not even a member of the pack, and they're giving me actual responsibilities that matter." We talked over dinner at our dated kitchen table.

"And Rachel? Is she only another pack responsibility?" Mom had a twinkle in her eye as she spooned in a bite of noodles.

Wolf perked up at Rachel's name. "I mean, I guess so. I don't know how she could be anything else? She's human."

"And this is a problem?"

My eyebrows lifted. "Well, human-werewolf relationships aren't exactly sanctioned."

"Maybe they could be?" Was it my imagination, or were Mom's cheeks flushing ever so slightly?

"Mom?"

The noodles and broccoli on her plate suddenly had her full attention.

"Seriously? Is there something you want to tell me?" I hedged, unable to stop the teasing note in my voice. Neither Mom nor I had dated—ever. It wasn't something that fit in, or was allowed, in the Kentucky pack.

"Well, nothing yet," she said. I nodded, a smile hiding in the corner of my mouth.

"All right. Keep your secrets then."

"He's wolf."

My head snapped up. "Who?" I wasn't teasing anymore.

Mom looked me in the eyes. "Jonathan Stone."

I sat back in my chair, dinner momentarily forgotten. Wolf nodded his head approvingly. He liked Jonathan—a man who'd spent time in the Army Rangers and who was now leading drills with the Wolfe pack in preparation for skirmishes against Victor's pack that we all knew were coming.

"Say something, Alex." Mom was the only one who ever used any variation of my first name.

"I hardly know what to say. I don't know what to feel. We've never been here before."

"Well, nothing is remotely official. I just…I like him. He's steady, dependable, kind."

"I appreciate you telling me. I've got to run patrols with him in an hour."

"Oh. Sorry. I hope it doesn't make things awkward. I wanted to let you know."

"Does…is he interested, too?"

"Maybe. I'm not the world's greatest at this sort of thing," she admitted ruefully. I nodded, filing all this new confusing information away to process later. And to watch Jonathan Stone a bit more carefully.

****

An hour later, it was time for me to head out for patrols. I stepped outside into the twilight, shutting the door snugly behind me. The first stars were peeking out as darkness overtook the world. Forest flanked our little rental house on all sides. It was secluded. Taking a full breath, I scented the evening. Crisp, chill air slid inside my chest, and I held it like a promise. I was going to run patrols for the Wolfes. My fingers shook as I took my shirt off and undid my pants. The possibility—the very real possibility—of belonging, of mattering, to a pack made me giddy.

I left my clothes and shoes in a pile on the sidewalk beside the house and craned my neck up to the moon, only barely becoming visible as twilight bled into darkness.

My eyes slid shut, and I let Wolf have his head. Fur raked through my skin, sending a tingling rush over my whole body. My wolf ears pushed out as my human ones receded. My bones crunched, backbone cracking in two as my tail extended. Claws scraped lightly against the concrete of the sidewalk as my paws emerged. My front paws clacked as the nails poked through, and my body bent over so that I was on all fours. Canines descended, gnashing through my gums as my jaw lengthened and my face contorted into its animal shape. Wind rushed over the thick fur of my ruff and teased the delicate whiskers around my nose.

I heaved a mighty shake to rid myself of any lingering humanness. Pointing my nose to the moon again, I took another inhale. All the smells of the forest exploded and intensified around me, sharp, pungent, and calling for exploration.

With another shake of my head, I loped off toward the designated meeting spot for patrols. I was the first to arrive. I sniffed the immediate perimeter then sat on my haunches and waited patiently. Cade Rivers, Sam's best friend, and Cade's dad, Steve, came trotting up a few minutes later. They nodded to me, and we exchanged customary scenting, refamiliarizing ourselves with each other. I heard Jonathan before I saw him. One single twig snapped to give his position away. We all turned our heads as Jonathan's big outline approached. He was a dark wolf riddled with grey. Almost as dark as me, though the very ends of my fur had reddish tips. Cade and Steve were both shadowy phantoms in the twilight, too. Cade was nearly as black as his human hair, while Steve had some silver at his muzzle. We were all perfectly camouflaged for running patrols in the dusky woods.

We took off at a good clip, Jonathan taking the lead, the rest of us fanning out behind. Wolf breathed deeply and processed all the scents and information. Forest, dirt, loam, crisp leaves that strangely reminded me of the pumpkin spice latte Rachel had me try. And that led me to thoughts of Rachel.

I was jerked from my tumultuous thoughts as the wind changed and a blast of coppery, tangy blood filled my nostrils.

With one high-pitched yelp to alert the others, I turned and cautiously approached the source of the smell. It wasn't long before I found blood. Lots of blood. It was human. I recoiled as Wolf momentarily exulted in the smell of the hunt and I jerked his will, terrified of this part of myself. Another few feet and I saw a hand all silvery and mottled with dark brown blood, sticking out of the underbrush.

Chapter 9

Rachel

A sense of foreboding cloaked me like a shroud when I woke up Thursday morning. There was nothing I could explain. Joanie was doing well. So well, that the plan was to have her released into a rehab center over the weekend. My parents were still deciding on which one and making calls to check for openings. Clary was planning to fly out tomorrow mid-morning, and life as we now knew it would move on. My clock read six forty-seven, and if I was going to make it to school showered, fed, and with concealer over the raccoon-like circles under my eyes, I had to haul myself out of bed. I was warm and comfortable, but the ominous feeling seemed to hang in the air, just above my bed. As if I would catch it like a disease if I moved. My phone buzzed, and I reached for it, a crease forming between my eyebrows.

Meg. —*They found Shelby Atwood. She's alive but barely.*—

My mouth dried like old bread. I punched Meg's speed dial.

"Rachel?"

"Meg. Every detail. What happened? Are you safe?" My voice sounded like a chain smoker's from the early morning and the terror that seized my throat.

"I'm fine. Don't worry about me. Sam's here. There are extra patrols going. The patrol came across Shelby late last night—she's in the hospital now. She's still alive, but only barely, from what I was told. She's lost a lot of blood."

"Which I guess we already knew," I said.

"Right. She's got slash marks though—definitely wolf—across her abdomen and on her legs. There are some superficial ones across her neck, too. They weren't sure if the marks were meant to keep her alive, or to let her bleed out slowly. It's awful," Meg finished on a shudder. I shuddered myself.

"Ugh. This is so messed up." I felt small, sitting there thinking about Shelby, wrapped up in some horrible plot bigger than herself. I knew what was going on, but I wasn't a part of things. I was just on the outer fringe. I didn't know if it was safer here, or if it would be safer to be a werewolf and be on the inside. I sighed. Selfishly, it didn't matter to me. I wanted to be a wolf and have that closeness, that bond with an extended family.

"You okay this morning? Have you called to get an update on Joanie yet?" Megan continued. I could hear some clinking in the background and figured she was getting her required morning coffee.

"Not yet. I need to though. I had this sick feeling in the pit of my stomach this morning, and I was having trouble getting out of bed, so I haven't yet," I confessed.

"I'm so sorry, Rachel. My news didn't make it any better."

"No, but I'm glad you texted."

"We're going to get through this, Rachel. We'll go

to the ends of the earth *together* if we have to. You're not alone."

The corner of my mouth tipped, thinking back to the time we were in early elementary and had stolen one of Clary's zombie movies and watched it even though we weren't supposed to. We'd been scared silly and had solemnly promised each other that if the end of the world came on our watch, we'd go to the ends of the earth together.

"To the ends of the earth."

"Is Kyp still coming to get you for school?"

"Yes. He should be here soon. He told me yesterday he'd prefer to drive me to and from school."

"Good. I feel better knowing you're not driving it by yourself. But you should know something else. Kyp and Cade were both on the patrol that found Shelby."

"Oh, poor Kyp! And Cade!"

"Yeah. I imagine it was pretty gruesome." Meg sounded as sad as I felt. "Also…how is Kyp?" Her voice trailed up at the end of her sentence and I snorted.

"He's fine, I suppose, aside from recently uncovering a nearly-dead girl in the woods. But as for 'Kyp and Rachel' I don't think there's anything to tell. Although, I have appreciated him hanging around and being incredibly helpful. Who knew he was so good in a crisis?"

"Just checking." I could hear the smile in Megan's voice.

"You'd be the first to know." I grinned. "See you at school."

"Go get a shower and get dressed. I'll bring you coffee with a breakfast sandwich and meet you at school."

****

Kyp was right on time and had to wait ten minutes while I finished gathering my life together and all the paraphernalia that went with it so we could get to school. I didn't give him more than a good morning when he got to my house, not wanting to explain any sympathetic actions to Clary should she be in the vicinity.

"Oh, hi Kyp. You're taking Rachel to school today?" Clary's voice drifted up the stairs as I shoved stuff into my backpack. Crap. I hadn't told anyone that Kyp would be picking me up and bringing me home. It had completely slipped my mind once Joanie woke up last night. It hadn't been important. But it was on Clary's radar now, and I was sure there would be questions.

"I'm sorry I'm late this morning. Megan called me first thing and we talked too long." The words rushed out as he turned the engine over a few minutes later. "And she told me about Shelby. Kyp, I'm so sorry," I said quietly as I reached over and put my hand on his arm. He blinked a few times.

"Thanks. It's definitely something I won't be forgetting," he said with a thick swallow.

I bit my lip and then frowned as my gaze snagged on the trashcans that were out of place at the end of our drive, almost like someone had run into them and hadn't put them back correctly. "Yeah. It's awful. First Mr. Steinbach, now Shelby. What do you think Victor wants?"

"Probably to spook us more than anything right now." His answer was matter-of-fact. "Why fight if fear can do the job for you? Picking a few lesser targets sends a bigger message and requires less effort on Victor's behalf."

"Well, it's working. I'm definitely spooked."

Kyp glanced over at me. "Me, too." Meeting his eyes for a fleeting second before he turned back to the road, I understood more of his motivation for wanting to pick me up for school. I shivered. I didn't even have any neighbors within eyesight.

"Did Sam ask you to keep an eye on me since everything is heating up?" I was considered an honorary pack member, a lot like Jennifer Kypson. We were in the know, but we weren't werewolves. We were accorded some special privileges, but we were not official members of the pack.

"He didn't have to. I volunteered." He sent me a sideways grin that I wasn't sure how to interpret, but it did send little tendrils of heat through my middle and uncoiled some of the dread.

****

School was abuzz with news of Shelby. Principal Angelo made a special announcement during homeroom. I was called to the office during fourth period. Mom called the school to speak to me directly so she didn't get me in trouble on my cell.

"Rachel, fantastic news. Assuming everything continues on the trend it's going, the hospital is going to release Joanie tomorrow, straight to a rehab center. Your dad and I have been discussing all the options and talking with her doctors. We've made a decision, but we'd like to talk it over with you. Do you have anything that you can't miss the rest of the afternoon? I wouldn't take you out of school, but we're fairly pressed for time, and this is a big decision."

The alarm that had dissipated during the ride to school with Kyp surfaced fresh, clawing its nasty talons into my gut. Why did they need to discuss things further with me? What happened to Joanie?

"No, of course. I can come. Oh, but I rode to school with a friend today. Sorry, can someone come pick me up?"

"Yes, we'll be by in a few minutes. We're out getting a drive-thru lunch and on our way home." She trailed off and I felt there was something more she would have added to that sentence if I had all the pieces of the puzzle.

"Sure, Mom. I'll wait in the office. Grab me a burger and a chocolate shake?"

"You bet. We'll see you in a few. I love you."

"Love you, too, Mom."

I passed the phone back to Ms. Nelson, the sweet secretary who had been at the school longer than anyone could remember. She hadn't aged a day since 1985, and neither had her wardrobe. Her colorful plaid skirt swished softly as it brushed against the bottom of her desk.

I took a seat in one of the beige vinyl-covered chairs and pulled out my phone. I shot a quick text to Kyp, and one to Megan, letting them know what was going on. After that, I just sat and waited. I bounced my foot. I jiggled my leg. I nibbled three fingernails.

Mom finally waltzed into the office in yesterday's clothes and with the barest minimum of makeup that I'd ever seen on her in public. She smiled weakly at Ms. Nelson and signed me out.

"I got you that chocolate shake," she said, her voice wobbly, as she gave me a big side hug on the way out the door.

"Great!" I forced fake enthusiasm into my voice.

****

Once we were home, Mom, Dad, and I sat down at the table. Clary had stayed at the hospital with Joanie. I sipped the chocolate shake that turned to gelatinous sludge in my mouth and stuck in my throat.

"When are they releasing Joanie?" I asked, unable to wait longer.

Dad cleared his throat. "We wanted to talk to you specifically, Rachel, because this will impact you the most," he said directly. I clenched my fist under the table. "We've checked a dozen programs and have made calls and talked to all the doctors and checked out the success rates, and we've found one that I think is going to be Joanie's best shot at beating this."

My heart felt heavy in my chest. Why would this need so much discussion involving me?

"Then, of course, she should do it. What's the catch?"

Dad's brow knit. "It's a completely family-involved program. Your mother and I would go with Joanie to the rehab center. Success rates are four times higher when both parents are heavily involved in the rehab program with the…addict." He stumbled on the word.

"That's great that the success rates are that much higher. Would you take your work with you and do it during the day there?" Dad's work could all be done remotely. Mom had been a housewife for years. There was no reason they couldn't both be involved in Joanie's recovery. No reason they shouldn't both be involved if it could boost her recovery that much.

Mom and Dad shared a glance that made an unhappy fluttering start in my stomach.

"Yes. I would work from there. The problem is that the program is in Colorado. Your mom and I would be gone for at least two weeks." He said it gently, concern stamped on his face. My eyebrows lifted.

"That's not so very long." I hoped my voice didn't sound as hollow as I felt. "And if you guys moving to Colorado for a few weeks is what it takes for her to get better, then that's what you have to do. I'll be fine here." I tried to sound reassuring. I wasn't afraid of them going to be with Joanie for a few weeks. I was afraid of being here alone with Victor Atwood and his posse at large. I doubted my parents had even seen the news about the murder this week or about Shelby being found. I wasn't about to mention it as a deterrent. I wanted Joanie to heal with my whole heart. If this was her best shot, we had to take it. As a family.

"When we realized this was a serious possibility, we called George Carmichael," Mom continued. Megan's grandpa still lived alone in Rock Falls in the house where Megan grew up. "He said he would love to have you while we're gone. If this is okay with you," Mom added with finality. "If you're uncomfortable with this, one of us will stay here with you. We can't go off to save one daughter and neglect the other." Tears stood in Mom's eyes, and I could see how hard this decision was for her, especially right now with emotions high and sleep low. Quickly I got up and wrapped them both in a hug.

"You have to go and do this for Joanie. Don't worry about me at all."

"My brave, brave girl," Dad whispered as he

stroked my hair.

****

That night was a flutter of activity. George Carmichael was delighted at the prospect of my staying with him. Mom and Dad were packing everything they'd need for themselves, plus everything they thought Joanie might need or want, along with things like old photographs they thought might be helpful in her recovery process. I wrote out a long letter to Joanie, telling her how much I loved her and some of my favorite memories of the two of us together. I didn't know what else to say, but I wanted her to know how much she meant to me, even if I didn't have all the right words.

****

Megan called me later that night to check in. I'd texted her the minimum details earlier.

"Rachel. I'm so sorry I'm only now calling you back. Dominic called Austin Thornehill, the Alpha of the Thornehill pack from upstate New York. They're going to start moving into the area in the next few days. The rest of us have been working on fighting skills and different maneuvers. Anyway, I feel like a crappy friend that I couldn't respond to your text when you sent it. Sorry. But I'm here now. Tell me everything."

I sighed. My body felt heavy. "Mom and Dad are leaving first thing in the morning, like at four thirty, to go out to the facility. Clary is flying out tomorrow morning. She's got a friend dropping her at the airport so I can get to school on time since Mom and Dad will be gone by then. I was doing some research on the rehab process. It sounds solid. I can totally see Joanie thriving in that sort of environment once she's got the junk out of her system enough to focus on anything." I groaned. "Megan, this *has* to work. I can't even think about the possibility that it won't."

"Rach, we're not even *considering* the possibility that it won't. Joanie is going to beat this. We're going to help her every step of the way when it's in our power to do so. And I'm here for you. You're getting the crap end of things, too. It's okay to be mad about it."

My eyes slid shut. It felt so good to have that validation come from someone else. A tiny part of me *was* angry that my parents were leaving me to be with Joanie for weeks, even though the largest part of me *wanted* them to go and for Joanie to get well.

"Thanks for saying so. I'm not really ready to be mad yet. I'm still too exhausted from it all. I'm sure I will be angry later, though. When everyone is gone. Speaking of, what are your thoughts on all this—and about my coming to live with Grandpa for a while?"

"I haven't actually called him yet. I know he'd love to have you. I called you back first. You know you're always welcome to stay here. The cabin addition will be done in about two more days, and there's plenty of space. There's even a second bathroom now." I could hear the smile in her words over the phone line.

"Thanks. The second bathroom is definitely enticing. I may stay out there a few nights, depending on how things shake out."

"For sure. There are extra patrols that run in Grandpa's vicinity, too. We don't know how much Victor knows about our pack, and who we love. Me, especially, since I was a target for at least part of this. So, Grandpa's house is well protected. I wanted you to know. If you feel safer here, in the middle of the pack, I totally get that, too. Plus, I'd love to have some good, quality girl time. We haven't had much of that since HarvestFest."

My belly churned, thinking of the one night I'd spent at the cabin and seeing Meg and Sam in the same bed. How awkward and out of place I'd felt.

"I'm glad Grandpa has extra protection. I'm sure I'll be fine there—although I'm all up for some girl time." I tried to keep my voice light.

"You name the time and place."

"Sounds good. I should probably go help finish up the packing. I need to give this letter I wrote to Joanie to my parents, too."

"See you tomorrow, Rach."

"Night, Meg."

****

I was awake before dawn to kiss my parents goodbye. Clary took them to the airport and to go say goodbye to Joanie while I got ready for school. I'd said my goodbyes to Joanie yesterday evening after the decision had been made for the Colorado rehab. Joanie was a mess. But she was breathing, and mostly coherent. I nursed a cup of coffee and watched the sun rise.

A clanging noise made me jerk.

"Stupid raccoons," I muttered, assuming they'd knocked over the trashcans again. A louder clanging sounded like the metal cans had been flung over. The mental image of all the trash I'd have to pick up sped through my overtired brain and it triggered a sudden flash of rage. Without another thought, I stalked to the front door and threw it open, intending to give the scavenging vermin a piece of my mind.

What happened instead was that Honeydew, wretched little fur ball, shot out into the yard, and started barking loud enough to raise the dead, trying to scare off the raccoons from her territory.

"Honeydew!" I shouted, grumbling to myself when the stupid animal charged across the yard and into the fringes of the woods that bordered our property.

"Honeydew!" I screeched again, thinking how Clary would kill me if I managed to lose her precious dog hours before she was flying back to Seattle. I darted straight across the yard after her, not even shutting the door properly behind me.

"*Honeydew!*" I hollered. "Who names their dog *Honeydew* anyway?" I muttered contemptibly as I tromped through the brush. I could see Honeydew's little tufts of brown and white fur jumping up and down farther into the woods, near the gravel road that led out the back way to the highway. I growled in frustration, realizing that if she hit the gravel road, she'd have a much easier time running away from me than having to hop over dead brush and limbs taller than her in the forest. Increasing my efforts, I leaped over a few fallen trees and was about at the road when Honeydew suddenly stopped barking. My heart kicked up another notch and I ran as fast as I could, afraid something might have happened to her.

Just as I reached the gravel road, there sat Honeydew, happily munching away at something on the ground.

"You little devil," I started, but was abruptly cut off when something dark was flung over my head and rough hands grabbed me from behind.

I screamed and thrashed, adrenaline pounding

through my head and spangling bright spots inside the bag over my head.

"Shut up."

"I've got her. Let's get her to Lenny and get out of the cold. I'm done waiting for her after sitting out here all week."

My blood froze and I gouged my heels into the ground, making it as difficult as possible for the two men who had me gripped tightly between them. It had to be Tall One and Short One. How could I have ever been naïve enough to assume Lenny wouldn't come after me after what I'd done to him?

Swirls of light flashed across my eyes as panic seized my chest. My breath was coming too tight, too shallow. My stomach dropped and I knew I was going to faint. The last thing I heard was the screech of a van door before the blackness swallowed me.

Chapter 10

Kyp

Rolling out of bed, I stretched. I pushed away the mental image of Shelby, lying in a pool of her own blood, slashes covering her torso, leaves and muck covering most of the rest of her, her eyes pale and staring up at me, blinking once and nearly scaring me out of my skin. Wolf growled inside me as I shook my head, trying again to clear the image.

A hot shower took away some of the chill that clung to me and a toasted bagel and sausage patty along with the note Mom left telling me to have a good day cheered me. As did the thought of seeing Rachel soon. Mom's interest in Jonathan made me wonder if something could be possible between Rachel and me? She didn't seem to mind my mixed blood at all. That was more than I could say for any other girl I'd ever thought about. Maybe I should pay more attention to the twinges and flutters I got when I was near her.

Swallowing down a glass of orange juice, I headed back to my room and grabbed my phone off the nightstand, unplugging it and pulling up the home screen.

Two percent battery.

I frowned and looked back at the cord, shaking my head in disgust when I realized the plug had been knocked loose from the wall and hadn't charged my phone at all overnight. There wasn't anything I could do about it now. I didn't have a car charger. I jerked the plug out and wound the cord up, hoping I could manage to charge it sometime between now and when school started. Sam and Dominic had no other way to contact me. I silently cursed my inability to connect properly with a pack—not that it would have mattered anyway, Wolf reminded me, since I wasn't officially a pack member yet. But I would be. The date was set for next Wednesday night. The most important day of my life to date. I got giddy just thinking about it. This was what I'd wanted my whole life. A place to belong. A pack to come alongside. People who didn't care about my hybrid genes. Sometimes I felt like I needed to pinch myself to make sure it wasn't all a dream.

I pulled up in Rachel's driveway, my truck idling as Wolf came fully alert, and the hair on the back of my neck prickled and a tremor rocked my arms.

Something was not right here.

Rachel's door wasn't shut. Honeydew sat happily on the porch, chewing something resembling a stick of jerky. I glanced around. Rachel's house wasn't as secluded as mine, but there were no visible neighbors. Her long drive led out to a gravel road before it hit the main street. Trees and underbrush surrounded the manicured lawn on every other side. It was too still.

I got out of the truck, all senses on high alert, listening for anything that would tell me what was going on. I picked up nothing but the chatter of birds and the whistle of the cold wind through the treetops. Bounding up the steps, I scooped up the dog and poked my head inside the door.

"Rachel?"

No answer. I already knew she was gone. I put the dog down and shut the door firmly behind me so she wouldn't get out again. I needed Wolf. Checking my surroundings again, I heard and saw nothing out of the ordinary. Just the stillness.

Within ten seconds, I'd stripped and shifted to my wolf. I scooped up my clothes and shoes in my mouth and put my nose to the ground. My heart pounded when Wolf quickly picked up Rachel's scent mixed with the smells of two others. The others were slightly familiar, and tumultuous churning in my gut warned me I was too late.

Wolf ate up the trail, which ended at a gravel road. I traced the road, back and forth. It must not be used overmuch. I ran my nose over the surface several more times before silently blessing old automobiles in general as I realized the only fresh vehicle smell would be easy to trace. It had an oil leak. Oil that needed to be changed. Badly. It was distinct, timeworn, and corroded. I'd be able to follow it, even if other vehicles had traveled the same road recently.

With an urgency I felt down to my bones, I ran.

Chapter 11

Rachel

Throbbing. Aching. Pain. All over. My head. Excruciating. I tried to lick my dry lips and cracked my crusted eyes open. The weak light sent a lancing pain shooting behind my eyes, so I clenched them closed again and then regretted shutting them so fiercely as it sent another wave of agony rolling over my scalp. I must have bashed my head against something hard when I passed out.

Squinting, I was able to glance around. I was in a tiny dilapidated stone building. Only a few feet by a few feet, old and ready to cave in with a stiff breeze. The breeze did gust then, and I shivered. Something clinked. With a horror that brought bile to the back of my throat, I realized that I was *manacled* to the wall. Bands of metal encased my wrists with heavy chains that went to screws the size of my fist, firmly embedded in the rock wall that suddenly looked far sturdier than it had at first glance.

My breath was coming too quick and too shallow. Spots danced in front of my face and I knew if I didn't get a grip, I was going to lose it all over again. I couldn't afford to have another fainting spell. No matter how warranted it was. I took a big breath through my nose and pushed all the air out slowly and measured through my mouth. I did it again. I'm not sure how many times I repeated merely breathing while clinging to consciousness.

When I stopped, my knees were shaking, and my fingers were nearly numb with cold. I was wearing a shirt and a hoodie with jeans, but it wasn't enough to keep out the November chill.

Lenny. What was Lenny going to do to me when he came? My knees knocked harder together and I forced myself to stay upright. My mind fled to a dozen horrific things that he could do to me. Panic clawed the back of my throat and I fought for control of my breathing again.

I could tell the sun was mostly overhead by the way the light came through a few holes in the adjacent wall, so I knew I had to have been wherever it was for an hour or more, assuming my judging of the sun's position was correct. I tried to calculate how far they might have taken me from my house and how far away it might be for them to retrieve Lenny and bring him back here so he could inflict his torture.

A whimper escaped and I sucked in my bottom lip, trying to contain the noise.

Get a grip, get a grip, I chanted to myself.

Something clattered at the entrance to the shed. My body froze as a board scraped against the threshold. I willed myself not to cry, to face my future with quiet dignity and as few hysterics as I could manage.

The door creaked on its hinges, driving my blood pressure up to dangerous new heights. Light flared at the corners of my vision. My teeth clenched as I squared my jaw and I faced the door as my heart careened inside my chest, banging my ribs and making my breath painfully stuttered.

A shadow filled the doorway, its owner still hidden from me. A step. Another. A dark head, warm brown eyes.

"Kyp!" I nearly shouted and then sagged in relief. The chains holding my wrists clanked together, echoing in the empty space.

"Rachel?" Kyp's eyes nearly popped out of his skull. "What happened?"

He was across the space in three steps, grabbing the chains that held the handcuffs to the stones, examining them for weakness as I did my best to hold tight to my vow of no hysterics.

"Kidnapped," I managed before I had to gulp back a sob. "Two guys, and maybe a girl driving, they grabbed me. Lenny. Party." I gulped, unable to form anything more coherent.

"Are you hurt?" His eyes raked over me quickly, head to toe, searching for obvious signs of injury.

I shook my head, my red curls wilder than usual. "No, but I don't know when they're coming back, and I don't know what they're going to do with me. They left to go get Lenny. Please, help me!"

"Of course, I'll help you," he retorted as he checked the handcuffs on my wrists. He messed with them for a minute more with no success. Nothing was budging.

"I need to go get help, Rachel. I can't get you out of these by myself, and my phone is dead."

My heart pounded in my chest like a stampede of elephants. Black dots swam before my eyes and I felt dizzy. "Please! Don't leave me, Kyp. I don't know when they're coming back, but if they get here before you do, that's the end of me."

His fists clenched at his sides, his fingers flexing in and out, his eyes shifting from my wrists to my hands to the chains on the wall.

My wrists! A sudden thought struck me with enough force to drive the air from my lungs.

"Kyp, you have to bite me."

"What?" He shook his head, clearly not seeing where I was going with this.

"If you change me into a werewolf, when the first shift comes, my bones will lengthen before they thicken again—they'll be skinny enough to slip the hand cuffs." *Just like Megan's shifts*, I thought to myself.

The color bled from his face. "Tell me you're not serious."

"Do you have a better solution?"

"I could go get help."

"And if you take too long? Then what? I don't even know how long I've been here."

He huffed a breath and ran both hands down his face, seeming to age fifty years in the one gesture.

"Rachel, do you even know what you're asking?"

I nodded, knowing I didn't have all the facts but assuming I had enough.

He looked me hard in the eye. "I don't even know if I *can* change you," he said quietly.

I refused to believe that. He was my last hope. Becoming a werewolf was my last hope, and not something I'd consider a burden after, though that was hardly my reasoning at that moment.

"You're plenty wolf enough to shift at will. That's good enough for me," I begged.

"Just say this works. This is a lifetime thing."

"I'm well aware of that." We were wasting time, bartering like this. My heart clacked painfully against my ribs.

"You realize this could cause a mate bond. That you will be stuck with me—possibly for life."

"Yes. And I do realize that I'm being totally selfish," I conceded, but at that moment, survival was top on my list.

"I'm less concerned about that right now," Kyp countered, his eyes intense. I could see the wheels turning in his mind, examining this from twenty different angles.

"Please, Kyp," I whispered.

"I'm the Omega. Not even legally that yet. I'm still Rogue. You'd be in the same position if I'm even able to change you. You could be stuck for life like this— with me. Are you sure you don't want me to go get help and try to find another way out of this?"

I didn't care if I had to follow him into the depths of a volcano at the moment. I'd happily follow him into the lion's den if it meant I escaped whatever torture and possible death awaited me at the hands of my captors.

"Alexander Kypson, you may be my last chance of getting out of here alive. I don't care if I'm shackled to you for life. I'd much rather be with you than dead or worse with one of them."

His eyes regarded me with the gravity of the Grim Reaper. He gave a curt nod and took his jacket off before yanking his shirt over his head.

"Um, what are you doing?" I stammered as relief and trepidation danced down my spine.

"If I'm going to bite you and possibly screw up both our lives irrevocably, I'm going to give you the best shot at becoming a wolf as I can. That means I have to be wolf myself. Clothes don't shift with us, as I'm sure you're aware."

I tried not to stare at his abs. At least if I did die in the near future, I'd have a pleasant last view. He was ripped. He wasn't a big guy, but his muscles were definitely toned and well used. And scarred. I was jarred out of my mental wandering as his fingers undid the button on his jeans. My face flamed.

"It's cold out there. You won't be able to control your shifts, and if your clothes don't make it, you'll need something warmer than your skin. I can wear fur if I have to," he said in reaction to my cherry-red face. I hadn't factored in the nakedness. Not that it was going to change my mind at this point.

When he stood before me in nothing but his boxers—thank goodness he left those on—he quickly removed my shoes and socks and then moved to my sweatshirt. I was already shivering with cold and anxiety.

"You sure about this?" His face was mere inches from mine. I nodded once and then swallowed hard as I felt his fingers on my bare skin as he slid my shirt and sweatshirt up over my head and down to the manacles on my wrists.

"If we can get your paws out, assuming you do change, before they rip the seams, you'll be able to wear these again. It's not going to hurt anything to have a spare set of clothes," he explained unnecessarily.

I shivered again, standing there with my sweatshirt and all bunched down around my wrists and the wretched manacles, freezing in my neon purple demi-cup.

"Purple is an excellent color on you," Kyp said nervously as he took a big breath and heat flooded his face.

A hysterical giggle wiggled its way out of my throat. "Shut up," I quipped.

He paused a second, staring at the button on my jeans.

"Just do it," I said through gritted teeth.

"This is not how I imagined getting a girl naked for the first time."

I felt the flush from my face stain my neck and shoulders. It was ridiculous that I could be this terrified, embarrassed, and self-conscious at once. His fingers were trembling as he undid the button and zipper on my jeans. I clenched my eyes shut as he tugged my pants down over my hips and slithered them off altogether.

My face burned even hotter when I glanced down and remembered that I was wearing my hot pink underwear that had *cheeky* stamped across the butt.

Kyp actually laughed out loud as his eyes skimmed my near-nakedness and read my rear end.

I glared at him.

He sobered. "You're absolutely sure you want to go through with this? If this works—and I really don't know that it will—this is it. Forever."

I tried to swallow past the giant boulder of fear lodged in my throat. I nodded. What other choice did I have?

"You've seen a shift up close before, right?" He gauged my preparedness for what was coming.

"Yes," I whispered. My nerves were ratcheted higher than they'd ever been.

"All right." He blew a long breath out his mouth.

"If this works, I'll try to yank the cuffs off your hands as your bones narrow. I'll try to get your sleeves off, too. We'll probably only have about three seconds to do it. If you can, jerk your arms backward. I'm going to bite you, then shift back so I have my hands. I have no idea if it will be quick, or if it will even happen at all." He chuffed another breath out and shook his hands out to the sides like he was flicking water off them. "If you shift, it's going to hurt. Like ten-times worse than the worst pain you've ever felt." His eyes softened and he took my hands in his. "Try not to scream. I…I'm sorry." He gulped. "You ready?"

I took a deep breath. "Ready. And, Kyp? *Thank you*," I whispered.

He nodded. "Here we go."

In horrified fascination, I shivered as Kyp's face contorted and changed shape. His shoulders rolled back into his spine. His face grew a muzzle and a snout. Ears sprouted and his hair lengthened to become fur. Another few seconds and a huge black wolf with red-tinged tips and soft brown eyes stood before me. It took my breath away.

He hunched his back legs, springing up so his front paws were braced on either side of my head. He ran his nose up the side of my neck, scenting me. Even in the middle of our current circumstances, the gesture was oddly intimate.

A rough tongue scraped across the curve of my neck, right where it joined with my collarbone. Kyp whined softly.

I squeezed my eyes shut and leaned my head away, shaking my curls out of the way. I took a deep breath as my heart raced.

"All right." The words strangled themselves from my throat. "Do it."

A warm breath whispered against my neck and then the hard sharp points of his teeth. He hesitated, his teeth resting against the bare skin of my neck. He inhaled and then four sharp stabs gouged into my flesh. I mashed my lips together, refusing to cry out. He held my flesh in his mouth for several seconds before running his tongue over the bite, then released me and shifted back to his skin.

It dawned on me that he was totally naked, and I practically was, too, but before I could be embarrassed, my vision swam and pin pricks started in my feet and worked their way up my legs, becoming nails and then daggers punching great holes into my legs, my hips, my belly, my chest, my arms. I swayed as fur poked through my skin like tiny shards of ice.

"Oh, crap. Oh, *crap*, it worked!" someone said near my head. "Don't fight the pain. Try not to scream. I'm right here. I'll get you out."

I bit down as hard as I could to keep from letting loose the guttural, primal noises of pain that rose in my throat. My shoulders heaved and my stomach lurched, spewing blood all over the wall just the other side of the figure in front of me. I wasn't sure what was real through the consuming flames of pain that licked at my body. I heard snapping, felt twisting, pulling, jarring, my body jerked, spasming as I was yanked. My head hit the wall but before I could sink down its rough expanse, my body curled in on itself, hands extending, feet morphing, pain coloring everything. Teeth cut through my mouth, filling my throat with blood and fear.

I couldn't hold back the agony building in my chest

and a foreign noise, something like keening and barking mixed together, came out into the quiet space. Pinwheels of light spangled at the corners of my vision. Then, mercifully, everything went black.

Chapter 12

Kyp

A string of words my mom would have washed my mouth out with soap for saying cycled through my brain. It worked. I had enough toxins to not only change Rachel, but to change her *instantly*.

As soon as I had my skin back on, my gaze flew to her face, and I watched her eyes cross and nearly roll back into her head. This was it. I had seconds to get her free of the cuffs.

Her shoulders heaved and her body shook. Tiny hairs poked through her skin and coated her in light auburn and silver fur. Her bones snapped and I knew that was my cue. The handcuffs were already in my hands, ready if the shift happened. I watched as first her elbows twisted, then her forearms, then finally, her wrists and hands changed shape. The second her hands started to thin I yanked the cuffs. They stuck farther up her hands, caught on her thumbs. I pulled harder, afraid I'd somehow pop a bone out of place that wouldn't go back properly as she continued deeper into her first shift.

Her whimpers filled the space and as her thumbs shrunk back into what was becoming her foreleg, I whipped the cuffs off, taking part of her fingernail on her right hand with it. She was free! We did it!

Quicker than I thought my trembling, fumbling fingers could go, I tried to get her sweatshirt off her, so she'd have something warmer than skin to venture outside in, but she collapsed.

This was not good.

Passing out during first shift should not happen. I grappled the sweatshirt off, the seams of the cuffs ripping as I forced it over her hands that were now large paws. Her body was limp and burning up. She had her wolf's legs and paws and her body was covered in beautiful silky fur, but her face was still more human than wolf, and her features weren't changing, only staying in a horrifying arrested state between wolf and girl.

"Rachel? Rachel, can you hear me?" My heart was racing, and fear caked the back of my mouth.

What had I done?

Were my toxins somehow corrupted with my human DNA? Was I killing her? Wolf jarred himself inside me, whining, furious, and scared at his inability to help Rachel, the one girl who had always been kind to me—the girl I suddenly realized meant much more to me than I'd thought.

Her body just laid there, feverish and limp in my arms as I cradled her against my chest. She felt too hot, even through her wolf's fur.

"Rachel! Rachel, you need to finish your shift," I said helplessly. Her breathing was labored and painfully raspy. My heart shriveled. I'd killed her. She wasn't going to survive this. Wolf rammed my chest from the inside. He snapped at me, and for a second, I kept my skin, but gave him my head. The grief over what I'd done was overpowering, and I surrendered to the wolf's instinct.

The second I relinquished my human side, Wolf rose within me, asserting his dominance. Without a conscious thought to do so, I spoke the first command I'd ever given.

"Rachel, you will finish shifting *now*." Icy waves of power crashed over my naked body, chilling me more than the frigid breeze that blew through the cracks in the shed. Wolf shook himself out, chest puffing in an uncharacteristic display of power that charged through my whole body, expanding and growing it, then settling. A surge of protectiveness for Rachel filled my chest, and I knew something dynamic had changed inside me.

Rachel whimpered in my arms, her head lolling back. Her eyes opened, unfocused, and then stared straight into mine. Her face contorted in pain as her mouth opened. With her jaw lengthening and her snout coming fully out from her face, her eyes rolled back into her head once more as her shriek pierced my ears. I grunted as her paws tried to wrap around my neck like arms might have, but her claws ripped three lines over my chest instead.

A violent tremor rocked her whole body as her shift finally finished.

We were both sweating and panting when she was through, but I was the only one still conscious. My brain refused to process what I had done, what had happened before my eyes. Not only had I bitten Rachel and changed her, I had commanded her. *And it worked.*

And I'd just screwed any chance I'd had at being accepted into the Wolfe pack.

With no time to dwell on these things, I gently laid

the beautiful auburn and silver wolf on the ground and got dressed as quickly as humanly possible. I gathered every spare shred of underclothes from the ground and wrapped the scraps up in Rachel's sweatshirt and jeans along with her boots and socks. I tied the sleeves together and made a pouch that I could sling over my shoulder. Taking one more glance around and satisfied that there was nothing left that I could do—Rachel's blood on the wall would have to stay, I ever so carefully scooped Rachel back into my arms.

I grunted again. Rachel was an attractively proportioned girl, shorter than I was and with just enough meat on her to make her deliciously curvy as I'd witnessed up close ten minutes ago. But her wolf couldn't have weighed less than two-hundred and fifty pounds. And right now, she was dead weight. I grimaced at the thought.

At the door, I listened. I sniffed. I could smell sweat, wolf, mold, dirt, and what I knew was my own scent—something vaguely reminiscent of cedar wood and juniper. I hoped my human DNA would cover the scent enough to simply be confusing, not identifying, should any other werewolf happen by. Not hearing anything, I stepped outside the shed into the cold. The temperature was dropping as the sun started to hide in the shadows of thick grey clouds. I sniffed again and nearly sneezed as a snowflake landed on my nose. Glancing up I saw tiny flakes swirling in their perfection, coming down to stick on the blades of grass.

****

By the time I got us back to Rachel's house, the snow was coming down in earnest. Honeydew was gone, but fortunately, the front door was still unlocked.

I assumed Clary had come and gone. Nudging the door open with the toe of my shoe, I breathed a sigh of relief as the heat hit me. I was sweating, carrying Rachel the nearly three miles back from the shed, but I was sure the heat would be better for Rachel than the plummeting temperatures outside.

I flipped the lock behind me, alert for any signs of predators waiting in the house. Sensing none, a breath gusted through my lips. I ignored the trickle of sweat making its way down my chest as it burned against the fresh cuts starting to dry stiff against my shirt. Rachel still hadn't opened her eyes, but her breathing wasn't labored, and she was nestled up against my chest. Wolf puffed himself out, sending a heavy feeling of protectiveness through me again. *Mine.*

Moving quickly into the living room, I laid Rachel's giant wolf carefully onto the couch, unable to resist letting my hand stroke softly over the silky red-brown fur of her ears. The protective surge I'd felt in the shed, and just now as I came through the door, flooded me again and nearly robbed me of breath as I stood there, gazing down at her, my hand stilled on her head.

I'd die for her, without thought. Wolf shivered, stretched, then paced within me. We had never felt this way about anyone. Not even Mom, and I knew I'd die without question to keep her safe, too. This was different. Wolf was careening around, almost frantically wiggling, like he was trying to get out of his own skin. I was jumpy and unsettled because of it. I closed my eyes and took a deep inhale through my nose and tried to calm down. It was like my wolf hit puberty all over again. Stretching, growing, maturing, gangly and uncoordinated, and feeling things that confused both of us.

The chair scraped over the wood floor as I brought it over beside the couch. I needed help. I didn't know what to do for Rachel. She just laid there, seeming to sleep peacefully, but I didn't know what might be going on inside her. Anxiety and guilt gnawed at my belly. Rachel made a soft snuffling sound and my heart hammered in my chest. I needed to find Rachel's phone. Or get mine and plug it in.

Wolf nudged me. His chest puffed out. *We are in charge. Command her to change.* The thought rattled around inside my head. It was both thrilling and terrifying to consider. Wolf nudged me harder.

"Rachel, you need to wake up. Now." The words were soft, escaping my mouth before I could pull them back. Tingling, cold, dominant power swept up my back and spread over my shoulders, leaving me disoriented and a little buzzed with the rush of it. A command.

Rachel's wolf groggily raised her head and yawned. She blinked at me a few times as my mouth dried to a husk.

"Rachel?" I whispered.

Her eyes focused and she cocked her head, blinked again, and then glanced at her paws still stretched out on the couch.

She yipped and her tail beat happily against the couch. She raised up on her front paws, looking eager to explore, not at all afraid. She tried to stand but promptly fell over the edge of the couch and landed in a tangle of legs and paws. Her tongue lolled out of her mouth as she tried to jump up again. She slathered a wet, rough kiss across my cheek as her huge paws landed on my shoulders, knocking me back into the chair, and then sending us both careening to the floor—the chair, me, and Rachel's giant wolf on top.

A laugh escaped despite my anxiety at the sheer puppy-like exuberance Rachel showed. Relief was hot on its heels as she danced away, awkwardly stumbling and ambling along the carpeted floor of her living room. Her head swung wildly from side to side, her nose rooting in the air as she took in all the new information that I knew had to be overloading her brain. She didn't seem to mind. She looked...exhilarated. Like she'd found some long-lost part of herself.

She jumped and pranced and stumbled for another minute while I watched on in utter awe. I absently rubbed the back of my head where it had cracked against the floor when Rachel knocked us over. Wolf nudged me. Dread spiraled down to my belly. Now what?

Chapter 13

Rachel

This was it. I was a wolf. A *werewolf*. I loved it. I loved every hair on my wolf's body, every sinew that stretched, every new muscle that bunched, ready for me to spring into action. To defend, protect, to belong. Megan had talked about being of two minds and not agreeing with her wolf, but I was experiencing none of that. Joy flooded my four legs and my four paws and beat steadily with every pump of my wolf's heart. We were of one mind. We needed no time to meld together. We were good. And we were safe. Kyp saved us. My wolf stretched her head toward him, relishing the way his brown eyes watched us with wonder.

I didn't want to shift back to my skin, but I didn't know how to talk to Kyp as a wolf. How to show him the gratitude that poured out of me. I realized the depth of what Kyp had done for me. He'd given me my life back. Literally. Lenny would have destroyed me. If he hadn't killed me outright, he would have killed off parts of me that I could never get back. Tears welled up and Wolf knew we needed to shift back to let them fall, to have that part of the trauma out of our system.

We were ready. *We'll shift back to fur soon. I love being in fur*, I told her. She bobbed her head even as the tears gathered at the corners of my large wolf eyes.

Seeming to understand my thoughts, Kyp grabbed the throw blanket from the back of the couch.

"Are you trying to shift back?" His voice was full of uncertainty and not a small degree of amazement. I bobbed my head.

I clenched my eyes shut and Wolf obediently returned full charge to me and I felt my fur recede. It hurt more than I expected, and the sound of crying grew deafening in my ears as my bones cracked and shrank back to their human form. My paws extended, joints separating, and claws seemed to cut me inside as they retracted, pushing my fingers out in their place. My chest heaved while my back arched as my tail slid its way back into my spine, curving and straightening in a way that nearly shattered my mind as spangles of pain danced across my eyes.

Suddenly I was sitting, whimpering, tears streaking my face, my hands clutching the navy afghan against my chest. Kyp was crouched in front of me, his concerned eyes glued to my face, his hand warming my shoulder where he touched it.

"Breathe, Rachel. That's it. Breathe in. Breathe out."

My breaths were short gasps, but it wasn't long before I was able to draw breath again normally. As soon as the metaphorical dust settled, my eyes swung to Kyp. His were the size of half dollars, his mouth slightly agape.

It didn't matter that I was clad in nothing but a blanket. I clenched it tighter around me with one hand and threw myself at Kyp, hugging him with all the strength I had.

He gasped in pain and I jerked back, confused.

Fresh blood seeped through his shirt.

"Kyp! You're hurt!" I exclaimed.

"Just a few scratches. They don't need stitches but should probably be cleaned soon."

"How do I ever thank you?" I whispered.

His eyes were touched with sadness as he smiled.

"You're safe. That's what matters."

Heat pooled in my belly as I felt my wolf nudge her head against me. We were forever in his debt. I'd never been more grateful to anyone for anything in my life. My hand gripped the blanket draped around me as my eyes skimmed the trickles of blood soaking into Kyp's shirt.

"I'll go grab the first aid kit." I jumped up, careful that the afghan stayed close to all my pertinent naked parts and rushed to my room. I threw on the first clothes I found—a drama club t-shirt and an old, worn pair of jeans. Skidding into the bathroom, Wolf raised her head and sniffed as I opened the bathroom mirror for the first aid kit stowed inside. She sniffed again and nodded her approval, though we wrinkled our nose as the smell of antiseptic hit. I blinked, unable to stop the smile that spread across my face as I realized Wolf was already actively present. My sense of smell was ten times what it had been that morning.

Kyp was huddled in the chair I'd knocked over a few minutes before.

"Woah. Kyp, what's wrong?" I tentatively reached out to touch his shoulder. His face had a sheen of sweat on it and his skin was one shade above grey.

"Not sure," he muttered. He took a steadying breath and shook his head like he was clearing away internal cobwebs. "I think I'm fine now. My wolf is acting kind of erratic." He dashed an arm over his forehead, taking the sweat with it.

"Here, let's take a peek at your chest." I put the box down on the floor and knelt next to Kyp's chair. I felt heat rise in my cheeks. "Um, you want to undo the buttons?"

Kyp snorted, realizing my embarrassment. To my relief, some color started coming back into his cheeks. He grinned good-naturedly and quickly undid the buttons on his flannel shirt.

"You don't have to do this. I've had plenty of experience patching myself up," he said as he slowly shrugged his arms through the sleeves.

I started as I stared at the three gashes across his chest and found myself biting my lip as I took in all the blood smeared from his shoulders to his navel. Wolf shuddered and whined in remorse. Momentarily distracted from Kyp's chest, I sought her in my mind. She sent me a clear image of her giant paws and I made the connection.

"Kyp," I gasped in horrified understanding. "Did I do this?"

He shrugged, slightly uncomfortable. "It's not like you meant to."

"I'm so sorry."

"It's fine," he said quietly, meeting my eyes. He glanced back down at his chest. "We need to call Sam and Dominic."

Wolf and I thrummed with excitement, thinking about seeing Megan and meeting the wolf part of her with my own wolf. The excitement took over and I suddenly felt twitching and knew I wasn't going to be able to hold back the shift. Honestly, I didn't want to. I wanted to exult in my new shape, take in all the new sensory information. Terror flashed across Kyp's face as he realized what was happening. I tried to reassure him that I was fine, we were fine, but my mouth elongated, and my canines poked through my gums before I could speak.

I squeezed my eyes shut as the pain ratcheted up my legs and I heard ripping and realized my clothes were fluttering to the floor. A groan escaped my throat as I felt my neck twisting and my spine realigning as my tail came out and my paws finished pushing themselves out.

Panting but euphoric, I was still a minute, shaking out my fur. I glanced up at Kyp and noted his face had lost the panicked expression, though he still seemed unsure of things. Trying to give him a wolfy grin, I rubbed my head against his knee to let him know I was absolutely fine. Wolf shook her head gloriously and I reveled in my wolf's skin.

"We need to get you to a dominant wolf," Kyp's voice held a note of worry.

****

An hour later we were sitting at Megan and Sam's cabin. Kyp had taken over and quickly swiped his chest with antiseptic and slapped some bandages over the gashes, borrowed one of my dad's old shirts, and stuffed me into his truck.

As soon as I had my fingers back, I texted Megan that it was an emergency and to meet us at the cabin. Kyp texted Sam, and I wasn't surprised to find that they'd beat us there, even though they'd had to sign themselves out of school before leaving.

"Rachel, what's wrong?" Megan exclaimed,

dashing down the steps as we pulled up, the tires crunching over the gravel. I closed the door of the truck slowly, suddenly nervous. What would Megan think? What would Sam think? I then realized I should be feeling much more traumatized after this morning's kidnapping. But all I could feel at that moment was relief, excitement at actually becoming a werewolf, and the unusual anxiety gnawing at me, looking at my best friend.

Megan rushed to me and threw her arms around me. On her next breath, she jerked back, her eyes like giant marshmallows around her hazel irises.

"Rachel? How…" Megan glanced at Kyp and my wolf lurched at the anguished expression on Kyp's face.

"Sam, I think we'd better talk," Kyp said quietly as Sam stood silently gaping between the two of us.

"Yeah. I think we'd better. Megan, are you okay with Rachel?" I didn't miss the underlying tension in his voice.

"Sure." Meg's eyes were still glued to my face, a hidden grin at the corner of her mouth. Sam nodded his head toward the cabin and Megan grabbed my hand and practically dragged me inside.

"Rachel?" She squealed as soon as the door was shut. "What happened? Why are you a wolf? I mean, I'm thrilled that you are, but…*wow*!" Her cheeks were high with color and she was practically frothing at the mouth in her excitement.

"Well, it certainly wasn't planned. It actually started with Lenny DiVen." Wolf champed her teeth at the thought of him and a ripple went over my skin, which Megan noticed sharply.

She immediately stilled. "Does your wolf need out

right now?"

"No, we're good. We're surprisingly of the same mind."

Meg gave a dry laugh, probably thinking how difficult her own transition with her wolf had been. "Sit down. I'll get tea started."

Chapter 14

Kyp

Sam didn't say a word as he trailed around to the back of the cabin and took a seat on one of the logs that ringed the sizeable fire pit. His shoulders hunched against the chill and he stuffed his hands into the pockets of his hoodie and glanced at me expectantly. I shifted uncomfortably on my feet. My heart was somewhere down around my ankles, and even Wolf was recoiling, aware that we had blown about ninety-nine percent of any chance we had at joining Sam's pack. The sudden wave of loneliness was overpowering.

But there was a glimmer that hadn't been there before. Rachel's face, smiling and shining brightly in my head, came to the front of my mind and I felt the glimmer grow stronger, and the loneliness receded. Still, I swallowed hard.

"Kyp. Rachel is now a werewolf. What happened?" Sam's voice held no judgement, only concerned curiosity. For that, I was thankful.

"It was never my intention to change her. The thought never even entered my mind." I gasped the words. My finger slid up and down my thumb as I sat down heavily a few feet away from Sam. "I didn't even think I could. My genes are so warped and..." I trailed off, still amazed that I'd had enough werewolf toxins to change her.

"Why? Why did you bite her?"

"You know I've been sticking close to Rachel—keeping an eye on her with Victor's pack roaming around. Especially after finding Shelby." I shuddered and forced the bloody image away. "I, I worry about her. Rachel's so involved in the pack, I was afraid they'd go after her, too, especially with her connections to Megan and you. Anyway, I was going to pick her up for school today, and she was gone." I paused. "I'll never forget that feeling of terror."

"It grabs you and doesn't let go."

I nodded at Sam's comment. He and Megan had faced their share of fear. He waited for me to continue.

"I followed her scent—Lenny sent some of his guys to kidnap her. I was able to follow an oil leak from their vehicle and found Rachel at an old stone outbuilding. They had her chained to the wall." My jaws clenched so hard my teeth ached. "Chained. To the wall." Wolf's hackles raised and I needed a deep breath to keep him from erupting right there by the fire pit. Sam growled deep in his chest, and I knew his wolf was answering mine in a mutual sharing of disgust for Lenny and his minions.

A bird flew up suddenly from some bushes several feet out and startled us both. I listened and sniffed while Sam did the same.

"Lot of traffic in the area today. Quite a few Thornehills are moving in today and over the weekend. The pack owns a few empty houses within the neighborhood they're going to use. It's got things busier than usual," Sam said.

I nodded again.

"What happened when you found her?"

A sigh gusted through my teeth, my blood boiling again at the memory of Rachel manacled to the wall. "There was no way I could get her out of the chains. They were big, heavy, nasty ones. I was going to go for help, though I wasn't sure what I could do. Neither of us had any idea of the time frame we had to work with and neither of us had our phones. Then she told me to bite her. She had to repeat herself. I had no idea where she was going with that." I gave a bitter laugh. "She was the one who had to explain to me—if she changed, then her bones would thin down enough to get the cuffs off." I shook my head. "I couldn't find any other option. I didn't really think it would work, anyway." My face flamed. "I stripped her down. I feel like the worst sort of creep." The words tumbled out before I could stop them. I felt guilty and needed absolution. I rubbed the back of my neck. "I've never done that— and I felt like I somehow...defiled her...seeing her all...unclothed."

Sam nodded in understanding and gave a sardonic chuckle. "I know what you mean. It's something you really want to see, but then feel guilty for looking and invading her privacy. I remember the first time Megan shifted. Lots of skin neither of us was prepared for." He winked, trying to put my mind at ease.

I nodded, feeling better knowing that this had happened to someone else—someone I respected, too. It wasn't like I hadn't seen a naked woman before. The Kentucky pack hadn't been particularly prudish. But Rachel was different.

"Was Rachel upset about that part?" Sam asked, a

crease forming between his eyebrows. I assumed Megan had been.

"Not particularly. She was uncomfortable, but not enough to stop and have me go for help." I couldn't help the flash of memory of her in that purple bra and bright pink underwear with the script on the butt. I cleared my throat. "Anyway, I shifted, and I bit her. *I bit her.*" I had to repeat—nearly to make myself believe it. "She changed right away. I think I started panicking then, but then she passed out only half phased. I thought I'd killed her," I whispered as a stone of emotion clogged my throat. "I *commanded* her to finish shifting. I've never uttered a command in my life. I'm the Omega. I have never been anything *but* the Omega. How is it possible she obeyed? I'm not *even* the Omega anymore. Right now I'm still Rogue." My hands tangled into my hair, tugging in confused frustration.

Sam had a faraway expression on his face, trying to puzzle this out, too. He shook his head then indicated I should continue.

"She shifted into her full wolf form," *She was a gorgeous wolf,* "but wouldn't come to. So, I carried her back to her house. I was desperate at that point and I commanded her to wake. She did." I shuddered, remembering the rush of power I'd felt, using a command.

"How was she when she woke?"

"In a word? Ecstatic."

Sam snorted. "Why am I not surprised? That sounds like the old Rachel. I think she's always been a little subconsciously tuned into the other-worldly side of things. Rachel was hardly even phased when she learned we were real."

We were quiet for a minute. Wolf nudged me and I felt my insides shrivel. Anxiety slithered through my veins, and I knew I needed to ask, but was loathe to end my ignorance.

"Has this completely screwed all chance of joining your pack?" I couldn't look at him as I uttered the dreaded words.

Sam angrily pulled at a tuft of grass, wadded it into a ball, and slung it away. "As far as I'm concerned, not at all." Sadness crossed his face. "But. It's not just my decision. A Changing Bite is still illegal in our pack. For what it's worth, I'll still vouch for you, but it's my dad that has the final say." He clapped me on the shoulder and Wolf and I gave a heavy sigh, relieved, but still full of dread.

Something foreign started scratching its way to my awareness. Wolf lurched up and I had the sudden compulsion to see Rachel.

"I need to check on Rachel," I blurted then jumped up and ran for the house without waiting for Sam.

Chapter 15

Rachel

I was dizzy. Wolf was dizzy. We were mid-shift, and our collective head was spinning like a top.

"Rachel, you need to calm down and finish your shift," Megan told me. Her tone told me that she was telling me something important, but Wolf couldn't quite figure it out, and I was too occupied trying to stay upright to pay her much mind. Suddenly, what felt like a tether in my mind snapped and a bleak howl rose in my throat. I could do nothing to hold it in, and a wild, heathen noise erupted, filling the cabin with a haunting, terrifying sound.

"Not good, not good," Megan chanted somewhere in the background. My back arched and all else was lost as I didn't so much surrender to the primal feelings coursing through me, as I succumbed to them. Horror filled us as Wolf and I realized that something deep, dark, and base was clawing its way up from the depths of me and was taking me down, dragging me under. I shrieked, fear snaking up my belly and wringing a desperate wail from my throat.

"*Rachel.*" That voice. *His* voice. Calm stole over me and my heart ceased its frantic beating. The darkness receded and Wolf and I were left quaking and shivering as the frigid tentacles of darkness that had a strangle hold on my heart released and went back to the deep.

Shaking my head out, Wolf and I righted ourselves. My vision cleared and I saw Kyp, white as a sheet, standing in the doorway with Sam behind him. I whined, pacing forward and bending my head to rub against Kyp's knees. My senses began returning to normal and I perused the room, locating Megan.

"I'm here, Rach." She made eye contact with me, then Sam. "Sam, she didn't react to my dominance at all." Megan was the equivalent of a Beta, since Sam was, and he was the one that bit her. Wolf cocked her head. Kyp was low man on the totem pole, therefore, I was that equivalent, too. Wolf should have reacted to Megan's dominance, but I'd felt nothing beyond the wild fear that took hold when the darkness tried to catch us.

"How is that possible?" Kyp asked. My wolf eyes caught when Sam's expression changed.

"Let's see if Dad is home yet," was all Sam answered.

Chapter 16

Kyp

Dominic Wolfe was in his study, filling out some paperwork for his law firm when Sam knocked on his door.

"Samuel, Kypson," he said by way of his typically blunt greeting. Dominic Wolfe was not a man to mince words. Sam nodded and we came fully into the room, sitting in the leather chairs opposite Dominic's desk. A faint clanking echoed up from downstairs in the kitchen where Mrs. Wolfe and Megan were with Rachel.

Dominic sniffed and raised his head looking at both of us, his eyes darting from me to Sam. Sam nodded nearly imperceptibly, and my skin crawled. They were having some sort of conversation about me using their link. I swallowed.

"I perceive something has happened. Best get it out." Dominic leaned forward and steepled his hands.

Sam and I explained the events of the morning. When the whole sordid tale was out, Dominic leaned way back in his chair, his hands clasped behind his head, his feet propping themselves on the edge of the mahogany-colored desk.

"Kypson, part of me really wishes you hadn't done that." Dominic sighed.

Something akin to shame burned in my gut. I was

sorry that this put my joining his pack in jeopardy—sorrier than I could express—but I couldn't be entirely sorry because my actions had saved Rachel. And I didn't regret that at all.

"I'm sorry this has complicated things, sir," I said quietly. My heart still wanted nothing more than to be a part of this man's pack, but I knew I had Rachel to consider now, too. And so did Dominic. "I know this wasn't in the plans, but is there any way you'd be willing to accept Rachel into your pack?" She didn't need to be Rogue with me.

Dominic steepled his hands again and met my eyes. "It's not quite that simple anymore." My eyebrows lifted.

"Sir?"

"I'd like having you and Rachel both join the pack. But it's not so simple," he repeated.

"Kyp, you smell different," Sam interjected. I wrinkled my nose. What did that have to do with anything?

"I always smell different. I've never smelled properly wolf or human."

"No, I know that. But your scent is changing. You're starting to smell all Alpha-y," Sam explained.

I rocked back in my chair, awareness only starting to dawn on me.

"You made your own pack when you bit Rachel," Dominic said.

Blood roared through my ears—Wolf's erratic behavior, the weird sweating and trembling, the glimmer that banished the aloneness—biting Rachel made me her Alpha. That's why commanding her worked and why she didn't react to Megan's wolf.

That's why my body was having these weird reactions. My genes were somehow mutating themselves. Wolf was changing. I was changing. Panic gripped my gut.

"Oh," was all I could stammer out.

Dominic burst out laughing and a glance at Sam confirmed his lips were quirked upward, too.

"It's not completely unheard of for an Alpha to surrender their power to another, although it's extremely rare, but I don't know if that's the wisest course of action," Dominic continued. "Something tells me that you were always meant to be an Alpha. You have to have Alpha somewhere in your bloodline for your wolf to assume the role. A strong one, too, I'd wager, since your mother is human. Also, when it comes to it, as I'm sure it will," his voice turned grim, "when Victor Atwood comes calling, it wouldn't be all bad to have three packs up against his one. Even if your pack doesn't have the numbers, it still carries the weight in the words if we can say we have three allied packs against his one."

I swallowed thickly. Responsibility sat heavily on my shoulders as I thought about everything this would entail. I knew I'd be responsible for Rachel after biting her, if the bite took. But being her Alpha? That felt so much weightier. I couldn't deny that part of me soared at the realization that I was my own. Responsible to no one else's whims. Capable. Accountable. Leader. Petrified. All the words and feelings that went with them swirled in my brain.

"I don't know what to say," I stammered.

"No bother. Think on it. Talk to your pack." Dominic winked. "If the both of you still want to join the Wolfe pack in a few weeks, we'll revisit the discussion."

I gulped and nodded, incapable of much else at that moment.

"What are we going to do about Lenny?" Sam asked.

I nodded my agreement. Lenny had to be dealt with. I would not allow him near Rachel again. Wolf puffed his chest out protectively.

Dominic twisted his lip as he considered the situation. "I think Lenny needs to visit the Sheriff's office. It is not good to have two enemies, and with his sights locked on Rachel, it's one more distraction we can't afford. Victor is the bigger threat. We need to deal with the smaller threat and remove it—even if it's not strictly wolf business. Sam, what do you think?"

"I agree. I think he's ruined enough lives. And Rachel is one of us now, so that makes it pack business?"

Dominic nodded at him.

"Kypson? She's your pack."

"He will not touch her again." I was surprised at the venom in my words. I hoped this Alpha stuff wasn't totally going to my head.

Dominic nodded and picked up his phone.

Lenny was in jail by that evening.

Chapter 17

Rachel

Mary Wolfe was the perfect hostess. She breezed about her kitchen getting Megan and me a quick lunch and chatted as if my suddenly turning up a werewolf were the most natural thing in the world. I swear, nothing phased this woman. I admired that about her. Sam got his lighter coloring from his mom. While Sam's looks favored his dad, where Dominic was all dark hair and eyes, Sam got Mary's blonde hair and blue eyes.

"It will be nice that you're officially a wolf now," Mary was saying as she sliced a sandwich. Diagonally, because it made it prettier, she'd said. "You have been so gracious and so involved with all of this process as Megan has become one of us. I feel like you're already one of the pack." Mary finished with a smile and flourish of her knife. I smiled back, warmed that Mary felt like I belonged, too. Megan squeezed my hand. She had been fairly sparking with excitement since we came in.

"It didn't feel right that you weren't a wolf," Megan confessed. "I'm sorry about the circumstances, but I'm so glad that we're not different this way anymore."

I smiled. So big that I probably verged on

ridiculous. The jealousy that had been rearing its head the past few weeks receded as I realized that Meg had felt the disparities in our situations more than she let on.

"Rachel, where are you planning to move?" Mary asked conversationally as she put a pile of sandwiches on the table.

"Move?" Alarm whispered through my gut.

"Your wolf," Megan answered gently. "Your wolf is going to have to have a dominant wolf nearby or that horrible feeling you felt earlier is going to take root. You'll go feral."

My belly clenched, thinking about that terrifying, gripping, tentacled sensation. Wolf nudged me inside. She didn't need out, but she did understand the need to be near a dominant wolf.

"I guess I hadn't gotten there yet. Too many other thoughts." I knew all about this phenomenon, I just hadn't applied it to myself. It was the whole reason Sam and Megan were together now. He had accidentally bitten her, and the only way to keep her wolf sane was for her to be with him. The constant proximity was one thing that had led her to fall in love with him.

"I'd hoped you'd be able to stay with us for a while," Megan interjected. "But your wolf didn't understand my dominance..."

"I'm sure the men will discuss it and find a good solution." Mary smiled brightly. "You're always welcome to the spare room here," she chirped. I smiled, trying to make it appear genuine.

"Thank you, Mary. Really. I appreciate it." The adrenaline from Joanie, my abduction, and the changing shifts were starting to catch up with me and I found myself yawning.

"You've got to be about dead on your feet. Do you want to try to shift one more time before you sleep? You're likely to sleep a good long while." Megan grinned and gave me a quick side hug.

"I think I'm going to have to crash soon," I confessed. Just then, we heard the door to Dominic's study open and three sets of feet moved toward the stairs. I marveled again that I could hear so much *more* than I ever had before.

It wasn't long before the men joined us at the table. Mary passed out paper plates and they helped themselves to the sandwiches. I watched Kyp carefully, but other than the quick once over he gave me to be sure I was all in one piece, I'm not sure he was comprehending much at all.

"Rachel, welcome to the wolf world officially," Dominic said around a mouthful of tuna fish on rye.

"Thanks," I said, unsure where this was going. Sam nodded encouragingly at Kyp. He took a big breath and then let his gaze meet mine.

"It seems that biting you has made us a pack," he said. I couldn't identify the emotion in his voice. "Apparently I'm your Alpha." He stumbled over the words, forcing them out.

"Well, that explains why your wolf didn't care for my instructions," Megan quipped. "You're higher up the food chain." She grinned.

I was part of Kyp's pack? Wolf smiled and nodded approvingly. Not part of Megan's pack? More emotions swirled inside me and I blinked a few times, trying to clear my head.

"Okay. So we're a pack. This is a good thing,

right?"

"I don't know yet," Kyp answered with a rueful smile.

Sam chuckled. "You'll be a great Alpha."

Kyp's mouth tightened like he'd swallowed something sour.

I couldn't help it when my eyelids started to droop right there at the table. Wolf was out of steam even though we'd only shifted a handful of times.

"Rachel, you need sleep." Kyp stated the obvious after glancing in my direction for the fortieth time during the meal. I nodded, too tired to even formulate the words to agree. I started fading in and out as the others around the table quickly began discussing the logistics of where I should crash. I drifted off entirely as arms scooped me up out of my chair and carried me to a soft surface where I was lost to the sweet darkness of restful oblivion.

Chapter 18

Kyp

Rachel was so much lighter as a girl than she was as a wolf. She was practically narcoleptic in her sudden sleep as I quickly moved from my chair to help her.

"Just take her upstairs to the guest room. Second on the left," Mary said with a motherly smile.

"You need help?" Megan asked.

"I'm good," I replied softly as I scooped Rachel up. Not only was she lighter as a girl, she was a lot curvier. I desperately tried to keep my cheeks from flushing as her chest pressed against mine.

We quietly made our way up the stairs and I put her down gently on the bed, but then frowned. I didn't want her to be cold. I turned down one side of the blanket then scooped her up again and was going to put her back down under the blanket when she nuzzled her head against my neck and shoulder. It sent my pulse spiking and my heart beating triple time. Wolf smiled and nudged me. *Our pack.*

Sweat broke out on my forehead again and another wave of the sick feeling I'd had earlier swept from my stomach up my spine and then receded. I wiped my forehead on the tail of my shirt, belatedly realizing it was Rachel's dad's. Wolf nudged me. I understood that it was my body changing, acclimating to making and secreting new chemicals that marked me as an Alpha. With a deep inhale that brought Rachel's smell of *kindness* and a new layer of something more distinctly floral to my nose, I pulled the blanket up to her shoulders and let myself brush a few pieces of red hair from her face.

Alpha. I was her Alpha. I didn't know how to be an Alpha. Wolf nudged me again. Although, with my time in the Kentucky pack, I did at least know a few things that made a bad Alpha. With one more lingering glance on Rachel's face, I shut the door softly behind me and made my way back down the stairs.

Mary and Megan were loading the dishwasher while Sam collected the glasses from the table and Dominic was throwing away the rest of the paper plates.

"I think she'll be out for a while." I wasn't sure what I should do next.

"Kyp, I've been thinking. Now, you are your own Alpha, so you don't have to do this, and I won't be offended," Dominic started while anxiety began churning around like tumble weed in my gut. "We've got several empty houses that the pack owns here in the subdivision. The Thornehill pack is already moving into several of them for the time being. There's a small house still open down at the end of the street. It's not big, but it would probably be serviceable for you, your mom, and Rachel, while she's still unstable. It's yours if you want it."

My eyebrows lifted at such a generous offer. Quickly I ran through scenarios. Rachel and my mom would have tons more protection inside the figurative walls of the Wolfe pack's territory. That alone was reason enough to accept.

"What do you want in return?" Nothing had ever come free with the Kentucky pack.

Dominic's eyebrows rose. "I wouldn't mind an alliance with your pack." He grinned, and I was both flattered and chagrined. He was giving me room to spread my metaphorical Alpha wings but giving me the security of his own pack to fall back on. Wolf snorted, convinced we were good to go in our new role. I wasn't so convinced.

"You sure? That's really generous. My *pack* doesn't have much to offer you at the moment."

"Being able to say that there are three packs allied against Atwood sounds a lot better than just two."

"I'll talk to Rachel when she wakes up. I don't want to spring this on her, but, yes. I'll call my mom. We still have half our stuff in boxes anyway. It wouldn't take much to transfer it here. I'd feel better if both she and Rachel had the added security from your pack. Our rental house is pretty isolated. We'll stay in the empty house at least a few nights until Rachel's wolf settles." Wolf nudged me. It was completely within my rights to decide for both my mom and Rachel, but I didn't want to be that sort of Alpha. I wanted to take the considerations of the rest of my pack into my decisions.

Dominic nodded.

"Say the word and we'll get a crew together and go out and move your stuff over," Sam offered. Megan bobbed her head enthusiastically.

****

Mom didn't take any convincing at all to move into the Wolfe neighborhood, which was a nice stroke to my

Alpha ego.

"Yes. If you think this is the safest thing right now, then I'm all in," Mom said over the phone once I'd given her a summarized update on what had happened. She'd been shocked to say the least, but her faith in me gave me confidence. I wanted to let Rachel sleep off her first shifts, but I also wanted to get Mom moved into the house tonight if possible. I didn't want Mom out at our rental house alone, but I couldn't leave Rachel either. In the end, Dominic suggested one of his pack go out to help Mom get her things and escort her back here. Having no better option and grateful for the support, I readily agreed.

Jonathan Stone happened to be available. Wolf narrowed his eyes. I needed to sit down with Jonathan at some point if he was going to be coming around more.

Chapter 19

Rachel

The barest hint of grey streaked through the shades as I slowly opened my heavy eyelids. Wolf stirred within me and I smiled widely, saying hello. She rubbed her head against me as I stretched. A tiny groan escaped as the muscles in my arms and legs felt like ropes tied too tight that refused to budge.

"Rachel?" a gravelly voice sounded from somewhere below me. Wolf perked her ears forward.

"Kyp?" I was bewildered. I remembered eating lunch at the Wolfe's house and feeling so tired. "Where are we?"

"You fell asleep at the table yesterday at Dominic's house. You're in the guest room."

"Oh." I digested this. "Why are you here?" My voice came out all high and funny sounding as I was trying to put together all the pieces of the hours I'd obviously slept through.

"I didn't want you to be alone. I, I'm trying to figure out how this Alpha thing works and what you need from me for your first shifts. New territory for both of us." His voice was rough and tired sounding, but his words sent heat rippling out from my middle to my extremities.

"Have you been on the floor all night?"

"Yeah. I've got a pallet. I'm fine." Guilt still had Wolf nudging against me again. She shook her fur out. She needed out. I wanted to let her out.

"I think I need to let my wolf out," I whispered into the dark. His head popped up over the side of the bed. It was too dark to see his face well, but I could make out the faint outlines of concern flitting over his forehead.

"Should we try sneaking outside so you can have a proper run?"

Wolf danced in excitement.

"Definitely." I grinned.

****

Under the last rays of the moon's light, I raced on four legs across an open meadow to the fringes of the forest, Kyp right next to me. The smells, the crunch of old leaves under a layer of lacy frost, the wind as it dragged its fingers over my ruff nearly sent me into rapture.

I shook my head, letting the feeling of every new, foreign sensation bury itself into my memory. My first run as a wolf. I was a little sad that Megan wasn't with me, but not even that could dampen the excitement coursing through me. Kyp barked beside me and I turned my attention to the faint trail he nodded toward.

We followed the old deer trail, meandered around a creek, and leaped over fallen logs. Nothing in my life had ever been so fulfilling, so thrilling, or so perfect.

As the sun hit the tops of the trees, I knew I wanted Megan to share this with me. Packs were supposed to have a mental link, but I didn't know if Kyp and I would share one, since he'd never been able to properly use his mental link with his old pack. I tried anyway.

Let's go get Sam and Megan, I thought to him. Kyp

stopped and cocked his head at me. I tried again. He stared at me, his sides pulsing with his breathing. He scratched his paw on the ground, and as I watched, I realized he'd written an M. I bobbed my head up and down, assuming he meant Megan. Finally, he nodded and took off back the way we'd come. About fifteen minutes later we were within eyeshot of the cabin.

Just then a group of three light-colored wolves loped by in the distance. Kyp visibly bristled and took a step in front of me. My heart slammed against my ribs until I saw Kyp relax his shoulders and the fur on his back laid down. His nose was cold and wet against my muzzle as he nudged me. Instinctually, I knew he wanted me to follow, rather than get too far out ahead.

We made it up to the cabin door and I scratched my massive paw against the side of the house, not wanting to break the screen.

Sam answered the door, his hair rumpled and his eyes still tired.

"Rachel!" he smiled. "Meg, I think it's time for a run," he called back into the cabin.

The four of us spent a glorious hour running and exploring together. When Wolf's belly rumbled, I knew I needed to stop to eat, though it was the last thing I wanted to do. I'd never felt so free. Thoughts of Joanie, of Lenny, of everything else troubling and painful, fell away in the face of being a wolf, wild, untamed, able to go and do without thought or care. Muscles pounding, lungs expanding, wind whipping my face.

My belly growled again and Kyp nudged me. Even without the use of words, I knew he was telling me to head back.

Back at the cabin, Megan went in first and tossed

both Kyp and me spare robes that Dominic's pack used. They were roomy enough to accommodate a wolf while spacious enough a wolf could wriggle out of them without the need for opposable thumbs. The robes she handed us were a dull grey. I giggled when she came out in a hot pink one.

"Ravishing, don't you think?" she laughed with me.

"Without doubt."

"Come on. I've got bacon and eggs in the fridge. Why don't you make some batter for French toast while I do the meat?"

I glanced at my hands. They were covered in dirt.

"Yeah. It'll take a while to get used to the dirt. I'm a lot less dirty after runs now than I was when I started." Megan shrugged. I did, too. A little dirt wasn't going to hamper my enjoyment of being a wolf.

****

"Rachel, how would you feel about moving into the neighborhood for the time being?" Kyp ventured as I popped another piece of bacon in my mouth. I was ravenous. Who knew being a wolf was such hungry work?

"Where?"

"Dominic has given our pack—meaning us and my mom—the house at the end of the street to use. With the Thornehills moving into the area, it seems like the smart place for us to be. You need to be near an Alpha." I watched with interest as his cheeks stained the faintest shade of red. "And I need to feel like you and Mom are protected."

"And you'd be near me," Megan said with a smile.

"Sure. My parents aren't going to be back for at

least two weeks." I swallowed as a sudden stab of emotion twisted my belly. Grief was weird. And it totally sucked. "So, we only need to let Grandpa in on the plan, so everyone is on the same page in case my parents call his house."

Megan nodded sympathetically as I finished.

"Why don't you call your dad?" Kyp suggested, accurately reading my need to check in on Joanie and my parents. I nodded.

"Here. Use my phone." Sam passed his over. I cleared my throat then got up and moved to one of the couches in the room. I didn't mind if everyone else overheard, I just wanted a little space.

"Hello, Ken Crumb speaking."

"Daddy, it's me. I'm on Sam's phone. Forgot to charge mine." I cringed as I improvised.

"Sweetheart!" Dad's voice had a solid quality to it that had been missing in the past week.

"How was your flight out? Everything go okay? How is Joanie?" My words tumbled over themselves.

"It was good. We're good. Joanie is good. Will be good." His words came out in a rush. "We're getting settled. Sorry we didn't call last night. Did you get my text? I never heard back."

"Yeah, sorry about that. Forgot to charge it," I said again, hoping he didn't hear the tremor in my voice at the lie. He was too preoccupied to pick up on it, and we talked a few more minutes about the facility and how the program was going to work. Some of the knot in my chest began to ease.

"I hope this works," I whispered as I hung up the phone.

"It will," Megan whispered back as she plopped

down next to me.

****

The rest of the weekend was a blur of packing, moving, meeting new wolves, and continuing to get acquainted with my own wolf. By Sunday evening, I was confident that my fur would be fine staying tucked away at school Monday.

"I wish I'd been so lucky," Megan said with a smile as we finished up the dinner dishes Sunday night. Kyp and I had spent the evening with Megan and Sam at their cabin, having a quiet dinner. I was still reveling in my new furry side and savoring the acceptance of becoming part of a pack. Kyp still seemed nervous and unsure of himself, struggling more with his transition into an Alpha than I was with my transition into a wolf.

Chapter 20

Kyp

Monday was bright and clear with the promise of some wintery sunshine. I stretched and grimaced as my back popped. I laid still for a moment in my old bed in my new room at the house at the end of Dominic's street. It was a strange feeling to be my own Alpha with these protective, dominant surges that flashed through me periodically, but to still feel so inadequate and unprepared. I'd never been anyone other than the lowest of the low. And now here I was, in a borrowed house, on borrowed pack land, with my own pack—even though it was only two strong. Mom had gotten in late after her shift and I could tell she was still asleep. There were rustlings down the hallway, and I knew Rachel was moving around. I swallowed as my blood moved a little quicker at the thought of her only a few feet down the hall. Unbidden, images of her clad in that purple bra and *cheeky* underwear flitted through my brain. I blinked, trying to clear them from my mind's eye. Those were not the sort of thoughts I needed to be having about my pack member…especially as the shower started. I groaned softly, understanding that this was going to be even harder in some ways than I'd thought.

"Do you care if we both drive this morning?"

Rachel asked as I dropped into the kitchen for a quick breakfast.

"No, that's fine. Why?"

"I really appreciate everything you have done and are doing for me," she quickly clarified as she glanced up and must have seen the confusion on my face. "I...I was hoping for a few minutes to myself. I haven't actually been alone since I changed, and I thought it might be helpful to just be me and the wolf for a bit."

"Oh. I can understand that."

"Please don't think this is me being ungrateful, because I'm not," she protested, her cheeks flushing slightly. My breathing hitched. She was so hopeful, and it only added a layer to her beauty.

"Of course." I smiled, unable to stop myself as my fingers reached out and brushed her arm. "I get the need to be alone."

She smiled, relieved. "Thanks. But you're still going to follow me, right?" Her forehead scrunched in concern.

"Definitely. Atwood is still out there." She nodded and her face relaxed. Wolf puffed up his chest, filling me with confidence that just my word of assurance could give Rachel such peace of mind.

"Good. You ready?" She snagged a granola bar from the box on the counter. We'd put things away later. Evidence of our recent move was still scattered all over the house.

"Yep. One sec," I said as my eyes skimmed a note my mom had taped to the refrigerator.

Kyp and Rachel, have a great day at school! Be safe. Kyp, please call Jonathan Stone on your way to school. Love, Mom

A phone number was scribbled on the bottom of the paper. Wolf's hackles prickled.

"Everything good?" Rachel touched my arm and my hackles smoothed right down.

"Yeah. Let's go." She gave my arm a quick squeeze and we tromped out the door, locking it behind us.

I followed Rachel out of the subdivision and quickly punched the phone number Mom had left on the paper.

"Hello?" the deep voice answered on the second ring.

"Jonathan? This is Kyp." I tried to keep my voice neutral, unsure where this conversation was going and unsure how I needed to react.

"Ah, good morning. Thanks for calling." He cleared his throat and I grinned, realizing that this seasoned man on the other end of the line was nervous about talking to me. Jonathan continued, "I wanted to ask your permission formally, both as your mother's protector and as the Alpha of your own pack," he cleared his throat again and I felt a zing of power course through me as Jonathan acknowledged my status, "if it would be all right with you if I started escorting your mom to and from work. I don't like the thought of her going in alone, but I didn't want to cross any boundaries, or overstep myself."

I was silent a minute. Emotion rushed through my chest. "Yes," I finally answered. "Yes. I'd like it if you did that, Jonathan."

"Thank you. I'll coordinate schedules with your mom."

"Jonathan," I said before I could stop myself, "are

you *interested* in my mother?"

There was a brief but pregnant pause on the other end. "Yes."

"Noted," I replied.

Chapter 21

Rachel

The day had gone fantastically. The time to myself
in the car that morning had been like a day at the spa.
Not even thinking about Joanie could keep me from
glowing with satisfaction. Wolf was present with me,
and perfectly behaved. I was anxious to let her out for a
run once I got back to pack lands that afternoon, but I
needed to finish up a few things first.

I told Kyp at lunch that I'd meet him by my locker
after school so we could follow each other back home.
As co-president of the drama club, there were a few
things I needed to straighten out and bring home with
me to organize for the spring musical we were already
planning, and I'd put it off with everything else going
on. I didn't have to be at play practice tonight, but there
were still some other things on my mental checklist.
And I needed to move back toward normal—at least,
whatever my new normal was going to look like being a
werewolf, and having Mom, Dad, and Joanie halfway
across the country for the time being.

Jennifer was still on her shift when Kyp and I
pulled into the driveway and just as I took my keys out
of the ignition, my phone dinged.

—*Come up to the cabin. I've got dinner started.
Miss you*—

My insides warmed at the text from Megan. We'd seen each other at school, but I felt it down to my bones that we hadn't had enough best-friend-time the past few weeks.

—*Let me check with Kyp*—

—*Bring him, too*—

I smiled and grabbed my backpack and purse and shoved open the door. Crisp air hit my nose and Wolf rose within me, scenting, exulting in the way my senses spread out and understood the world in such a vastly different way than ever before.

Kyp smiled at me as he stuck his key into the lock on the door.

"Megan just invited us up for dinner. Want to go?"

"Sure. When do they want us?"

"Probably right now." I groaned. "Although I have a few homework things I *have* to get done tonight. Most of my teachers are done with their leniency." I sighed dramatically. It's not like any of my teachers had been devoid of mercy, but I was still a student and I did have things I had to get done to keep my grades where I wanted them.

"That's fine. I've got some physics to do tonight, too."

"I'll never get things done if we go over there first. I'll just want to sit and talk and be with friends and run around in fur all night."

Kyp chuckled. "So text Megan back and tell her we'll be over after homework is done."

"I suppose. You're doing a great job with this Alpha thing and making sure all the things get done," I teased. His smile faltered slightly, and I wondered if I'd said the wrong thing.

Chapter 22

Kyp

Megan and Sam were excellent company as usual. Megan had made some sort of stir fry that was better than any take-out. We were just finishing dinner, pushing back from the table, when Rachel's whole body tensed.

"Ooh, guys, I don't mean to eat and run, but I've got to let Wolf out. Now." Even as she spoke, Rachel raced toward the new addition that had become Sam and Megan's bedroom. I stood, Wolf on high alert and I felt my face flush as I heard the soft patter of clothes hitting the floor. My belly squirmed.

A minute later Rachel's wolf poked her head out of the door, and I felt a stirring in my gut looking at her. *Mine. My pack.* The words heated me up from the inside out, making my flush darker. I desperately wanted to be what she needed as her Alpha.

"Meet you outside?" Meg smiled at her best friend. Rachel gave us a toothy grin and bobbed her head.

As we all took quick turns shifting into our fur, I wondered if Rachel and I would be able to communicate the way we had earlier. The thought sent excited shivers down my forelegs and set my paws dancing on the cold ground beside the steps of the cabin. I decided to try it out.

Race you to the third tree on the right I thought at her. She swung her head around and her wolf eyes narrowed. She looked back to the tree in question and back at me. I tried to send a picture of us running toward the tree.

Yelping, Rachel wagged her tail and turned her body to face our course. She crouched and glanced expectantly at me. Triumph swept over me, realizing that we *had* communicated with some sort of mental link.

A quick bark and we were off. I could have beat her easily. She was still getting used to running as a wolf, but I slowed some to keep pace with her. Rachel glanced at me with slit eyes, and I chuffed out a breath as she realized what I was doing. She bared her teeth and nipped playfully at my shoulder and my heart sped up. I wanted to knock into her and nuzzle her neck. Wolf pinged my brain and I realized with no small amount of shock, that translated into human terms, I wanted to kiss her. The realization gave me such a pause that I stumbled over a clod of grass and Rachel went shooting ahead of me, circling the tree and coming back as I stood panting, waiting for her, since she'd won. Sam and Megan loped up beside me and I was glad they were there to distract me from my thoughts that were seriously going haywire regarding Rachel. *Mine* echoed softly in my brain, but I shoved it down. I was well aware she was my pack now. But I wasn't sure how appropriate it was for me to want to kiss her...though now that I had recognized the desire, it lodged itself like a live coal under my skin.

A picture of Rachel's cell phone suddenly flashed through my brain. Rachel yipped, and I realized she wanted to go check in with her parents. I gave a bark in return and we loped back to the cabin. Meg and Sam followed, though not close. It was clear they were enjoying the near-frigid air and the crisp moonlight as it dappled over the ground. It was an excellent night for a run. The air was perfect for carrying scents and the way the cold ruffled through my fur was one of my favorite things about late fall. But Rachel needed to check in. She was my pack. And I wanted to kiss her. I shook my head with the barest hint of a growl to clear the image. My heart still raced. Not from the quick run.

Chapter 23

Rachel

I fell into an easy rhythm the rest of the week. Living with Jennifer and Kyp wasn't nearly as awkward as I'd been afraid it might be. Jennifer was almost like a cross between my mom and Clary. Part of her was the concerned mother figure, while the other part of her was like another fun older sister. It was a comforting combination that I realized I needed. And Kyp was the perfect gentleman. He made sure my needs and his mom's needs came before his. He did a perimeter check of the house every night. He opened the doors for me. He let me have the shower first and never complained about my taking too long or using too much hot water. He was careful about touching me—especially when we were at the house. It was almost as if he was afraid to touch me at all if no one else was around. And I found that I wanted him to. Particularly when no one else was around.

School went like clockwork. Kyp and I rode to school together. Then he hung around and helped out as a volunteer on the sets after school while I worked with Luke on the finishing touches the winter play and rehearsals. The play was set to run the week before Christmas break, and for once, we were ahead of schedule. We needed to finish up the sets and finalize two scenes. Our drama group was exceedingly responsible this year and everyone knew almost all their lines and all cues were nearly finalized.

I knew Thursday afternoon was going to be busy with set work. We were tackling the more complicated set for Scene III, so I made time to check in with Dad before I got tangled up in the project.

"Sweetheart!" Dad's voice was happy but still strained.

"Hi Daddy. How is everything?"

"It's going. Slower than we'd hoped. Joanie is…being stubborn." He sighed and my heart fell to my toes.

"Why is she being stubborn? She realizes she almost died, doesn't she?" I tried to keep the anger out of my voice. I wasn't entirely successful. Kyp came around the corner then and I waved to him distractedly. He saw my phone and must have read my frustrated expression because he came up and quietly touched my elbow, silently offering his support. Wolf relaxed, and the human part of me might have melted a little, too.

"She is being stubborn. She was born stubborn, that girl, but she's broken, too. Her body and her mind have been through as much torture as we have, only on a much more intimate scale," Dad reminded me. My eyes slid shut as I pinched the bridge of my nose, trying to quell my own irritation and remember that this was all a process. Joanie wasn't going to just recover overnight.

"I know. Sorry."

"It's all right, Sweetheart. I know it's hard. How are you doing? School okay? Staying with Grandpa working out?"

"It's fine. We're getting ready to work on the big set components tonight, so that should be fun." I tried to deflect the living arrangement question. I filled him in on a few details of the sets.

"We'll make sure we're back for the play," he promised. "We're hoping Joanie will be progressed far enough along that we'll be able to come home by Thanksgiving."

"That'd be great, Dad," I said, my stomach clenching. I missed my parents, but how was I going to explain my need for nighttime runs in fur? I did not want to be that girl who snuck out behind her parents' backs at night. Although, I was hiding plenty from them now. I shivered and Wolf nudged her head against me in sympathy. It was a complicated situation. We said our goodbyes and I hung up with a long sigh.

"What happened?" Kyp asked quietly from my side, where he'd stood patiently the entire time.

"I'm frustrated with Joanie, and then I feel guilty for feeling frustrated with her." I blinked rapidly as I felt tears prick the back of my eyes. I did not want to cry right now.

Kyp didn't say anything. Didn't try to tell me everything was going to be all right. Didn't whisper platitudes to me while he held me and stroked my hair, although I might have preferred that. He took my hand, holding it firmly, grounding me to the present, and pouring his strength into me through our linked fingers. Wolf leaned toward him and I took control of myself with a calming breath.

****

The evening wore on, and it wore on me, too. Though the set was coming along nicely, and rehearsals happened with few hiccups, I felt incomplete somehow. My eyes kept tracking to Kyp, to see what he was doing, to see if he was watching me. Then I'd blush and go back to my task at hand. Wolf wasn't helping. She wanted out. And she wanted Kyp's attention, too.

"Rachel, do we have any more of this green paint?" Anthony called about five o'clock. There were a few things we were trying to finish up before all heading home for the evening.

"I think there's some backstage by the props room. I'll go check," I offered.

The back of the stage was dark. The paint had to be way back in the back corner. It couldn't be in the well-lit portion where everyone was working on the sets. I was grumpy and I knew I needed to get over it. I wanted to go home and let Wolf out. My foot tangled in a forgotten pile of rope used to hoist the different sets and I felt like cursing. I held it in and proceeded back to the recesses of the stage behind the curtain. There was just enough light peeking through the door to the classroom to make out the different shapes of the props.

"It's awfully dark to be back here by yourself."

I yelped and Wolf startled as a dark figure emerged from between two fake palm trees. My arms swung wide and I tripped over another pile of set rope but this time I couldn't catch myself, and I went tumbling headlong into the shadowy mass.

"Oof!"

I crashed into the man and landed on top of him. I dragged in a lung full of air and startled, wide-eyed, as the narrow strip of light showed me Kyp's face.

"You scared me to death," I hissed.

"Yeah. I got that," he quipped. His hands had

wrapped around me in our rapid descent and I was suddenly acutely aware of their presence on my hips. One of my arms was braced on the floor beside his head, the other gripped a shoulder of nicely rounded muscle.

I knew I should move and get up, but something in his gaze held me there. My heart rate increased, and not from my sudden spike in adrenaline. I licked suddenly dry lips. Wolf went all giddy.

It then became apparent exactly what sort of effect I was having on him, positioned as I was. My eyes went wide, and I blushed to the roots of my hair. His eyes were steady, but his Adam's apple bobbed as he swallowed hard and his face heated. His fingers gripped my hips tighter, not pulling me into him, but I could feel the wanting in his hands. Kyp's gaze darted quickly to my mouth and back to my eyes.

Adrenaline rushed through me and without another thought, I planted my lips on his.

I was too stunned to do anything more. I kissed him. I kissed Kyp. I *was* kissing him. I was *kissing* Alexander Kypson!

His lips were unsure but did not pull back. I was stunned, totally shocked. Kyp was kissing me back. Nerves attacked my stomach, sending it spiraling through my midsection. A thousand thoughts flew through my brain. I hadn't been kissed much. Was I doing this right? Would he notice? Would he care? We were *kissing*! Should I open my mouth? Did he want me to open my mouth? My whole body felt hot, quivering with excitement, and through his thin T-shirt I could feel the muscles of Kyp's body beneath mine, flexing as he maneuvered into a spot where he could better reach my mouth.

Before I could even decide how to respond, he was pulling away, and I hadn't moved. I'm not even sure I breathed. His body didn't relax beneath me, but one of his hands left my hip and carefully tucked an errant curl behind my ear. My heart was hammering in my chest, my hand reflexively gripping his shoulder tighter. Wolf sighed in contentment, basking in the attention. She gave her full approval. He looked back to my eyes, unspoken questions there in the shadowed light. I took a shuddering breath and glanced at his lips. I wanted to feel that again. I wanted to feel *him* again as he pressed his mouth to mine. We were friends. Friends who were obviously attracted to one another. I glanced back up to his eyes, not moving, wanting *him* to kiss *me*, my impulsivity be cursed, but unsure how to ask. Apparently, he got the message. His hand slid down my side back to my hip, leaving a trail of tingles in its wake as he inched his mouth closer to mine. I met him half-way, wanting him to know that I was a willing participant, wanting him to know that I wanted this, too. That I hadn't kissed him because I had no impulse control.

Time slowed as we kissed. It wasn't a wildly passionate kiss, but it was *good*. I stretched my body out, trying to find a better angle to reach him and he grunted, breaking our lips apart as his right hand slid up to my side. I started to pull back, embarrassed, realizing that I'd inadvertently pressed against him in a place I probably shouldn't have, my face flaming all over again.

Kyp didn't let me get far. His hand slid the rest of the way up my back and tangled into my hair and the base of my head, tugging me back down to his lips. His kisses were sweet and gentle. He wasn't pushy, but he was definitely making a move well beyond the friendship line. The line I'd crossed first. Pleasant heat poured through me. *He kissed me back.*

He pulled away slowly. I was breathing harder than I liked to admit. His face was still solemn, but his eyes held an intensity that warmed me to my toes.

"Rachel, did you find that paint yet?" Anthony called from just the other side of the curtain.

In one movement, Kyp had flipped me over, straddled me for one second, placed one more lightning-fast kiss on my cheek and hauled us both to our feet.

"Um, yeah. I'll be right there!" my voice came out unnaturally high.

Kyp's lips curved upward slightly at the edges.

"Come on," he whispered. "Let's go find that paint before someone else comes looking."

He tugged my hand, releasing it as I moved after him. Other than a new warmth when he glanced at me, he was acting like nothing out of the ordinary had happened. We were just back to being friends. I was more than a little thrown-off balance by his behavior. Had he wanted to kiss me? Did I foolishly make another impulsive move? Even though I'd been thinking about it for days? Had he just been excited in the moment?

Chapter 24

Kyp

Blood pounded in my ears and roared through my veins as I gulped and forced my face into a mask of politeness as we grabbed the paint and headed back toward Anthony. We'd kissed. My first kiss. My first kiss was Rachel. I was pretty sure I was going to spontaneously combust from the pressure of happy emotions galloping through me. Wolf puffed up his chest and urged me to formally Claim her. As far as he was concerned, as part of our pack, she was mine for keeps. Possibly in ways other than just a part of my pack. I swallowed down a flurry of nerves as I glanced over at Rachel, talking calmly to Whitney about where some bush was supposed to sit on the set. Her cheeks were still flushed, and if I wasn't mistaken, her hips had a little extra swing in them. I hoped both were my fault.

My first finger rubbed over my thumb, the only outward sign that my insides were all tied up in knots. I didn't know what to do now. I wanted Rachel to be more than a friend, more than a pack mate. The familiar awkwardness of not knowing what to do or how to act rose and clawed at my belly. Wolf snorted. I shook my head. Animal instincts were a little different than proper social etiquette.

Things wrapped up in the next few minutes as I

watched Rachel give a few last orders for the evening. Once she was done, she turned and looked up at me where I was standing off to the side and out of the way, leaning lightly against the wall. Her green eyes were like shiny orbs, large, innocent, and questioning. I felt the corner of my mouth tip up and a hot rush fell over me as her whole face lit up with her answering smile.

Once our coats were on and we were walking out the doors to the cold parking lot, I let my fingers drift near her hand, brushing against it ever so slightly. I saw her glance at me in her peripheral vision, and color rose in her cheeks again. With one more hard swallow, I grabbed her hand and held on, hardly daring to breathe until I felt her body relax beside mine as we covered the short distance to my truck.

We still said nothing as I opened the door for her, and she hopped up into the cab. She paused with her fingers on the handle and glanced at me. Her smile was big as the great outdoors, and I felt myself responding with a solid internal jerk toward the sunshine on her face. Closing her door, I rounded the truck and hopped in.

"So," I finally said as my fingers crept over the middle seat to tentatively grasp her hand again. She immediately flipped her palm up, intertwining our fingers and my shoulders lost some of their stiff posture. I turned out of the parking lot toward the house.

"So," she said back, her voice sounding breathless in a way that shot heat down my limbs.

Just then, a loud trilling sounded, and Rachel's nose scrunched up.

"Sorry, that's Meg's ringtone. I should get that in

case anything new has happened." I nodded and sadly let go of her hand as she dug in her purse for her phone and swiped it on.

"Hey Meggie," she chirped. She reached back over and took my hand again and my heart banged a few extra times against my ribs.

Chapter 25

Rachel

"Rachel! Are you leaving play practice, or is this a bad time?"

"We're on the way home," I responded, absolutely squealing in delight on the inside and bemoaning the fact that I couldn't spill my guts to her right there. That would have been awkward with Kyp sitting right beside me. Also, Kyp and I really needed to talk. Probably before I rehashed every possible detail with my best friend. "What's up?" I think my voice came out a little high on the end.

"Well, I was hoping that you, Raven, and maybe Cindy would come up to the cabin Friday night. Sarah Thornehill officially came down from New York today. She'll be starting school with us Monday, and I thought it might be nice to welcome her and for her to get to know a few of us. You remember Sarah, right?"

I'd met Sarah at HarvestFest the month before. She was the daughter of Austin Thornehill, and as such, she was the Thornehill pack's Beta. They'd been in town to conference with Dominic about rumors of threats. Those threats turned out to be real as Victor Atwood aptly proved not long after.

"Sure, I remember. That should be fine. I don't have plans that I know of." I felt the pressure of Kyp's hand on mine and felt suddenly guilty. What if Kyp wanted to do something together...as a couple...Friday night? "Actually, let me just check with Kyp," I told her. I mean, he was my Alpha, too. I probably should check in with him?

"Megan is having some of the girls over Friday to welcome Sarah Thornehill. Is that okay?" I asked him, unsure.

He hesitated only a moment before nodding. "Sure. At the cabin?"

"Yes."

"That's fine. It'll be well-patrolled."

I squeezed his hand, hoping he understood that I wanted to spend time with him, too, if he did.

"What time? Do you want me to bring anything?"

"Just come up as soon as you get done with practice. I'll have snacky stuff for dinner. I'm feeling the urge to bake, so there'll be cookies or cake or something, too. Probably chips and cheese dip, meatballs, that sort of thing."

"Are you okay?" I asked her, realizing I hadn't actually asked her how she was doing the past few days. I'd been so preoccupied with my own life. Shame curdled in my belly. Megan loved to bake. But especially when she was feeling stressed. I had planned to stock the kitchen of my current house over the weekend with dry goods. I baked to ease stress, too, and there was some serious kneading calling to me. Maybe some scones, too, as my hand tingled where Kyp held it.

"I'm holding it together. We've been training every night. We should practice some moves this weekend. You think your wolf is good and settled for that? I know it's hard to make everything synchronize at the beginning. You're so much better at this than I was starting out."

I smiled. Wolf and I had never had trouble melding our minds together. It had taken me awhile to get the hang of coordinating four legs to walk or run, but we were doing pretty well. It certainly wouldn't hurt me to learn some defensive measures.

"That sounds good. I'll check with Kyp," I added, knowing he'd be in favor of my learning to protect myself, even if he didn't ever plan on me needing to.

"Fantastic. Any new news on Joanie?"

"Dad said she's being stubborn, so everything is taking longer than they were hoping."

"I'm so sorry, Rach." Megan let out a heavy sigh that didn't quite miss the receiver.

"Me, too. Hey, I'll see you in the morning, yeah? We're almost home."

"Okay. I'm excited about it!"

"Same!"

I hung up and slipped the phone back into my bag.

"Sorry about that. I was looking forward to where that *so* was going to lead." I turned to Kyp as he turned into the road that would take us to our house. A smile twitched his lips as his hand squeezed mine lightly.

"Yeah? I was kind of hoping you might have a *so* of your own you wanted to mention," he answered lightly. I felt myself blushing again. I *had* kissed him first. I suddenly found myself tongue tied. I cleared my throat.

"Let's just wait til we get to the house," Kyp said.

"Okay." My voice was breathless.

Chapter 26

Kyp

I couldn't pull into the driveway and park fast enough or slow enough. Part of me wanted to race into the house and just plant my lips on hers forever. Wolf liked that idea. The other part of me, the insecure part, wanted to put on the brakes. I had no idea what I was doing. I knew I wanted to do more of it, but I didn't even know if I was any good at kissing or not. I desperately wanted to be good at kissing. I was way out of my comfort zone and not sure how to proceed. But the truck was parked. There was nothing else to do but go inside and talk. And maybe kiss.

Fumbling the keys out of the ignition, Rachel didn't wait for me to open her door but met me by the path that led to the door. I unlocked the house and held the door open for her. Mom wouldn't be home for a few more hours. Her shifts were a lot of strange hours this week. One of her crew mates was sick.

Glancing at the clock, my stomach realized it was 6:00 the same time my eyes registered the time.

Rachel grinned. "I'm not trying to put off this conversation, but let's call and order a pizza. I'm starving, and it sounds like you are, too. My treat. Mom and Dad told me the other day to make sure I do something fun for myself." She smiled.

"Pizza sounds great."

She dug a card out of her purse and handed it to me. With a smile that was both shy and cheeky, she bounded up the stairs.

I ordered while she changed into sweats and then we went to the living room and sat awkwardly on each end of the couch.

"Um," I began eloquently. Wolf chuffed and nudged me firmly. "Rachel, I really like you. Like, a lot more than I probably should."

Her eyebrows rose. "Is it a bad thing for you to like me?"

"Well, I'm your Alpha. I don't know if that's a line I should cross." I drifted off, completely unsure of myself or where the boundaries for us should be. I scrubbed a hand on the back of my neck.

"It sounds like you've already crossed it. And you did kiss me back."

"And I sincerely enjoyed it." That nervous fluttery sensation began working its way up my throat.

"I really like you back," she whispered, and my heart soared.

I swallowed and my finger began rubbing over my thumb. "I've never done this before," tumbled out and seemed to suck all the air out of me. There it was. My insecurities laid bare. Wolf appeared unaffected. He was confident in his instincts, and his instincts said Rachel was *mine*. I wasn't sure if it was an Alpha instinct or something else, but it was confusing to feel that and the intense attraction I felt for her swirling around all muddled up together.

"Never…had a girlfriend?"

I guess my insecurities hadn't been overly clear. I

shook my head.

"No. It wasn't something I was allowed to do in the Kentucky pack." My Alpha had kept me on a tight leash. Besides, no one there had wanted to sully themselves by dating a half-breed. Her eyebrows drew together, and she frowned.

"I know I've never met your last Alpha, but seriously. I detest him."

My heart thumped at her words and I couldn't stop the smile that stretched across my face.

"Kyp," Rachel brought me back down to earth. "Is there some wolf law that says an Alpha can't be involved with a pack member?"

"I…I have no idea. I think every pack pretty much makes up its own laws. I mean, there is the universal and instinctually preserved law of keeping our species an absolute secret, but otherwise? I have no clue."

"So," she drew the word out, "if we're our own pack, and you wanted to, say, date a pack member, then you'd be the only one stopping yourself. Right?"

I chuckled, following where she was going. Just then the doorbell rang.

"Stay here. I'll get it." We were in a well-protected area, but my Alpha hackles still rose with the thought of danger lurking at the door, bearing pizza or not. It was just a poor pimply-faced guy. Not a trace of werewolf scent on him. "Thanks, man," I said as took the warm boxes from him and nudged the door shut. I put the pizzas on the counter and locked the door.

When I glanced up, Rachel was leaning against the doorjamb to the living room. Watching me, her face unreadable, her green eyes sparkled as the light from the kitchen fell softly across her face. Wolf lunged. His desires were clear.

"Rachel," I whispered, "do you want to be with me?"

"Yes."

Chapter 27

Rachel

Megan and I texted for hours that night. Way later than we should have. But I had to fill her in. There was no way I'd be able to wait. I'm pretty sure I heard her squealing all the way up at the cabin at my news. We texted about Kyp. We texted about me. We texted about the new *us*. I pumped her for information about dating. I hadn't done much of it. She had all sorts of helpful tidbits. I fell asleep smiling and woke up feeling lighter than I'd felt in weeks.

Kyp had kissed me once more last night. Quietly, just a brush of his lips against mine, before I shut my door to put on my pajamas and text Megan like a crazy woman. My lips were still tingling.

"Morning," Kyp said shyly as he handed me a cup of coffee and poured himself a second one.

"Morning," I whispered back. A shiver worked its way down my spine as our fingers brushed. I giggled when I realized he was grinning like a fool. This was new territory for both of us, and there was something special about that.

He chuckled, too, and put down his coffee then reached for me. I nearly scalded myself in my haste to put my cup down then dash into his arms. He didn't disappoint. His arms came around me in a way that left me feeling safe, protected, and in no doubt of his feelings. His quick intake of breath as his hand hesitantly skimmed the curve of my waist sent little spangles of excitement tripping through me.

Chapter 28

Kyp

Blood pumped through me with a vengeance as my hand lightly slid over that curve that drove me wild. The image of that same curve totally bared in the shed the day she'd been turned flashed into my mind and I felt the breath leave me. My hand roamed from her waist to the small of her back and back again, sending my pulse spiking even higher.

Mom's door opening upstairs jerked me back to the present. I pulled Rachel in for one last squeeze and felt her curves pressed up against me. Swallowing, I let her go, but kept my hand lightly on her waist, wanting Mom to know.

She walked in all rumpled and with slight shadows cupping her eyes. She immediately zeroed in on my hand as Rachel hid behind a giant gulp of coffee.

"Morning, Mom."

"Good morning." She suddenly became more alert as her gaze swung to my face.

"Morning, Jennifer," Rachel added softly.

"So, um, Rachel and I," I started, unsure how to phrase it. Were dating? Were seeing each other? I didn't even know the right word.

"Are together," Rachel finished after my slight pause. I glanced at her, appreciating her word choice.

Together. Not alone. Together. Wolf preened.

Mom's smile reached her eyes and banished any remaining sleep.

"That's fabulous. Really. I'm delighted for both of you." I could see her brain whirring as she looked at us, her smile still in place.

"Mom, what is it?"

"I...I was just thinking that some ground rules might be in order, since you guys are both living here for the time being."

Rachel's phone rang loudly from the tabletop.

"Sorry, it's my mom. I'll go take it to the other room." She snatched it up with a smile and ducked her head as she went into the living room.

"Kyp, I *am* happy for you," Mom said quietly as she slid her arms around me for a quick hug.

I couldn't stop smiling. "Thanks, Mom."

"I don't mean to be a buzz-kill, but you know why you need ground rules," she whispered, concern evident in her voice.

"I know. And we'll definitely set some. But we've got to go, or we'll be late. Did Jonathan bring you home last night?"

"He did. And yes, he's taking me to work later today, too." She smiled, her eyes taking on a dreamy quality.

"Wow. I think you've got it almost as bad as I do," I teased her.

She chuckled. "Maybe. Have a good day. Love you."

"Love you, too, Mom."

Chapter 29

Rachel

Mom called that morning simply to tell me to have a good day, and it brightened my mood even more. I was able to briefly tell her that Kyp and I were dating. Once she remembered he was Jennifer's son, she was delighted. Mom was happy that I was happy. And she already liked Kyp. I was floating. I swear, there were helium balloons attached to my limbs.

"Holy smokes, Rachel," Megan said as soon as she found me at my locker before first hour. "If I didn't know you better, I'd say you were high," she teased.

"High on love?" Sam quipped as he came up behind her.

I laughed even as pleased embarrassment wiggled in my belly. Sam smiled and nodded at Kyp who was standing behind me. Close enough that I could feel the heat radiating off him.

"Here." Meg handed me a giant homemade chocolate heart wrapped in pink cellophane. I snorted and tucked it away in my purse.

"These may have to be a customer special when we open our bakery," I said.

Megan grinned. "I've actually been researching the business classes at a few community colleges in the surrounding area. We should make time to chat about

165

our game plan. We've got to start getting stuff in after Christmas."

"I know." I bit my lip. Things had gotten so far out of whack, that I'd honestly not spared our future baking business, *Nutmeg and Crumbs*, a single thought.

"Hey," Meg said, catching my arm, "you've had bigger problems. I can deal with this end of things. I'll sift through stuff and bring my findings to you and then we can make our decisions together."

I smiled gratefully. The sudden weight that had dropped on my shoulders lifted.

The bell for first period rang and we scattered to our classes, but not before Kyp gave my hand a quick squeeze. As I drifted down the hall toward class with Megan, I stumbled as images of Kyp kissing me behind the curtain last night filtered through my thoughts.

"Rachel, you okay?"

"Yeah." My cheeks heated as I realized the thoughts weren't my own. Kyp was sending them to me through our so-called link. The smile almost broke my face.

"Rach?"

"We're working on figuring out this link thing," I said and glanced at her.

"Must be some pretty good thoughts to make your face turn a shade of tomato." She chuckled.

"Shut up. Like you're any better with your conversations with Sam," I retorted as I felt my blush crawl down my neck as we sank into our seats just as the final bell rang.

****

The set was nearing completion. It was spectacular! It was one of the best sets the drama club had done in years. I sighed in contentment. I walked on stage and surveyed all our hard work. We just needed to finish the greenery on a few trees and paint the sides of the final few plywood bushes, and then we could move on to finishing up the costumes. A few kids milled about, the rest of our members still trickling in.

"Rachel?" Kyp called from backstage.

"Yeah?" I called back as I adjusted a branch on the nearest set tree.

"Are you sure that green paint is back here?"

"I just saw it a few minutes ago."

Whitney rolled her eyes. "Guys. They can't find anything, even if it's right in front of them."

I grinned at her. "Are you sure?" I hollered back to Kyp. I tried not to roll my eyes like Whitney just had. "I just saw it back by the door of the classroom before I came up here."

"I still don't see it."

"Kyp, it was just there," I called back, wondering how he could possibly have missed it. I arranged a cluster of leaves to appear more natural.

"Can you come help me real quick?"

Whitney sighed and gave me a pointed look. "You should have just gone and gotten it yourself the first time." She went back to adding foliage to her branch.

"Be right there," I answered and gave my branch a final pat. Fizz erupted in my belly as I walked toward Kyp and Wolf danced around in anticipation.

My knee-high boots were soft soled enough that they didn't make much noise as I traipsed backstage, behind the two sets of velvet curtains toward the far back corner.

I saw the paint cans before I saw Kyp. My

eyebrows wrinkled as I looked at the green paint cans, clearly stacked neatly together, right where I thought they should be. A noise directly to my right drew my attention.

Kyp snaked one arm out, grabbing my hand and tugging me against him. It was so unexpected that I toppled into him, and his other hand wrapped around my waist. Without waiting for permission, his head lowered, and his mouth covered mine in a sweet kiss. His lips were warm as he held me closer. I could feel his heart pounding beneath my hands splayed on his chest. He didn't try to deepen the kiss, but ended it instead, pulling back to rest his forehead against mine.

"I've wanted to do that all day," he groaned softly.

I was tingly all over and a little lightheaded. My lips curled up as heat pooled in my middle. Wolf flopped on her belly in satisfaction.

"It was harder to get you back here alone than I thought it would be," he whispered, a grin in his words.

"If I'd known *green paint* was code for *let's make out*, you might not have had to work so hard." I poked him gently.

He craned his head back further so he could see my eyes, searching. "Really?"

I lifted an eyebrow at him.

"So, if I were to tell you I still couldn't find the green paint…"

Butterflies swarmed up my spine. I glanced at his lips and back to his eyes. Wolf nudged me on, telling me to act on my instincts. So I did.

Reaching up on my tip toes, I tangled my arms around his neck and stretched up to kiss him.

Chapter 30

Kyp

Kissing Rachel was the best thing I'd ever done. Her total acceptance made me feel complete in a way I never had before. Coupled with my new status as Alpha, I had reached a pinnacle I'd never even thought to aspire to.

But that brought a wave of insecurity crashing through me. I was the Alpha. And I wanted Rachel. I somehow had to keep those two things separate but functioning together.

Her lips slowly rubbed against mine, and I swear my blood ignited. I pulled back slightly, searching her face. Looking for any hint that she saw the struggle going on inside me.

"Green paint is good," she quipped.

I snorted. "I think I could get used to finding green paint. Frequently."

She smiled, her eyes twinkling mischief. "Come on. If we get the set stuff done, we can go home. I'm sure we could find some *green paint* if we looked hard enough." She winked.

My stomach dropped to my toes. That was dangerous territory. Not because I didn't want to kiss her, but because my mom wouldn't be home until late. And as the Alpha, I had to keep things in order.

My insides churned uncomfortably as I was taken back to another time—a darker time—back in Kentucky.

****

Avis Briar was the prettiest girl in the pack. With long blonde hair and curves earlier than the others our age, she was the top of the junior pack hierarchy. In the overall pack, she was just stuck somewhere in the middle like all the rest of—well, not me. I was the Omega. The runt. The excess baggage no one wanted.

Avis was my first real crush. I was thirteen, she was fourteen. I made no move, only watched her from the shadows. But I'd never really liked someone before. I wasn't as good at hiding that as I was hiding everything else. I learned quickly.

The teenagers—most of them older than me, though I'd been able to shift into fur longer than they had—gathered at the river one evening.

The fire flickered, sparks flying upward into the dark night. Stars sprinkled the sky and there was a hum of mosquitoes by the river water.

"Kiss her!" One of the guys laughed and pushed his friend toward one of the girls.

"Get away, you hairy idiot!" the girl screeched, not actually wanting him to stop. She playfully batted his shoulder as he leaned over and sloppily covered her mouth with his.

I turned my face away. It felt awkward to watch and I took no pleasure in it, although I was curious. I hadn't even been invited to come with the others, but no one had said I couldn't come. And I got so lonely that sometimes I was desperate enough for any scrap of attention they'd throw me. Tonight was one of those nights.

Curling my knees to my chest on the outside of the circle, just close enough to feel almost included, but not so close that the others took notice, I observed.

A few other couples broke off and went into the brush together while everyone else continued talking and laughing. Avis sat across from me on the other side of the fire. Occasionally I'd steal glances at her. Her hair shone like gold in the firelight and her teeth sparkled when she smiled.

As the loud talking and laughter died down, a quiet buzz of chatter surrounded us. I stole another glance at Avis and was surprised to find her watching me. One eyebrow arched lazily, and a tiny smile curled one side of her lips. Her perfect lips. Heat rushed through me and I was afraid the other wolves might hear my increased heartbeat.

Gracefully, she unfolded her long legs from under her and crossed them at the ankle. Still Avis held my gaze. My mouth dried. She reached out her hand and crooked her finger at me then patted the grass next to her.

My eyes grew wide. Hope and fear mingled in my belly. Her chin raised, daring me to come over to her. Avis had never been mean to me the way many of the others had. Was it possible she could like me back? Wolf made a noise deep in his throat, wanting her acceptance badly.

Heart thundering and palms sweating, I rose and slowly entered the circle of light cast by the dancing flames. Avis smiled up at me, coy and inviting. I licked my lips. All talking died away and Wolf prickled inside me, suddenly wary now that we were the center of attention.

At that moment, the couples who had left the group earlier sprang from the brush. Two of them grabbed my arms and pinned them behind me while another yanked my head back by my hair.

I was in trouble. I clenched my teeth tight together so the whimper building in my chest wouldn't escape. Wolf gnashed and tore against my skin, wanting out, wanting to protect us. I forced him back down. It would only be a bloodier confrontation if I let him out. He snarled and howled inside me.

Avis rose on her long legs, lightly padding three steps to me. Dread settled like lead in my stomach.

Without warning, her fist shot out and punched me in the gut. I wheezed and strained against the bigger wolves holding me.

"What makes you think you can look at me?" she asked. Her voice was cold and dripped venom. Wolf recoiled inside me and any hope I'd tried to secretly harbor that someday she might like me withered to ash. "You are dirt. You are nothing. You will never be one of us. You will never be a werewolf. You are a dirty little inbred whelp. Your mother is a whore and your father never wanted you. Knew you were worthless. If you ever touch me, or look at me again, I'll gouge out your eyes with my fangs."

Each word cut deeper than the last, far more painful than the blows that then rained down on me. I'd been black and blue for days. But the emotional scars left that night went far deeper.

****

I shook my head to clear the hated memory and focused on Rachel's face.

172

"Hey, where'd you go?" she asked softly. Her green eyes searched mine as her hands found mine, grounding me to the present. To her.

I hoped I was enough.

Chapter 31

Rachel

The double doors of the drama room swished shut behind me, a folder full of loose sheet music and stage notes for play practice clasped in my hands. I was trying to hurry. Jennifer's car was in the shop, so she'd borrowed Kyp's truck. We'd come in my car and I wanted to be sure we got to the auto shop on time. I was having trouble getting a few obstinate pieces shoved back into their proper places, so I didn't notice when I nearly ran smack into two guys by the water fountain, a few paces away from the doors of the choir room.

"Hey, there she is." One of them elbowed the other. My nose immediately told me they were wolves, though I didn't know their names. They were vaguely familiar—from the Thornehill pack probably. Maybe their parents planned to stay for a while and had enrolled them in school already. Definitely younger than me, but definitely much larger.

"Hey?" It came out sounding like a question as I returned their stares.

The blond one lounging against the wall pushed off, his height impressive at somewhere over six feet. His hands were shoved into his pockets, feigning disinterest, but his eyes were bright with…anticipation? His eyes raked over me and Wolf immediately raised her hackles. Unease and irritation slid down my spine and coiled tight like a spring wound taut in my belly.

They came a step closer, and I started to feel boxed in. My hands started sweating while Wolf crouched, uneasy as well. I glanced around. There was no one left in this hallway. It was just the three of us.

"Well, come on," the fatter one with brown hair said.

I lifted an eyebrow. "Excuse me?"

"Come on. We want to see, too."

"What are you talking about?" I had no idea what they were going on about. "Did you want to look over the sheet music for the play? You'll have to wait for the spring production tryouts." I held up the folder in my hand apologetically.

They glanced at each other, sharing a sly glance and a chuckle.

"You're funny," the blond said. "Quit messing around. Somebody will come down here eventually."

"Sorry, guys, no idea what you're talking about, but I've got to go."

"Now hold on," the chubby one said, taking another step into my space. He was close enough to touch and that was way too close for my comfort. I felt myself involuntarily back up a step. I was wishing I'd taken Kyp up on his offer to meet me at the drama room instead of at my locker before heading to the auto shop.

"Come on," he said in an almost whiny voice. "Seriously! The Rogue said he got a free show!"

Rogue—Kyp? He wasn't Rogue anymore. What did Kyp have to do with any of this?

"One quick peek. It's not like you're keeping secrets if you're sharing them with the Rogue," the blond said.

"See what?"

They shared slightly confused glances.

"You know," the shorter one said, lowering his voice to a whisper even though no one else was around. "Your boobs."

"*What*?" I shrieked. "Back off and leave me alone. I don't know what you heard, but clearly, you were mistaken. There have been no free shows, nor will there be." Wolf was snarling and simmering barely below the surface.

The plump one grabbed hold of my arm and my adrenaline spiked. He wasn't amused. He was pretty ticked off.

"I heard him. The Rogue said you let him strip you bare. I'm a whole lot higher up the social ladder than he is. My turn."

Shock had me rooted to the spot. Kyp told people *what*? Hurt, betrayal, anger, and then icy fear twisted my gut as I tried to yank my arm out of the boy's grasp and couldn't.

"Let go of me," I tried to say, but it came out strangled and barely above a whisper.

The blond one walked up. "I know what to do."

I didn't like anything that sentence implied, and I tried to wrack my brain for anything helpful. Wolf was preparing for a full-scale launch, but if I shifted here, I'd still be at the mercy of these two. Random wolf inside the high school attacking two teenage boys? Or three ruthless wolves descend upon the hallways of Rock Falls High? The headlines would be fantastic.

"Hold her," he said. Fear escalated to panic at that, and before I knew what I was doing, I kicked out hard and caught the brown-haired boy soundly in the groin. He dropped like a rock and grabbed his crotch.

"You little," the rest was lost as he curled in on himself, holding his injured body parts. I didn't stick around to offer consolation. I wheeled around the blond boy and gasped painfully as a chunk of hair came out at the roots as he grabbed for me and mostly missed. I didn't slow down, and I jetted down the hallway.

"*Stop!*" the waves of power rolled over me and had me stumbling against the wall. Adrenaline mixed with panic and fur rippled over my hands in fear. Panic gripped me with indecision as a few fuzzy dots hovered at the edge of my vision. My fight or flight response was muddled somewhere in between and rooted me to the floor. I was sure Mr. Wolfe would take care of this once the events reached his ears…but I didn't think I'd make it unscathed for that long. That thought kicked my heart up yet another notch and my breath came in tight pants. I would not go down like this. I would not be humiliated or used in this way. I gritted my teeth and glared at the boy as he marched toward me. Something wild broke free inside me, something both foreign to me and to the wolf and together we embraced it. I shook my head.

Power coursed through my veins. I had no idea what was going on, but suddenly I felt invincible. With a monumental effort and a shake from Wolf, I threw off the restraints his words had drawn around me. Wolf lunged inside me, and my flight response kicked into high gear.

"*No!*" I spat out as I turned on my heel and raced down the hallway, catching only a glimpse of the boy's stunned face as I turned the corner. He wasn't chasing me, and I didn't slow down. I caught a few odd stares by the last few stragglers as I ran to my car, fumbling to get my keys out of my purse while I dashed across the parking lot.

My car beeped as I clicked the unlock button. After nearly yanking the door from the frame, I collapsed into the front seat, shaking so uncontrollably that I almost couldn't hit the button to lock the doors. Jamming the gear shaft into drive, I lurched out of the parking lot and onto the street.

Tears dripped down my face as I turned to go straight to the cabin. I needed my best friend. I had just been harassed and nearly forced to do something against my will. But most of all, I was betrayed. By the one person I was deeply coming to care for—the one person who should care for me as part of his pack, even if he felt nothing else.

He had kissed me—was he only using me, too? My heart cracked as a sob shuddered out of my throat. I careened around the corner, out of sight of the high school. I had kissed him first. Maybe he didn't really like me. Maybe he just wanted a free boob flashing, too. I sped down the back road. Away from Kyp. Was I wrong about everything I thought I knew about him?

****

My face was a soggy mess of streaked mascara and red patchy blotches from my crying jag, which I wasn't sure was entirely over, as I pulled into the gravel drive at the cabin. I shut off the engine as Meg opened the door, her face going from pleased to shock to alarm in about two seconds.

I opened the door as she reached my car.

"Rachel, what's wrong?" She dragged me into a

hug before I was completely on my feet and I collapsed against her, the tears coming on again. Wolf didn't ask to be let out, just nudged me and howled inside, commiserating the feeling of complete betrayal.

"Is it Joanie?" she whispered.

I shook my head. "Let's go inside and I'll try to explain." My voice was wavering and rough.

Sam poked his head out the door, took one look at me, and his eyebrows practically disappeared into the hair flopped over his forehead. He said nothing, just held the door open for both of us as we stumbled through together.

"Girl time?" Meg asked quietly as we came into the kitchen. I nodded miserably.

She glanced at Sam. "Girl time," she said more clearly. He nodded and swiped his phone from the kitchen table and snagged his calculus book as he shoved the phone into his back pocket.

"Rachel, anything I can do?" he offered. I shook my head. There was a lot he could do, and at some point tonight, I'd need to tell him what happened, but I needed to talk to Meg first. She would understand this on a level no one else would. Best friends were like that.

"Okay. Meg, let me know?" She nodded at him and he ducked back to drop a quick kiss on her lips before he shut the door behind him. They were so obviously in love it was almost sappy. Normally, I'd silently approve of their obvious affection, but today it was irritating as the knife of betrayal twisted in a little deeper when I thought about what Kyp must have said about me to those two guys. With the same degree that I cared for him, in that second, I hated him with equal ferocity.

Wolf growled inside me.

"Come on," Meg said as she pulled out a kitchen chair for me. I sank into it as she pulled down two large mugs from the cabinet and put the kettle on the stove.

"I hardly know where to start," I croaked. "The two guys who tried to force me to flash my boobs, or the fact that *Kyp* told everyone I'm good for a free show, or that one of them tried to control me and force me." I glanced up. Meg's eyes were wide, her lips parted, her hands frozen around a plate of sugar cookies she was bringing to the table.

"Rachel," she said aghast. "Tell me *everything!*"

And I did. I didn't leave out anything. The tears came again in torrents as I worked through the fear and anxiety and heartbreak the thoughts dredged back up.

I was about halfway through the tale and hadn't even gotten to express my hurt and anger at Kyp's part in all of this when there was a knock at the door.

Meg's eyebrows drew together. She started to get up. Then I sensed it. I sensed *him*. I waved her back down, my anger boiling over into a fiery rage that threatened to consume not just me, but also the man at the door. Wolf added to my inner pain, gnashing her teeth at the thought of the coming confrontation. I stood up so fast that the chair nearly tipped over behind me. I stalked to the door and threw it open to reveal Kyp's very worried face. *He should be worried!* I thought.

"Rachel! I was so wor—"

Slap!

He didn't finish the sentence because my palm connected solidly with his jaw. His head jerked back before wild eyes focused on mine, bewilderment etched across his face.

"How dare you!" I choked. I was so angry I couldn't even get the words out. "Of all the nasty things you could have done. You took the most vulnerable moment of my life and twisted it into something horrible and then spread it around the entire pack that, what, I'm the person you call when you need a good time?"

Hideous images of that afternoon, the faces of the two boys, being backed into the corner and threatened, hammered my skull and I couldn't make them disappear fast enough. I channeled the fury they caused into my next words. My voice broke and a huge sob worked its way up my throat and the last of my resolve crumbled as I uttered the three words I was sure would never be true again.

"*I trusted you.*"

I didn't wait for a reply. I didn't wait for anything. I slammed the door in his face and sagged to the floor in a heap, my hands covering my face as tears, snot, and anguish covered my cheeks. Kyp and Rachel were so done. I couldn't see any way to resolve this kind of breach of trust. I didn't care if he was my Alpha. I'd transfer packs just as soon as I could stop the tears from tracking down my cheeks.

Meg's arms slid around me, and I sobbed into her shoulder, the fear, the anxiety, the hurt all leaked out through my eyes until I felt hollow. The only other time I'd been this upset was when I found out about Joanie. And if I was honest with myself, I wasn't even so much upset about what happened in the hallway this afternoon anymore. I was upset because it was *Kyp*—and until two hours ago, I'd been quickly falling in love with him.

Chapter 32

Kyp

I stood there, stunned, jaw smarting, the door slammed in my face. *What happened?*

Stumbling as I backed down the steps to the gravel of the driveway, I slowly turned, wondering what to do next. Obviously, something major had gone down. And Rachel thought it was my fault. I took a deep breath as painful flashbacks of the fire pit and my first crush wormed their way into my brain. I shook my head. Rachel wasn't Avis. Wolf was just as confused as I was.

Images started flitting into my head. Gasping in shock, I realized that I was seeing Rachel's thoughts—memories. What had happened to her. Wolf stood and snarled, the faces of Rachel's tormentors clearly pictured in my mind's eye. My blood boiled and a growl ripped from my throat. I didn't care who they were. Rachel was mine—my pack. Turning on my heel, I marched toward the neighborhood below the cabin. No one was going to mess with my pack. No one would touch Rachel again.

Getting ahold of myself about halfway down the gravel road to Dominic's house, I yanked my shirt off over my head, dragged my shoes and pants off, heedless of any eyes that may have been watching.

Tipping my head to the moon, I let the change fall over me, relishing the sharp sensation of fur along my back, and the piercing of my fangs as they jutted through my mouth. I'd be using them soon.

Scooping my clothes in my mouth, I took off back down the road at a fast clip. My anger built, fueling me, sending a steaming cloud of fury roiling through me.

Images continued to float through my brain, some the same ones I'd seen already, others new pieces of the story.

A low growl slipped between my teeth. Whoever the two guys were, they reminded me of one reason I'd hated living in the Kentucky pack. They used people. I was done being used, and no one in my pack would be used against their will either.

Houses came into view. Clenching my teeth at the need for skin, I shifted back and quickly dressed. Unsure how best to proceed to find my targets, I took a quick stroll down the sidewalk.

Luck was with me and I hadn't gone more than a block and a half before two shapes matching the ones in my head emerged at the mouth of the woods at the far side of the subdivision.

Sniffing, I caught their scents and approached. They glanced up from whatever had them occupied as I drew nearer.

"Who are you?" the tall one asked.

"The Alpha. You messed with my pack."

The fat one sneered.

"I don't know what you're talking about."

"Tell me about after school today." My voice echoed with restrained power and Wolf puffed his chest inside me, straightening my back and widening my stance.

A growl meant as bravado but interlaced with fear tinged the air as the pair of them turned fully to face me.

"There are two of us and one of you. I don't care if you're an Alpha." The blond one clenched his fists.

A smirk bearing no amusement twisted my lips. "I'll take my chances."

Chapter 33

Rachel

I had calmed enough to drink a cup of steaming herbal tea. My eyes were swollen and puffy. I'd washed the last vestiges of makeup off and all that remained were the red blotches that said I'd recently cried my eyes out. I took another sip of tea and glanced up at Meg.

"What is it?" she asked.

"I feel guilty. Horribly guilty."

"For what?" she sounded surprised.

I sighed, silently cursing my over-active conscience and my reckless behavior. "I slapped him. I realize he absolutely deserved it after breaking my trust and my heart all in the same afternoon, but that doesn't mean I needed to lose control, haul off and hit him." Wolf snorted.

"Well, I wasn't going to say it, but I was pretty surprised when you did. Although, I don't think I was as surprised as Kyp was."

I gave her a weak chuckle before dropping my head to the table and groaning. "Meg, why would he do this? The worst part of it isn't even the nasty rumor—it's that *he* spread it! No one else knew how I became a wolf! I, he bit me…and then we were together. I wanted to be with him more than I've ever wanted to be with anyone. Boyfriends and girlfriends are supposed to be able to share secrets—so are Alphas and pack members! I mean, I told you, but I tell you everything. And I know you didn't go blabbing it around that I get naked for people just because. Seriously? Can you even picture me randomly flashing some guy?"

"Not remotely. I'm so sorry any of this has happened. But I still find it hard to believe that Kyp did this. It doesn't seem like him."

She was about to say more but there was another knock at the door. Wolf perked up, her ears pricking forward. Why was *he* here? Meg glanced at my stony face and went to the door.

"Hi, Kyp," she greeted him tentatively after a sharp intake of breath.

"Please tell Rachel that no one is going to bother her about this ever again. And that…just tell her."

"I will. Are—"

"Thanks," he cut her off. I couldn't see him from where he stood on the porch, but he sounded a little off. Guilt flooded my belly again. I told myself I shouldn't feel guilty. This was his fault. I was the injured party. I shook my head. Anger still seethed under my skin. But that still wasn't excuse enough for my actions. I rose stiffly from the table as Meg shut the door. She glanced at me and grabbed my jacket from the back of the couch and handed it to me. She knew me so well.

"Go easy on him until you have the full story," she whispered. That did nothing to ease the knot of tension rammed against my breastbone.

My arms slid into my coat as I stepped into the night. Kyp wasn't very far away and he turned when the door creaked.

The moonlight shined down on him and I caught my breath. I understood Meg's words then. Kyp's face was a mess. His lip was split, and he had a gash above his left eyebrow. He saw me standing there, mouth open like an idiot, and one of his arms reached over to clasp his other. He said nothing, and his face gave away nothing. My boiling rage lowered to a simmer as curiosity slowly overtook my other emotions.

"Kyp," His name came out strangled through my confusion and anger. He took a tentative step closer. "I'm sorry I slapped you." But that was all I was sorry for. Even still, I couldn't force the words *we're through,* out my lips. My heart cracked all over again looking at his bruised face.

He bobbed his head once, expression still impassive.

"Can we talk?" he asked slowly like he was talking to a wild animal, which, I supposed, wasn't that far off the mark.

I nodded stiffly. I would let him have his final words—which had better include a major apology—and then we were over.

He glanced around. "Somewhere a little more private?" I wasn't sure exactly what he had in mind. There weren't presently a ton of options. My car was still sitting there in the driveway though, and while it wouldn't be particularly warm, with the doors shut, it would offer some measure of privacy. Maybe sitting in the cold would speed up this conversation and then we could get on with our respective lives.

I inclined my head. "My car is unlocked."

He waited for me until I was even with him so we could walk the remaining steps to my car together. I refused to look at him even as guilt, anger, and apprehension churned in my gut. Before I could do it myself, he reached out and opened the back door of my car for me. I glanced at him, trying not to outright glare, and crawled in.

My breath plumed in little white puffs and I pulled my knees up to my chin as Kyp slid in the other side.

We sat there a minute, neither of us quite meeting the other's eyes, neither of us quite sure where to start. Eventually his eyes flitted to my face and he took a deep breath.

"I'm so sorry about what happened to you today." Anger sparked through me, shaking off some of the chill.

"Then why did you start the rumor in the first place?"

He appeared genuinely confused. "Rachel, I didn't tell anyone anything. I told Sam and Dominic what happened, but that's it."

My mouth pinched shut as unease slithered its way down my back. I wasn't buying it. "Are you serious? Jerkface One and Jerkface Two said you told them I was good for a free show." I spat the venom-laced words at him.

He sighed and ran a hand gingerly over his face.

"I gathered. Actually, I made them tell me exactly what happened. I told Sam, in a fair amount of detail, what happened the day I bit you. I wasn't sharing details to hurt you, I was sharing details to try to explain what happened, and to maybe salvage my place in his pack. But that's it."

"You didn't tell anyone else?" My small bud of guilt was blooming into a sizeable plant. He shook his head as an expression of genuine hurt reached his eyes.

"I thought you knew me better," he said quietly, his eyes not quite meeting mine. Wolf nudged me hard within. I *did* know Kyp better. Though Wolf and I had been so blindsided by anger and anxiety that we'd ignored all rationality. That plant of guilt turned into vines that were threatening to strangle me. I wasn't so sure that I was the injured party anymore. My anger morphed into shame. It appeared that I'd done far more wrong to Kyp than Kyp had done to me. I was ashamed. Tears pricked the back of my eyes again and I blinked rapidly to keep them at bay.

"What happened to you?" I whispered, afraid my voice would break if I said it any louder. He glanced up at me, his mouth thinning.

"I guess you heard me telling Megan. You won't be having any more trouble from Jerkface One and Jerkface Two."

Heat slid through me and understanding dawned as my shame curdled in my belly. *I* was the reason for the gash and his bloody lip, not to mention the bruise I could now see purpling over his jaw. He'd fought for me—for my honor. I had abused him with my anger, and he had still gone off to protect me. He was still acting as my Alpha. A good one. He had kept my secrets and protected me the best way he knew how. The tears gathering at the back of my eyes couldn't be contained anymore and a few of them slid down my cold cheeks.

"Rachel, don't cry," he said softly.

"I'm so sorry, Kyp." A sob was working its way up my throat. How did I even have tears left? My reservoir wasn't dry yet, because more tears followed. I felt horrible. How could I have mistreated Kyp so badly?

His hands twitched, hesitating. Finally, he said, "Come here." He eased an arm around my shoulders, and I let him pull me into him, though I was certain I didn't deserve his comfort at the moment. His other arm wrapped around me and rubbed up and down my arm as I pressed my face into his jacket.

When the tears started to dry, I ventured another question. I did nothing to move out of the circle of Kyp's arms, even though I wondered if I should have. I may have ended our relationship with my anger, though I only wanted him more than ever now. Wolf whined inside me. I couldn't lose Kyp. "How did you know who the two guys were?"

His hand stilled its circular motion over my elbow. My belly tensed as he didn't immediately answer.

"After you slammed the door, I started walking toward the woods, trying to figure out what had just happened when pictures started filtering into my mind." A shudder rippled through him and he winced. I sat back afraid I was pushing on a sore spot. His arm slid away, but his hand rested close to mine. Not actually holding it but touching on the seat. He looked me in the eye. "I *saw* what happened to you today."

"How is that possible? We've never shared a mental link." I gasped, remembering the horrible mental images that had popped into my head as I'd given Kyp an earful earlier in the evening.

"I don't think it should be possible," he replied. "I was barely ever able to link with my Kentucky Alpha, even more rarely with his Beta. We don't have a mate bond, so I think this might be some sort of weird half-breed aberration. I guess because I was the one to change you. Maybe because we're our own pack. Maybe this is my half-wolf version of an Alpha link. It took me a minute to realize what was going on. Everything was fuzzy and hazy at first, but the more I concentrated on it, the more the whole picture came together." His eyes searched my face, and his lips drew down as he raised his hand and let it hover before softly touching my hair. "How's your head?"

"You saw him pull my hair out?"

He nodded, heat flooding his face, although I was pretty sure it was from anger and not embarrassment.

"I took some pain killers a while ago."

"Rachel, I'm sorry."

I shook my head. "No more apologies. It's done, and you've done more than your fair share to right the situation. But how did they so misconstrue what happened?"

He grimaced. "That's why I wanted to talk more privately. I told Sam out by the fire pit. Neither of us could sense anyone else, but there was a bird that took off suddenly that startled us both. I'm sure it was the other two wolves that frightened it. I confirmed that the blond one overheard part of the conversation, but clearly missed the context. He told his buddy, and that's how it started. They didn't tell anyone else, just assumed things. They'll be going back to New York in the morning."

"I'm sorry I doubted you, Kyp." I hiccupped. "Has this…have I ruined everything?" I forced the whisper out.

He bit his lip, staring at the floorboard, some internal war waging within him. Wolf crumpled to a heap as he didn't immediately respond. After what felt

191

like an age, he spoke. "I," he swallowed, "it's hard for me. To open up to people." He glanced back up at me. Vulnerability was stamped across his bruised face, but he continued, struggling to get the words out. "You know more about me than anyone. When I first moved here, you were the one who went out of your way to make me feel comfortable in this foreign world of werewolves that you'd only just discovered. You told me about your sister. And then you asked me to bite you." He stopped, swallowing hard again.

"Save me," I quietly corrected, my fingers nudging his. He gripped them, and I could feel his shaking slightly. Were they shaking because he was breaking up with me and it made a part of him sad? Was he nervous?

"Change you," he amended, "and...that brought another level to our friendship—to our *pack*. You know me because you want to. Even after all the stuff that's happened over the past few weeks. No one's ever done that for me before. There have always been strings attached to every relationship I've had with anyone aside from my mom. I've always been the outcast, the runt, the Omega, the Rogue. And while I've accepted that—it is what it is, and I am who I am—you were the first person that genuinely didn't care about any of that."

The magnitude of what my doubt and anger cost him struck me like a blow. What had my quick temper and my inability to rationally think through a situation done to him?

"But after tonight," he continued. My heart withered, drying up to dust as the dam of my never-ending tears was near to bursting again. "I think it might be good to take a step back. I'm still wrestling with how to be an Alpha, how to *be* in a relationship." He looked up and met my eyes, mine with tears puddling in them, waiting for him to finish killing the relationship I'd so unwittingly sabotaged.

"Are you breaking up with me?" The words were like a knife going straight through my chest. His eyes gentled.

"Rachel, I don't want to break up with you. I care about you more than I've ever cared about anyone. But I think if we're going to do this right, we need to take things slower—figure out how to be a pack, how to trust each other without question."

I nodded. I *needed* Kyp. "Can I hug you?" I felt the need to ask. One side of his mouth raised. I leaned forward on my knees and wrapped my arms around him as much as the tight confines of the car would allow.

"I was wrong, Kyp. You are so much more than any of the labels anyone has ever put on you. I'm so sorry I hurt you."

"Rachel," he murmured as his hands came around me. One slid to the base of my head while his other wrapped firmly around my waist. He leaned his face into the crook of my neck but then jerked back.

"What's wrong?" I asked, loosening my hold around his shoulders.

"Sorry. I don't want to get any blood on you."

I leaned in and kissed his cheek before I thought better of it. His eyes widened and I blushed. "Sorry. Slower."

His thumb brushed over my chin sending gooseflesh prickling down my arms. Wolf sighed. She was content knowing we hadn't lost Kyp. The human side of me was still concerned, but not panicked anymore.

"Come on. I know your mom knows a lot more about this than I do, but you can tell me what to do and we'll see if we can patch you up inside the cabin."

Besides, as I glanced out the window toward the yellow porch light, I realized how foggy the windows had become. We'd start all sorts of other rumors if we weren't careful.

"All right, but I don't think it's anything that won't heal on its own in a few days."

"Does it usually take that long?"

"One of the perks of only being half." His lips gave a sardonic twist.

"Sorry," I started.

"Don't be, Rachel. I know you didn't mean it like that."

I smiled and reached over to give his arm a quick squeeze. He grinned back, and I could have sworn that his eyes flitted ever so quickly to my lips, but I could have been mistaken in the darkness of the car. Maybe I hadn't completely killed off the best thing in my life.

****

Meg was furiously scrubbing a cookie sheet at the sink when we walked back in.

"Rachel, I was about ready to come looking for you myself! Is everything okay?" I nodded as Kyp came in behind me. "Kyp, are you all right?" she exclaimed as he walked into the light of the dining room, his face streaked with dirt, several shades of purple on his jaw, and the two bloody spots fully visible.

"I'll live." He grinned lopsidedly.

"Can you grab the first aid stuff, Meg?" I asked as I pulled out a chair for Kyp.

"Sure." She crossed the room and grabbed the white box from the top drawer in the far dresser. "If everyone is okay, I'm going to step out just a sec and give Sam a call. Rachel, you need to tell him what happened."

I nodded.

"If he's free, go ahead and have him come up. I'd like to discuss a few things with him, too," Kyp added.

Chapter 34

Kyp

It didn't take Sam long to get back to the cabin. And it didn't take long for us to give him the short version of what happened that day.

"Woah. And you took both of them on in a fight?" Sam asked, his eyebrows shooting up. He glanced at the stark bruises on my face.

"I did. It's been a while, but it wasn't unusual for the Kentucky Alpha to pit two or three bigger wolves against me. It was part of my *training* he said." I couldn't help the bitter note that slipped into my voice. It had been part of their *entertainment*, but in the end, it had made a competent fighter out of me. I could hold my own with wolves much larger than me, and with more than one wolf at a time. As was evidenced by the fight I'd just won with the two idiots who confronted Rachel. After fifteen minutes, they'd flashed me their underbellies like white flags of surrender.

"I'm impressed," Sam said.

"I also made it clear to them that they were to leave the area by tomorrow morning." I wasn't sure if that was overstepping myself since I wasn't in my own territory—even if I'd had any—but as Rachel's Alpha, I felt justified. No one was going to screw around with me or mine, now that I could help it.

To my relief, Sam nodded. "We don't need wolves like that hanging around. They'd just be asking for trouble. We've got enough of that. I'll speak to Dad or their parents if you want the added support. Immature wolves aren't going to help our cause. Austin Thornehill will back that up, too. Especially since they're his wolves."

****

I laid awake in bed a long time that night. Thoughts of Rachel, Avis, the two wolves that had accosted Rachel, and then my fight with them all jumbled in my brain. I rubbed my chest to relieve the tight knot of tension lodged beneath my ribs.

Rachel's reaction—and her quick belief that I would betray her like that—sat heavily on me. Her lack of trust in me both as her boyfriend and as her Alpha soured in my belly. Should I even be her Alpha? I was certain she deserved better—someone who actually knew *how* to be an Alpha, someone who could properly care for her and look after her. Her lack of faith in me had rocked my own perception of myself. I was floating on a sea of doubt and had no anchor.

Maybe I should rescind my Alphaship and beg Dominic to take Rachel into his pack. I'd leave. Go my own way. Find some dark corner of the earth and just live out the rest of my days as a wolf.

Wolf snarled inside me, puffing out his chest. He flooded my head with images of Mom. I couldn't leave her. I had a responsibility to take care of her. And Rachel. Wolf stood up straight, displaying his dominance, reminding me that *we were the Alpha*. He sent images of Rachel to the front of my mind. The way her green eyes sparkled when she looked at me. The

AJ Skelly

way she'd kissed me that night behind the stage curtain. The way she'd felt, all curve and kindness.

Shaking my head, I rolled onto my side. A floorboard creaked and I wondered if Rachel was still awake, too. Part of me wanted to go check, to pull her into my arms and soak in the feeling of hers coming around me. Would she kiss me again? Would she hold me back? Did she need me? Could I be what she needed?

The night passed with fitful sleep.

Chapter 35

Rachel

Kyp had managed to get his mom's car back from the shop while I had my escapade—unwittingly attempting to destroy our relationship with my impulsivity and anger yesterday—so today we rode together in his truck.

Tension crackled the air between us. Wolf whined, dying a little on the inside as Kyp—still my boyfriend...I thought—drove, looking straight ahead, a line creasing his forehead as his eyebrows nearly met. Wolf nudged me. This needed to air.

"Kyp," I ventured before my courage could leave me.

He startled and glanced over at me. "Yeah?"

I wet my lips. "I'm still sorry. About yesterday."

His face softened as his eyes went back to the road. "I'm sorry you got hurt," he said quietly. Unease slithered in my belly. Was he also sorry we had all this weirdness between us now? Did he regret not completely breaking up with me?

"I hate this tension between us," I blurted.

Kyp glanced at the clock on the dash and then pulled off the road. We weren't quite in town yet, and wide meadows sparkled outside the windows as the early morning sunlight hit the frost.

Kyp looked at me, a helpless expression on his face. "I don't know what to do," he finally admitted.

"About what?" I bit my lip, afraid the death knell of our relationship was coming now that he'd thought more about it last night.

He shrugged, glancing back out the front windshield again. "Any of it. I don't know how to be your Alpha. I don't know how to be your boyfriend." He drifted off, not looking at me. Wolf nudged me. I knew Kyp well enough to know he was having a crisis of confidence. But maybe it meant that his thoughts were pinwheeling more about his own behavior, rather than mine.

"Kyp, you are a wonderful boyfriend. Not that we've been doing this very long, but still. You are an amazing friend. And you've protected me and saved my life several times already. How can you think you're not a good Alpha?"

His shoulders sagged.

"I still want this. Do you?"

His gaze tore from the glittering frost to my face. "I do, Rachel. I just don't know how."

"I don't know how either, or know any different, for that matter." I gave him a small smile. "Can we figure it out together?" I reached my hand across the seat, palm up.

Slowly his slid on top of mine, gripping it tightly. "Yeah." His voice was hoarse.

****

School was exhausting. It dragged. And dragged. By the time play practice rolled around, I just wanted a hug and a cup of coffee.

We still had the stupid greenery to finish. Every

time I saw a bush or clump of ivy, it made me think of green paint. And how badly I wanted Kyp to kiss me again. We'd tried to be normal at school, but there was still this underlying tension that we just could not seem to get rid of. I didn't know if it was me or him, but it was there, and I still hated it. It was better than it had been, but almost like a third person in our relationship.

"Rachel, are you sure this is the right shade of green? I think we used a darker one yesterday. Doesn't this look lighter to you?" someone called as they waved a paintbrush over a plump bush. It was the last straw. I wanted to snap.

"Ask Luke." I took myself backstage to collect my tattered emotions and be alone for just a moment. I was going to combust under all this pressure.

"Hey." Kyp's voice was quiet as he materialized from the shadows.

I swiped a hand over my face and dragged my red curls away from my eyes. "I really need a hug," I blurted.

"I have one of those." A smile teased his mouth, though his eyes were serious. "But I think they work best if both parties hug the other at the same time."

"Agreed," the word slid from my lips in a rush as I reached my arms up around his neck. His hands tentatively encircled my waist. "Nnmm. You have to give it with your whole self. Otherwise, it doesn't count." I squeezed him extra tight and felt it when he let go of whatever awkwardness that was holding him back. His arms tightened and he took a shuddering breath against my hair. Tension ebbed from my shoulders as we stood there, arms around each other, trying to silently mend what had gone wrong between us.

Kyp's phone vibrated. I frowned, irritated at the intrusion. I wasn't done with my hug yet. I was going to ignore it, but Kyp pulled back.

He scowled. "It's Sam. Have to take it," he whispered. His voice was rough. He quickly released me, leaving me cold in the absence of his arms, and fished his phone out of his pocket.

"Hey," he said into the phone, his face and voice showing none of the displeasure I was feeling. My insides writhed. Was he glad for the intrusion?

Kyp's expression shifted. His eyebrows rose and his mouth thinned. Sam was quiet enough on the other end that I couldn't hear the conversation, even though I was close to the phone.

"All right. We'll be right there."

Unease gathered in my belly and roused Wolf. Something was not right.

"What's wrong?" I asked as soon as he hung up the phone.

"I'm not sure, but something's up. We need to leave. Now. Greenery will have to be finished by other people."

Chapter 36

Kyp

Sam hadn't said what was wrong on the phone, but his voice had been tight, and it hadn't been a request to come.

"I need you to come to the house. Now," he'd said. Wolf pricked his ears forward and sent all my new Alpha senses to high alert as we exited the back of the school. Some of my hearing and smelling had improved as my body changed and adapted to my new role.

"Kyp, what's wrong?" Rachel asked as she walked beside me to the truck.

"I don't know. Sam just said we need to get to Dominic's house immediately. I was listening and scenting."

"Oh. Sorry, I didn't mean to interrupt," she said quietly and grabbed my hand. I glanced at her, relishing the feel of her skin against mine. Her eyes were distant, and I could tell her wolf was coming to the fore to do her own perimeter check.

I opened the truck for her and smiled when I realized she'd scooted over to the middle seat rather than sitting by the door. I wanted to kiss her again, but I was still feeling insecure about a lot of things, and Wolf was pulling me to hurry to get to Sam.

Duty won and the truck rumbled to life.

A few minutes later we were parked in Dominic's driveway. Another dark SUV was already there next to his car.

"Do you know who that SUV belongs to?" Rachel asked.

"No, I don't. Maybe someone from the Thornehill pack?"

"Probably. Maybe it's Austin Thornehill's. Megan said they were coming down today."

I knocked on the door, my arm touching Rachel's and filling me with heat, despite what were probably grave circumstances waiting for us inside.

"Kyp, I'm glad you're here. Hi, Rachel," Sam said in a rush as he ushered us into the house and toward the living room.

Dominic, Austin Thornehill, and his daughter, Sarah, were seated.

"Austin," Dominic said rising, "I don't know if you've met our other allied Alpha, but this is Alexander Kypson."

Austin rose, as did Sarah.

"It's nice to meet you," Austin said, his blue eyes shining genuinely. I had met Sarah at HarvestFest but had only seen the Thornehill Alpha from a distance. I understood now where she got her light-colored hair, though her eyes were green like celery.

"Just Kyp is fine," I answered as I crossed the room to exchange customary scenting. I glanced back at Rachel. "This is Rachel. She's my pack." I couldn't help the note of pride that crept into my voice. I could tell Rachel was uncomfortable, but she came forward and exchanged scents with Austin.

"I think you've already met my daughter, Sarah?"

"We did meet briefly at HarvestFest. It's nice to see you again, Sarah," Rachel said with a smile.

"You, too. I've never had a better Russian Teacake than the one I had at your booth," Sarah commented with a smile, curiosity lighting her green eyes. Rachel had been fully human the last time Sarah had met her. Neither Sarah nor Rachel said anything. I didn't know if Dominic had told them anything or if he'd left it to me to handle my own pack business. Such as it was.

"I'm glad you liked it." Some of the unease dropped from Rachel's shoulders.

"We're here because there's been another development," Dominic broke in, ending all pleasantries before Sarah had even exchanged scents with either Rachel or me. "Victor Atwood has killed again."

The blood froze in my veins as Wolf stood fully, his chest puffing, every instinct driving me to protect Rachel. My finger began to worry over my thumb to keep myself still and not physically reach out and grab Rachel. I held back a shiver of relief when she stepped closer so that her shoulder touched mine.

"Who was it?" Rachel asked, her voice hushed.

"Sharon Murdock," Sam said. "He left her driver's license right on top of her slashed chest, though part of her face was missing like Mr. Steinbach's."

The floor began to spin and for a second I thought I was going to throw up. Wolf snapped his jaws.

"Mom." The word left my lips in a frozen hush as I scrambled to get my phone out of my pocket.

"Kyp? What's wrong?" Several voices spoke over one another, but I ignored them, holding Rachel's hand like a vice and praying for my mom to pick up her phone. I only called her at work if I meant it, so she'd pick up if she was able.

"Alexander? What's going on?"

"Mom, where are you?"

"I just got back from a call out. I'm getting ready to walk into the lounge."

"Listen to me. You are sick. Too sick to continue your shift. I want you to go to the ER waiting room. There are always people there and there's a guard on duty by the metal detectors. You wait there until either Jonathan or I come to pick you up. Do you understand?" If I hadn't been nearly panicked out of my mind at that moment, it would have been bizarre to hear myself ordering my mother around. But she didn't question it. She accepted it and my judgment.

"All right. Are you safe?" She breathed heavily.

"I'm fine. I need you to be, too."

"Love you. I'm feeling aches and pains coming on now."

"Love you, too. See you soon."

I clicked the call off, my heart still racing in my chest.

"You know Sharon Murdock?" Dominic questioned, one black bushy brow raised in surprise.

I shook my head. "No. But she's on Mom's crew. She called in sick this week. Mom has been covering some of her hours." I gulped. "I either need to go get her or call Jonathan." My voice held a finality that surprised even me. And I realized that I was placing a lot of trust in a werewolf I didn't know overly well. But Mom trusted him. I reminded Wolf that Mom had good instincts.

"Of course." Austin nodded, gaining a rapid

understanding of the situation. "That may mean that Atwood is abducting his victims and holding them before committing the murders."

My gut rolled again as I punched Jonathan's number.

"This is Stone."

"Jonathan. It's Kyp. Can you go pick up my mom at the hospital? Right now?"

"I'm leaving as we speak. Can I ask what's wrong?" I glanced at Dominic who nodded, his wolf-enhanced hearing having no problem picking up the phone conversation in the otherwise silent room.

"Atwood has murdered a member of my mom's crew."

I hung up the phone and realized my hand was shaking. I stuffed the phone back in my pocket and raised my eyes to meet the concerned gazes of everyone else in the room. Wolf nudged me and I straightened. Rachel squeezed my hand, and I felt my heart slow down a notch.

"Who found her?" I asked, glad there was no tremor in my voice.

"I did," Dominic answered stiffly. "Sam, too."

I glanced at Sam. His face was grim.

Dominic cleared his throat. "We are going to have to go on the offensive. I'm not sure yet how, but this cannot continue."

There was a murmur of agreements.

"Who's with the body now?" Sarah asked.

"One of our boys from the police. We have to let the police handle it officially, but at least we'll have a hand in it and all the police knowledge."

"Who's your man?" Austin asked.

"Gordon Rockwell," Dominic answered.

Sarah's eyebrows creased, trying to place the name.

"You remember Jake? You probably met Jake and Cindy at HarvestFest," Sam interjected.

"Oh! Gordon Rockwell is Jake's dad," Sarah clarified. Sam nodded.

Sudden images of Sam's cabin flitted across my brain. I blinked, then glanced at Rachel as I realized she was using our link. I focused and my mind saw Rachel sitting at the cabin table with Megan. Her emerald eyes were huge in her pale face. I bobbed my head, understanding this was too much for Rachel right now. I got it.

"Sam, is Megan at the cabin right now?"

He nodded. "Amalie Rivers is with her."

"I think I need to join them," Rachel said. Her freckles stood out against the paleness of her skin.

****

Once Rachel was snugged away with Megan and Amalie, the two Alphas, their Betas, and I set off to the location Gordon Rockwell had sent us. We needed to go on the offensive, and to do that, we had to find more information.

The plan was to split up and track back toward Victor's pack without getting too close. We needed evidence.

The place Sharon had been dumped reeked of blood. My stomach heaved as Wolf took in the tangy odor. It woke a place inside me that demanded power and my newly onset Alpha genes seemed to enhance that darker part. And that concerned me. I gave Wolf's will a good shake to remind him that I was in charge, even as an Alpha pair, *I* was still the Alpha. Insecurity gripped me afresh. Shaking my head to rid it of the inept feeling, I focused my senses back on my surroundings.

We spread out, noses to the ground. The police had been all over this area already when they'd taken the body, and it was hard for me to pick up a clean scent of wolf. The other wolves found it before I did.

Sarah's snowy wolf gave a quick yip and pawed the ground in front of her. The rest of us quickly moved over to where her white paw scratched at the dirt. I sniffed and caught the muskiness of wolf buried under the wet dirt and blood that seeped into everything. Dominic nudged me over and ran his nose across the whole area. His hackles raised. He must have recognized the scent. Sam growled low in his chest. Dominic looked up sharply at Sam who pointed with his nose to a small cluster of trees in the opposite direction. Austin and Sarah veered over and sniffed. Glancing at each other, they nodded and turned to the rest of us.

Wolf grumbled silently inside. I wished I had a working link. Although it was getting better with Rachel. I still felt alone out here, Alpha though I was, among these two established wolves with their pack mates. Technically, Rachel was my Beta, since she was the only other one in my pack. But I was glad she hadn't come for this. This was too much for her on top of everything else she was dealing with.

The wind whistled through another knot of trees to my right and a smell caught my nose. I couldn't identify exactly what it was, it just smelled *off*. It wasn't a normal forest odor. Barking, I got the others' attention and lifted my nose into the air, indicating they should scent as well.

The wind gusted again, and this time I got a nose full. What I smelled sent Wolf cowering and my blood turning to ice. I backed up, whimpering before I could stop myself.

Unable to communicate the full scope of my terror with the others, I did the only thing I could. I shifted.

"Run. It's a trap," my strangled voice choked out.

That smell was poison. I'd had it used on me once in the Kentucky pack after I lost a fight. As punishment, I'd had my hands dipped in a tar-like substance laced with wolfsbane and who knew what else. It had blistered my skin for days and separated me from my wolf until the blisters healed. It was excruciating. If they'd laid the stuff on the ground and one of us stepped on it, I had no doubt the same thing would happen. We'd be hobbled. Literally and figuratively. Victor could swoop in and snatch us up like a fat prize as we wallowed around in misery and pain, unable to shift to our wolves.

Dominic didn't waste time. He bulled his nose into Sam's side back the direction we'd come. Austin and Sarah turned as one and together we fled, careful to stay to our own scents so we stepped nowhere unnecessarily.

Back on Wolfe land, we slowed our frantic run, but not by much. Once we were seated in Dominic's living room, the moon was rising. My belly rumbled, and I realized I never ate dinner.

"Kyp, how did you know what that smell was?" Austin asked.

"I've had an unpleasant experience with it." I gave

them a brief description of what had happened to me.

Sam scrubbed a hand over his face. "He's a mastermind. If he could have taken us all out tonight, the rest of the packs would have been easy pickings."

"Did Jordan ever say any more about how Victor uses his mind control on his pack?" Dominic asked Austin about a prisoner from Victor's pack who had broken away from the maniac and taken refuge with the Thornehill pack.

"He didn't know how it worked, only that it did. Jordan said he wasn't even aware most of the time that he had been controlled but would sometimes find himself in strange situations or some place he knew he hadn't wanted to go. Sometimes he could feel it like a nudge and was still aware of what he was doing, and other times Victor just outright used command."

Ice chilled my blood once more. "How many people can he do this to at once?"

"His entire pack. All at the same time."

Sarah shifted in her seat, her eyes radiating hatred.

How were we supposed to defeat an invincible enemy?

Chapter 37

Rachel

Girl's night was exactly what I needed. Both to get my mind off Joanie's staggeringly slow recovery and the tension that was still present between me and Kyp. Things had felt better in the Wolfe's living room when we'd held hands out of desperation, but the talk of another body brought too many unstable emotions rising to the top. It was overwhelming and my head was still buzzing with excess emotion. And then there was Kyp. We weren't quite back to rights yet.

Amalie left to join a patrol near the cabin not long after I got there. I fished nail polish out of my purse. Because nail polish made everything better. Although, in retrospect, I did feel a little guilty leaving Sarah there by herself. I hadn't been thinking that she'd be coming up after the meeting—just that I needed to stop hearing horrible details before I spontaneously combusted.

"Rachel, can you grab the soda out of the fridge while I take these cookies off the sheet?" Megan said.

"Sure. Ooh, blackberry ginger ale! My favorite." I glanced at her and she smiled. She'd made my favorite cookies, got my favorite soda, and lit my favorite scented candle—pumpkin spice. "I appreciate all this, you know."

"You've had the worst few weeks of your life, and

I feel rotten. I haven't been able to go through it with you like I should." Megan frowned.

"Megan. You are the best friend ever. In the world."

Her eyebrows scrunched together. "Still. I feel like you've had to go through this on your own more than you should have."

"We've all had full plates. And on the plus side, I'm not sure Kyp and I would be, you know, Kyp and I, if you and I had been joined at the hip like normal." Although, if I were honest with myself, I wasn't sure we would come out of this with Kyp and Rachel still intact.

Megan's face relaxed and her eyes lit up. "I *am* glad about that. Are things going—" A knock at the door cut her off.

"That'll be Raven or Sarah," Meg commented, giving me a look that let me know she'd picked up on something. I squirmed internally.

"Rachel!" Raven greeted me as she came in, Sarah behind her.

"Hi, guys!" Raven, Cade's younger sister, had helped Meg and I decorate cookies for HarvestFest and we'd since become friends.

Before I could apologize to Sarah for leaving her behind, Meg jumped in.

"Sarah, I'm so glad you could come up. Well, I guess you came down from New York first," Megan amended. Sarah's green eyes took the room in at a glance, silently cataloging and assessing. It took her less than two seconds, but Wolf instinctively recognized what she was doing. Her face lit up as her eyes tracked back to Meg.

"Thank you for having me. I know our packs are allies, but it will be nice to make a few friends my own age."

"Sam says being the Beta can sometimes feel isolating," Megan offered as she took Sarah's jacket.

Sarah's blonde eyebrow rose. "He's not wrong." My insides squirmed harder. I was technically Kyp's Beta. And I'd bailed tonight.

"Well, Cindy had something come up, so it's just the four of us. We've got plenty of snacks."

"I brought the nail polish!" I chimed, trying to haul myself out of my blackening mood.

"Ooh, what colors did you bring?" Raven asked. She knew my penchant for wild colors.

I rummaged in my purse. "Turquoise, purple, hot pink sparkles, fire engine red, and, oh, I guess this one is still in here, too." I held up a bottle of Aurora Borealis polish.

Megan smiled wide. "That's the one I want to use." She turned to Sarah. "That's the polish I wore the day I married Sam."

"You all got married not that long ago, right? I mean, finding your true mate and all is pretty rare."

Megan glanced at me. I knew her becoming a werewolf had been a total accident, but we were sworn to secrecy. It couldn't get out that Sam had broken one of the werewolves' cardinal rules.

Raven chuckled. "Rare enough that every werewolf girl dreams about finding her true mate like human girls dream about finding their prince and their happily ever after." She smiled.

A secret, but sad smile hovered around the edges of Sarah's mouth and it made me curious.

"We had an unconventional courtship, but yes. We're mates, and we're still trying to figure out who takes out the trash and who does the laundry." She smiled again, her teeth showing and her eyes twinkling.

"So, what's life like in your pack?" I interjected, sensing that Megan was concerned about giving too much away.

Sarah selected the fire engine red and unscrewed the top. Red lacquer dripped like blood onto her nails. "My mom was killed in a raid by a group of feral wolves when I was young, so I don't remember much about her other than what my dad tells me."

I sucked in a hard breath.

"I'm so sorry," Raven murmured.

"Sarah," Meg breathed.

A fist lodged itself in my throat and I tried to swallow it down. My emotions were too high all the way around.

Sarah shrugged, a practiced move that told me she was used to hiding her real thoughts. "It's always just been me and my dad. We're a good team. He's a fair Alpha, and he lets me be his Beta. He doesn't try to keep me tethered and he doesn't try to keep me safe—within reason. I support him and he supports me. He's raised me to fight my own battles, and I do." She flexed her painted fingers. "But I've found sometimes that makes friendships a little strange. Sorry. Too much?"

"Not at all," Megan assured her.

Girl talk commenced, but I found myself wondering as I watched Sarah. Was I supposed to be acting differently? After all, I *was* Kyp's Beta. Did he need more from me? I knew I'd messed things up between us, but if I stepped up to really be his Beta, would that somehow mend the unsettling rift between us? Maybe he was upset because I wasn't acting like a Beta should. Uncertainty gnawed at my belly.

****

Saturday morning was spent doing laundry, unpacking boxes and helping Jennifer put the rest of the house in order. Kyp found excuses to be outside working on who knew what. Wolf whined. He was avoiding me, and it was breaking my heart.

About noon, Kyp got a phone call. Dominic had an update on Shelby—well, really just more of the same. She was still in a coma. Her body had healed for the most part, but she still wouldn't wake up. I wasn't sure how I was supposed to feel about her. Part of me hated her for what she did to Megan—or what she tried to do. But the other part of me wondered how much of what she did was because she was Victor's daughter. Eventually I shoved it to the back of my brain to think about later.

That afternoon, I laid down for a quick nap. Sometime later I woke but just laid in bed, processing. A quiet knock sounded on the door a few minutes after that.

"Rachel?" My belly quivered as Wolf roused, responding to Kyp's voice.

"I'm awake. You can come in." I covered a yawn as I sat up and rubbed my eyes. Adrenaline washed any remaining tiredness away.

Kyp opened the door but didn't come in. It was almost like he was afraid to be near me. I unfolded myself and went to him, hesitantly wrapping my arms around him for a quick hug.

He dropped a kiss on the top of my head, and my

skin flushed as he stepped back.

"I need to go over to Dominic's. We're going to go over new strategies and plan out a new patrol route. Do you want to come?"

Anxiety quivered in my belly. No. I did not want to go. But should I? Would it make things better if I did? Indecision warred within me. I wanted to support Kyp, but the thought of hearing all those details about Sharon's death or the unavoidable confrontation with Victor made me want to throw up.

"It's okay if you don't. I wanted to ask you. You have the right to be there if you want to. But I don't want you to come if it makes you uncomfortable."

"Do you need me?" *Do you want me?* I screamed inside.

His lips twisted up. "Yes. But not at the meeting tonight." His eyes were kind as he smiled down at me, careful not to touch me as he leaned against my doorjamb. Wolf whined. Kyp needed us, but did he want us?

"You sure?"

"I'm sure. If you want to come, that's fine. But there's nothing going on tonight that you have to be present for. You're overwhelmed enough as it is. It's okay if you stay here. Mom already left for work, but there are plenty of patrols running. Call Megan if you want. I shouldn't be too late. You won't be unprotected."

"Okay. If you're sure? I do have some homework I have to finish." I bit my lip, still wondering if I should go and hope my gag reflex held until the meeting was over.

"Sounds good. I'll see you in a while. Call me—or

try the link—if you need anything."

I nodded.

"Anything." He tipped my chin up with his finger. His eyes were intense, and my insides melted.

"I will," I promised.

For one glorious moment, I thought he was going to kiss me. Then he gave me a little half smile and the moment was gone.

"See you soon." With a nod, he trudged down the hall. Snagging my backpack, I clomped downstairs, too.

****

The phone startled me from my studying sometime later. College Algebra and I were just starting to get along well when the blaring ring of the phone broke any concentration I'd had. I glanced at the screen and scrambled to unlock the phone when I saw Mom's name pop up.

"Mom! Hi!"

"Rachel, Sweetie!" A lump lodged in my throat. I hadn't realized how much I had missed the sound of my mother's voice.

"How are you? How's Joanie?" I wasted no time in asking as I sat up on the couch and curled my arms around my knees.

There was a long pause on the other end. My belly cramped and my heart sped up. I clutched my knees tighter to my chest.

"There's been an incident," Mom started. She sniffed. I clenched my eyes shut against the pain of whatever she'd say next. I knew it would be bad.

"What happened?" I managed around the boulder clogging my windpipe.

She inhaled a teary breath. "Joanie relapsed."

Relapsed. What did that even mean?

"Is…is she okay?" I stammered. Mom choked on her words and the next thing I heard was the crackle of the phone being passed over to Dad.

"Hi, Sweetheart." His deep voice was gruff and charged with emotion.

"Dad, what happened to Joanie?" Fear was racing up my spine, threatening to lock me in place. Wolf paced heavily, every sense on high alert.

"She didn't come down to dinner tonight, and when your mom went up to check on her, she found Joanie…passed out on the floor."

I sucked in a breath as all the oxygen seemed to flee the room.

"We don't yet know how she got her hands on anything, or what all she took. There's going to be an investigation as this could impact other patients here, but for the time being, we feel we need to stay here to be with Joanie and help her through this second rough patch." He stopped and cleared his throat, and I knew he was struggling with his words.

"I'm so sorry, Sweetheart. We want to come home to you, but feel like if we do, we might break the last of our relationship with Joanie right now. You're the strong one. Are you all right? Can you be strong just a little longer?"

"I can be strong," I whispered as my insides withered into dust.

"That's my girl. Are you all right?"

"Sure." It was a lie, and my father knew it.

"I know how hard this is, Sweetheart. You're my brave girl. Hang on. Your mom is ready to talk."

"Rachel?" My mom had her fake bright voice on.

"Hey, Mom." I tried to force a cheerful tone.

"Honey, I'm so sorry. Sorry about all of this." She hiccupped. "We need to be here for Joanie if she's ever going to come back from this."

"Of course, you do. I'll be fine. Grandpa is taking great care of me," I assured her while trying not to feel guilty. Grandpa was still perfectly available to me, but it was much safer for both of us if I stayed with Kyp and Jennifer.

"Is there anything you need? You have the credit card. You get what you need. And do something special. Take Megan and some friends and go do something fun this weekend. Our treat. Please, do something to get your mind off of this. Do it for your dad and me," she finished in a whisper.

I was barely holding it together. Tears threatened as my eyes burned. I sniffed to keep them at bay.

"I'll be fine. And I will. Do something fun."

"Get your mind off this. We will come back from this. Together. As a family." Mom's voice broke then, and her sob echoed in the phone. "I love you, Sweetie."

"Love you, Sweetheart."

"Love you, too, Mom. Love you, Dad."

I stared at the blank phone screen for several minutes after we hung up. My heart shattered as I thought about Joanie, what agony our parents must be in as they watched her destroying her life this way. I wanted to believe Mom—that we could all come back from this. Be one big happy family again.

But I knew we couldn't.

The Joanie we loved was gone forever. A new Joanie had taken her place. She could get better, she could come back, but she'd never be the same again.

The old Joanie was gone. Just like the old Rachel was gone.

I was a werewolf.

Emotion spun my insides as I swiped my phone back on. I pulled up my favorites to place the call, needing my best friend to comfort me.

My thumb froze just before I hit Kyp's contact. I blinked and sucked in a breath. Hard realization whooshed the air back out. Despite everything—all the tension, all the anxiety, all the unsureness—I wanted Kyp.

When had I ever called anyone before I called Meg? When had I subconsciously reached out to Kyp before Megan?

Meg was still my best friend. Granted, her relationship with Sam did take up more of her time than it previously had, but it hadn't altered our relationship that much. If anything, we'd only grown closer together after I became a werewolf, too. Stunned, I hesitated a second as uncertainty rumbled through me, then hit Kyp's contact anyway. Wolf nuzzled me. She knew he'd come.

He picked up on the second ring.

"Rachel?" His deep voice was like a balm over the tattered edges of my frazzled nerves.

"Can you come back?" I hated that my voice wavered over the phone.

"What's wrong?"

"Joanie."

"I'm on my way."

True to his word, not ten minutes later, Kyp was on the doorstep.

He stood there in the doorway, dark eyes awash in

concern, brow drawn in, mouth turned slightly down at the corners.

"What happened, Rachel?"

I closed my eyes as I stepped back so he could come in. I smelled the fresh air that clung to his clothes as he brushed past me and tried not to think as his hand covered mine on the doorknob. He shut the door, and the lock clicked into place.

My head sunk against his chest. He hesitated only a second before his arms came around me and just held me.

Tears came then. I didn't even try to hide them. I needed someone else to be strong for a while. Kyp could do that. Kyp would do that.

****

I sobbed, getting tears and snot all over Kyp's jacket. Once my tears started to dry and the hiccups started, I looked at his jacket in mortification and started to pull back.

"It's fine," he said softly, seemingly reading my thoughts. We were still standing in the entryway, my sock-clad feet freezing on the cold tiles. Kyp hadn't said a word. Just let me cry it out, stroking my hair and letting me lean on him.

"What happened?" His voice was still quiet and gentle.

I took another step back, out of his embrace, and wiped at the remains of tears from my cheeks. A shuddering breath entered my lungs, and I blew it out through my mouth.

I knew my eyes were swollen, and my face probably resembled some over-grown, mottled strawberry. Kyp didn't notice it, or if he did, he didn't care. And that's exactly the sort of friend I needed at the moment.

"Joanie took something again tonight."

His brows drew together. "In the rehab place?"

I nodded miserably.

"Come on; let's sit and you can tell me as much or as little as you want." He shrugged out of his jacket and draped it over a kitchen chair as I led the way into the living room. The lights were low, the darkness of the room inviting. The shadows took me in, covering my vulnerability as I sank onto one end of the couch.

Kyp was right behind me, taking the other end. I finally looked at him. He was wearing a white and red wide striped waffle shirt and worn jeans with his tennis shoes. He looked comfortable, steady. His shoulders were wide enough to take some of this burden from me.

"My parents called just before I called you."

He nodded encouragement.

"Joanie didn't come down to dinner, and Mom found her in her room, passed out on some medication." I felt my mouth quiver, just saying what happened aloud. I glanced up and saw the pain that flashed through Kyp's eyes.

"I'm so sorry, Rachel."

"I...I'm so heartsick," I whispered, the confession tumbling from my lips. "Joanie is gone. She'll never be the same, even if she makes a full recovery. It's like our family has been tainted. Even if—*when*, because I refuse to believe that Joanie won't beat this—Joanie comes home, the whole dynamic of our family will have changed." I was silent a minute, warring with myself. Kyp's hand found my ankle curled up on the couch. His fingers rubbed my skin gently and urged me to continue. "And it makes me think about me. I'm changed, too. I will never be the same, and my parents have no idea how different I've become—how changed I am, and how I will never be the same Rachel they left. And the worst part is that I can't tell them. I'm completely torn between two worlds, neither of which I understand. I don't know the rules in one world, but I don't fully belong in the other anymore."

"Do you wish I hadn't bitten you?" The words were soft, yet I heard the ache behind them.

I looked up sharply. Kyp's face was unreadable, but his tone had been clear. "No. I don't regret it for a second," I told him firmly. I held his gaze long enough to ensure that he understood that I meant what I said, but then glanced away and sighed. "But I don't know how to let my family into this new world that I'm now a part of. I can't tell them. They can't ever know. It just leaves this sort of hole in my chest that I feel my parents should be able to fill...but I can't ever let them try. If they were to find out that I'm a werewolf on top of everything else with Joanie, I think that just might be the end of my family all together."

He squeezed my ankle.

"Go take a hot shower. I'll make popcorn. We can put a movie in, maybe try to take your mind off things for a while before I need to go run a patrol."

"Okay," I conceded. Kyp got up off the couch and extended his hand down to help me up. I grasped it and let him pull me to my feet, lurching to a stand so close to him that my chest brushed his.

The air charged with electricity and I looked up at his face. Something passed between us that superseded the lingering awkwardness. The tension built until it was a living, breathing thing in the scant space between us. His eyes flashed to my lips as his Adam's apple bobbed. I wanted him. Wanted him to make the darkness abate. Wanted him to want me like I wanted him. With my free hand, I reached up and tangled my fingers into his hair as my mouth found his.

He groaned a sweet, tortured noise against my lips but offered no resistance. Quickly dropping my hand, he wrapped his arm tight around me, his other skimming the curve of my hip to my waist. Sparks shot through me, filling me with heat, and fueling the growing *want* inside me.

We kissed. And kissed. Awkward at first but quickly finding a rhythm. My head was spinning, my heart pounding. The darkness receded and fell away under the pressure of his lips against mine. My body was on fire as my hands twined into his hair and his wrapped firmly around my middle. I wanted more. I wanted the darkness to stay away. Maybe. Maybe if we went a little further, I could hold onto this feeling—this euphoria. This dance along the abyss that kept me from teetering over the edge into oblivion. This forbidden dance that might keep us together.

I slid my hands from his hair, over his shoulders, down his sides. He made a noise deep in his throat that made the hair along my arms prickle. It sent a rush of emotion careening through me. Wolf nuzzled her head against me at his guttural response.

My fingers left him, and I tugged my shirt upward, desperate for more of *this*. His hands slipped onto my skin and Wolf whimpered—but not the way I expected. His hands tightened on my bare skin, and he jerked his face away from mine.

"Rachel, what are you doing?" His voice was husky and uneven.

"I…" I stammered, "Don't you want to?" My insides writhed as his eyes widened. Desire turned to ash as he swallowed and dropped his hands and took a step back. I wanted to die at that moment. He didn't want me after all. Shame, hot and potent, swept over me and nearly brought me to my knees. I'd seen rejection on other faces, read about it in books, but never until that moment had I understood the knifing, debilitating, ripping out of my guts. Wolf nudged me again, and shame flooded me anew as I realized there was a bubble of relief lodged in the middle of the turmoil.

"It's not a question of wanting to. *Of course, I want to*. Trust me, all systems are primed and ready to go." Kyp took another fortifying breath and raked his hands through his hair.

"Then what?" I whispered as insecurities added a new layer to my grief. Was I not pretty enough? I knew I was totally inexperienced, but I didn't think that would matter to him. He was just as inexperienced as me. Maybe it did matter. Maybe I just wasn't enough, and that was the bottom line. Despair clawed at me. Wolf nudged me harder. *We are enough*, she stoutly conveyed.

Kyp took another breath and opened his mouth, though no words came out. He was still breathing harder than usual, and he blinked a few times, apparently lost for words as I withered waiting for him to say something. Anything.

"Rachel. You are beautiful. You're the most beautiful girl I've ever met. But this," He moved his hand, indicating the space between us. "This is...I'm not ready. I don't think you are either."

My eyes filled as an invisible fist squeezed my throat tight.

"I know most people wouldn't think twice about hooking up, but I'm not most people. Werewolves," he started then paused and shrugged his shoulders, "werewolves take mating *very* seriously. I probably take it to more of an extreme than most." His gaze darted to mine, and I was surprised to see pain reflecting deep in their depths. "My mom got pregnant with me when she was seventeen. She was on a school trip. She was on the Academic Team and they were in some final championship where they met up with other schools in Washington, DC for some big tournament. There was a huge unsanctioned party the last night. Mom went and got drunk. She'd never had alcohol before but wanted to impress some guy from another school. She drank too much, and one thing led to another. She came home and found out she was pregnant with me three weeks later. She was able to hide the pregnancy until after graduation, but when she finally told her parents, they kicked her out. She worked and supported both of us on her own until I turned five.

"I can only assume it's something in my mixed DNA that forced the change on me so early. You know most wolves don't have their first shift until early puberty. Well, my first shift came at age five, right before bed on a Friday night. Scared my mom so bad, she nearly had a mental breakdown right there. But she pulled herself together and waited until I shifted back to my skin about ten minutes later.

"She knew she couldn't take me to a hospital if I was going to have any shot at a normal life, and she figured there must be more *creatures* like me out there and assumed my father—whoever he is—was one of them. She researched, and eventually, we found the Kentucky pack. We were beyond flat broke, desperate, and had nothing but a fragile hope that they could help us—help me.

"I was tormented because I'm a half-breed and born out of wedlock. Two things that just aren't done when you're a werewolf. My mom was snubbed by everyone. Made the butt of jokes, excluded, reminded daily of her status not only as a human, but as a human who dared to get pregnant and give birth to a half-were child without the father's consent or his protection as his mate.

"I will *never* risk doing that to a girl. The shame I've had to live with, the shame my mom has had to live with—all for one mistake. I will not make that same mistake. You're worth more than that. So am I, even though I don't always feel it. I'm your Alpha and I'm trying to be your boyfriend and probably really screwing up at both. I don't want to make it worse by doing something that we might both regret later.

"And that, Rachel, is why I will not do more than kiss you. Even though I want to."

I was speechless. He'd just laid his life's greatest pain before me. And he was right. I wasn't ready to do more than kiss. My first time shouldn't be because I was angry and upset. Shame crept over me and my head drooped.

"I'm sorry," I whispered. The words sounded as broken as I felt. I was ashamed, grieved, and afraid I'd just made things forever awkward between us. Again.

"It's okay," he said simply. Tentatively, he stepped toward me. I was too embarrassed to look up at him. He wrapped his arms around me and pulled me against his chest.

Chapter 38

Kyp

I held Rachel, my heart still pounding. I refused to let my hands slide down to the curve of her waist. I wanted to. I wanted her. I wanted to go down the path Rachel had started us on. Might have continued if Mom's earlier warning about needing house rules hadn't pinged in my brain. I swallowed. I needed rules. My entire life had been bound up in rules and I didn't know how to function without them.

Becoming Alpha had freed me from the chains of those rules, but it also took away their protection. I was now the rule-maker for my pack. For me and Rachel. I had to make the rules and enforce them. Wolf snorted. *Mine*. Yes. My pack. My responsibility. My girlfriend. Who I desperately needed to protect from myself as well as from her grief that made her do rash things. One more thing to add to the list of Alpha things to figure out.

****

Once Rachel was convinced that we were okay she went up to shower. I put a bag of popcorn in the microwave and sent a quick text off to Sam to let him know things were all right here. We'd been about done with the meeting when Rachel had called.

Thinking about my mom and my childhood made

me think uncomfortable thoughts about my dad. Whoever he was. I didn't know. Mom didn't know. All she knew was that he was an Academic Team guy named Tor from a different school and he'd oozed charisma, magnetism, and had a wicked smile.

And had obviously taken advantage of a teenaged girl while she was drunk. It made my blood boil. Werewolves didn't tolerate alcohol well. It made the wolf unpredictable and could cause a spontaneous shift. Therefore, I had to conclude, that he wasn't drunk when he took advantage of my mom. I hated him for that, but at the same time, yearned to know the man who had fathered me.

Would he like me? Would he be proud of me? Probably not, since I'd spent most of my life in the shadows, the lowest of the low of the pack. But I was an Alpha now, such as I was. Had he been an Alpha? Dominic said I had to have Alpha blood somewhere in my family tree, and strong blood, in order to become Alpha myself with my mixed genes.

Hearing the water still running and knowing Rachel would be a few minutes, I crept into my mom's room and took down her wooden box from her top shelf. The wood creaked against the hinges as I opened the box and found what I was searching for.

Mom had one picture of my dad. It was a snapshot of the two of them smiling in front of a monument in DC. My finger ran over the face of my father. My lips were shaped like his. My eyes were dark like his, but the similarities ended there. His hair was far darker, his chin and jaw more prominent, his nose sharper than mine.

I didn't look like my mom, but I didn't look much

AJ Skelly

like my dad either.

Wolf nudged me. We were our own. That conviction settled on me and some of the unrest in my gut stilled. I stared at the picture again.

What would my life have been like if he'd known Mom was pregnant? If he knew he had a son?

The water shut off upstairs, and with a sigh and one more hard look at the man who created me, I replaced the picture, closed the box, and put it back on the shelf.

****

We had decided at our meeting that we'd only send one Alpha out per night, reducing the overall danger to our packs. Saturday night was my night since it wasn't a school night. It seemed ironic that with everything going on, school still played a significant role in anything. But education was important. I knew that, and Dominic and Austin both felt that way, too. After making sure Rachel was okay, we watched a half hour of one of her favorite movies together. But after that, it was time for me to head back out for my patrol.

Cade, Gordon Rockwell, and two wolves from the Thornehill pack made up our group tonight.

Initially, the scouting went well. We ran the perimeter of the Wolfe lands and found only old traces of Victor's pack. Nothing fresh. We were about to head back when I caught a scent that had Wolf cocking his head to the side.

I nudged Cade and indicated that I was going a little way off the path to check it out. He nodded and I broke away from the group, not intending to go more than a few yards.

But when I scented the wet grass, that same scent teased my nose. It was faint with the water that had fallen on it earlier in the day. It was familiar, but I knew I'd never smelled it before. I followed the weak trail a few yards further. Wolf's ears perked up and my body thrummed into action. Ahead of me a twig snapped. I crouched low to the ground, invisible in the dark shadows of the underbrush.

The wind brought the smell to me again. Sharper, clearer. And not far ahead.

Willing my heart to slow its rapid pounding in my chest, I knew I was too far away from the others to risk barking for their attention. Wolf pressed me. I needed to find out who that scent belonged to.

It was a werewolf.

Silently I picked my way over spongy moss and soft grass that padded my heavy footfalls. I moved like a wraith through the brush until I was nearly upon the scent.

Careful to keep upwind of the wolf, I scanned the area.

I nearly yelped in surprise when a massive black wolf materialized not ten feet ahead, his back to me. I was undetected, silently thanking my half-human genes that made my scent all muddled.

In horrified fascination, I watched the black shoulders ripple, the fur receding as the giant beast lunged up on his back legs. Fur became skin as his tail disappeared into his back, straightening the man taller. With a mighty shake of his shaggy head, the rest of the wolf fell away and left a man in his mid-thirties standing naked in the moonlight.

The man turned his face up to the moonlight and my lungs froze. Moonlight cast across a face aged but unchanged.

The tread of a small truck jerked my eyes from the man. The truck slowed. I was close enough to see a young man, possibly in his early twenties, driving.

"Find anything, Victor?" the young man asked.

Victor?

"No one has found the poison yet," the naked man replied. He grabbed a shirt and pants out of the truck and slid them on.

"Back to the camp." The truck disappeared into the forest.

I stayed crouched on the forest floor. Too shocked. Too numb. Too terrified. Too unbelieving to move.

Victor—*Tor*—Atwood was my father.

****

That night I ran. I ran, and I ran, and I ran. Before I let the numbness take me completely, I found the others, shifted, and told Cade I had something I had to do. With my Alpha status, he didn't question me. I told him to tell Rachel to spend the night with Megan. And then I ran. The wolf led. I don't know how far we went. I think at one point I may have been near Canada. I ran until I couldn't. Until my legs gave out and my heart threatened to explode in my chest.

Sometime just before dawn, I found myself back near Rock Falls. There was a lake not far outside town, and after a long drink tasting slightly of fish, I sat still on my haunches.

At some point I shifted back to my skin and sat freezing, naked on a wooden bench at the lake's edge.

Chapter 39

Rachel

"What do you mean he just told you to tell me to spend the night at Megan's?" I grilled Cade for the third time.

"I don't know, Rachel." Cade held up his hands in defense. "That's just what he told me. He said he had something he had to go take care of and for you to spend the night at Megan's."

I bit my lip. I didn't like this. Something was wrong. I couldn't call him. His phone was here. I tried to use our spotty link, but he didn't respond. I paced.

"Come on. I'll go with you up to the cabin. I'm going to check in with Sam anyway."

Eventually I let him persuade me. I texted Megan and threw a few things in a bag.

"You want me to drive your car, or you want to drive?" Cade asked as I locked the door behind me. I left a note for Jennifer on the table.

"I'll drive."

I pulled onto the main road going through the subdivision.

"Did he say anything else? Look a certain way? Anything?" I pressed.

"He was distracted. But he's an Alpha now. You don't really question another Alpha's decisions." He glanced sideways at me as I bit my lip again.

****

"And that's it?" Meg asked, her reaction eerily like mine.

"That's it. Something is wrong."

"Is Cade telling Sam now?"

"I assume so."

"What does your wolf think?" Megan asked.

Wolf was pacing. She didn't like whatever was going on either. Something was off about the whole situation.

"The same thing I do."

Meg nodded. "I vote that if he hasn't made contact by morning, we go hunting."

Sam agreed with her as he walked back in the door having sent Cade back to his own house.

"He may have a legitimate reason for staying away. Maybe he just needed to clear his head? Becoming an Alpha is a big change and he's probably still coming to terms with it," Sam said.

"I hope that's all it is," I said. Secretly, Wolf and I worried that I'd pushed too far tonight. That this was somehow a reaction to my own crazy and the mistakes I'd made that he couldn't handle—not about becoming Alpha. Fresh mortification and concern churned like acid in my middle and sent ripples of unease through me.

"It's late. I think I'm heading to bed. You girls staying up to talk?" Sam covered a yawn with the back of his wrist.

Meg glanced at me. "What do you feel like?"

I felt like finding Kyp and giving him a piece of my mind, and then kissing him senseless.

236

"I think I'll try bed, too. I want to be up early."

Meg nodded. "Want me to sleep out here?" There were still three beds left out in the common room, even though Sam and Meg had moved their bedroom into their newly finished addition.

I smiled. "No. If you're out here, we'll only talk all night. Just no funny business loud enough I can hear," I forced a light tone that melted into a genuine smile as Meg's face heated. Sam cracked a grin.

"Wolf hearing and all," I pushed.

"Oh, shut up," Megan laughed.

****

I spent a restless night. I borrowed a book and tried to read for a while, but the words just blurred on the page. Wolf kept pacing. I'd let her out earlier in the afternoon. She wasn't needing out, but we both needed to know where Kyp was.

Finally, I drifted into a shallow sleep. Before succumbing, my last thoughts were to Kyp.

Where are you?

****

When I cracked my eyes open with the first rays of the sun, Wolf nudged me. Our heart beat steadily. We knew where Kyp was.

Chapter 40

Kyp

My head sunk into my hands, dread spiraling through me and sitting in my belly like lead. *Victor Atwood was my father*. I choked on the thought, bile rising in the back of my throat. Wolf whimpered and circled painfully. Neither of us wanted anything to do with the madman targeting the Wolfe pack, and possibly working on some master plan to dominate the world.

Bitter laughter erupted out of nowhere and I momentarily wondered if I was losing it. After all, I was the offspring of a totally crazed monster. I swiped a hand across my eyes and sniffed. What was I going to do?

The approach of a car sent Wolf scampering up to the front of my mind, but almost instantly, I knew it was Rachel.

Rachel. My heart pounded. *Rachel*. My chest ached and I felt feverish thinking about what this new revelation was going to mean for this thing trying to bloom between us. The sweet pain in my chest every time I thought of her. The rush that covered me head to toe every time we kissed. I couldn't imagine ever feeling this way about another girl. I couldn't imagine my life without Rachel.

But how could I keep her in my life now? I wasn't sure I could bear that either. I'd tried to slow things down so we didn't burn out before we had a chance to properly give us a shot, and so I could deal with my own insecurities. But I was her Alpha. She was my pack. Suddenly I wanted the responsibility. Wanted it like I never had. No one would try to protect Rachel better than I would. Because...I loved her.

Her car door opened and shut, but I didn't raise my head from my hands, my emotions and my thoughts a tangled mess. I felt her weight on the bench beside me and her smell of *rightness* enveloped me, making the ache in my chest open into a deep chasm. She tossed a pair of pants on my lap.

"How'd you find me?" I croaked, my voice hoarse and rusty. I tugged the pants on.

She didn't answer but put her hand on my bare shoulder. I glanced up then away before straightening. Still, she did not speak, but put her other hand over my thudding heart.

"Because I *feel* you. We're connected. No matter how many times I mess up, we always will be," she said softly. I slumped in defeat. She would not appreciate the new connotations her connectedness to me would bring. She didn't say anything else but wrapped her arms around me and hugged me tight. I resisted for a few seconds, then let myself melt against her. I needed her. I needed this last bit of closeness before she found out who I really was, and everything went up in smoke.

"And because I love you," she whispered. Something between a strangled laugh and a sob sounded from my throat.

"You can't," I croaked as Wolf jumped around inside at her admission and the rest of me wilted under the pressure created at the words I'd always longed to hear.

Struggling from her arms I raked my hands through my hair again, silently marveling at the conundrum in which I suddenly found myself. Rachel loved me. I loved her. And my parentage was going to crush it.

"I know you might not feel the same way, but why can't I love you?" Rachel asked, one red eyebrow arched upward, hurt leaking into her voice. Air gusted between my teeth. Might as well rip off the band-aid all at once.

"I found out something yesterday that will change the way you see me."

"I doubt it's enough to make me stop feeling this way about you."

A bitter laugh escaped. "Victor Atwood is my father."

Dead silence. I couldn't look at her, just stayed staring straight ahead at the water as the wind ruffled the surface into tiny wavelets.

"We can totally use this to our advantage."

My eyes leaped to her face. "What?"

Her face was animated, her eyes alight with that glow that seemed to reach out and pull me in.

"You're his son. You didn't know about him, maybe he doesn't know about you? I think that could give us an edge. The edge to get close to him without Victor calling the shots."

"You're crazy. Didn't you just hear me tell you that the world's most hated werewolf is my father?"

"Kyp." Her voice softened as she reached up,

hesitated, and cupped my face with one hand. "I don't care who your dad is. It doesn't change who *you* are. *You are you.* You've said that to me several times before. You are what you are, and it is what it is. So, your dad is a raging psychopath who wants to take over the world. That's not who *you* are."

My eyes filled with tears and I put the heels of my hands to them. I couldn't understand this girl. How could she love me when I was finding it hard to love myself with this newest revelation?

"I mean, it sucks that you're never going to have the relationship with your dad that Sam has with his and stuff but knowing who your dad is doesn't actually change anything about you. Just your perception."

With tears still making my vision blurry, I grabbed her face with both my hands and kissed her. Hard. I couldn't help myself. I loved her. She loved me. *Still.*

Her validation set things loose inside me that tumbled around and righted themselves back properly. Knitting me together in a way that I'd longed for but had been unable to do on my own.

Wolf sat resolutely and nudged me. *Mine.* None of my insecurities mattered anymore. I would embrace my Alpha—for Rachel. I'd protect her—from my own father—until my dying breath. Heat filled me as Rachel's arms skimmed my bare shoulders to my back, pulling me tighter, her lips soft but insistent against mine. *Mate*, Wolf nudged again. I acknowledged him with wonder, unable to wrap my brain around how it worked, but wanting it with every molecule of my dual natures.

I love you, I thought at her, unwilling to break away long enough to speak it. I knew she heard me when her kisses became more insistent and she pressed herself against me with not even enough room for air between us. Who moved first, I don't know, but thirty seconds later she was on my lap and we were kissing in a way I knew we couldn't keep up for long or my hands would be going places I'd feel guilty about later.

As if reading my thoughts—maybe she did—Rachel pulled back slightly, her face flushed, her eyes sparkling.

"Marry me when this is over," she whispered.

I laughed, unrestrained and full of joy. "Isn't the guy supposed to be the one that does the asking?" I said as I brushed a loose curl away from her face, my other hand still resting on my favorite curve where her waist met her hip.

"I heard your wolf. We agree," she said primly and raised an eyebrow, daring me to contradict her. I kissed her again, slowly, softly.

"I'd like to ask you officially at some point—you know—when I have a ring and your parents have a chance to get used to the idea. But, *yes*."

She giggled and hugged me tight around the neck. Wolf sat back in satisfaction, content that Rachel was going to be ours for keeps.

"I love you," I whispered into her hair.

"I love you, too."

Chapter 41

Rachel

Long minutes passed and we just held each other. Wolf and I were beside ourselves. The awkward tension was gone. Kyp loved us. And we were going to be married! I was already making a mental list. And then reality started to settle back in. The wedding would have to wait. At least long enough for my parents to come to terms with their daughter marrying so young. I didn't think they'd object at all to my choice, just the timing. Also, Victor Atwood had to be dealt with.

I pulled back just far enough that I could see his face, though I was still cozied up on his lap.

"How did you find out that Victor is your dad?" Some of the light left his face, but not all of it, so I knew he was processing and not in the outright denial stage. What a shock he must have been through!

"When we were patrolling last night, I smelled something. Familiar, but unknown. I followed it. Thankfully my scent is unique enough that it's not quickly recognized as a werewolf. Victor rose up barely three yards in front of me and shifted back. I saw his face. It's him. He's…he's my father. A guy picked him up in a truck and called him Victor. Mom has one picture of her and Tor from that trip when she got pregnant with me. It's Victor. He's older, broader, more powerful, but it's him. The second I saw it, I felt it, too. All the way down to my claws. Wolf knew it, too. It's why his scent was familiar. It's got similar undertones to my own. I was far enough away I couldn't call the others. I was too messed up to try to explain to them anyway. I am sorry I left you hanging in the wind last night. I shouldn't have done that."

"I'm so sorry," I said, trying to understand how horrible that must have been. His thumb moved over my hip.

"Me, too," he whispered back.

****

I knew I needed to be a part of the next round of meetings. Kyp needed me. He needed a Beta, and someone totally in his corner. His fears weren't unfounded. I wasn't sure what the other wolves would think once they learned that Kyp was Victor Atwood's son. I shuddered. What a crappy way to find out who your dad was.

I drove us back to the house, trying not to steal too many glances at Kyp's bare abs. My face heated as I tried to block out the accidental view I'd had when I'd first found him at the lake. I'd assumed he wouldn't have clothes on since he'd gone out as a wolf, which is why I brought the pants. But I kind of thought he'd still be a wolf...not fully human and fully unclothed.

"How do you think we could use this to our advantage?" Kyp broke the silence.

My lip found its way between my teeth and I chewed it a second before speaking. "Victor is smart. He's sneaky. We've never been able to catch him, and more than once he's tried to trap us or ambush us. He operates on a completely different level than our packs do. Normal werewolf laws don't seem to apply to him. He throws them all out the window and only does as he pleases. He's insanely dangerous and he has a freaky mind control thing none of us understands. But you're his son. If he never knew you existed, I don't know. He might want to meet you. Maybe we could set up a meeting where we finally have the upper hand."

Sneaking a glance, I could see his brain churning behind his eyebrows slung low over his eyes.

"Or I could go to him."

"What? No! That's not what I meant at all."

"Think about it. I'm his long-lost son. He knows nothing about me. Logically, I would go to him. Ask to join his pack."

"Kyp. Do you hear yourself?"

"Yeah. I do. I don't want anything to do with Victor, but I want his threat to end. And if I have to go in as bait to do it, then so be it."

I tasted blood and released my lip.

Chapter 42

Kyp

The other Alphas and Betas took the news better than I'd anticipated. There was some swearing, a lot of shock, and one broken decorative dish that had been knocked off Dominic's desk after my confession.

"You're sure, absolutely sure that Victor is your father?" Austin asked again.

"I felt it. Wolf felt it. His smell is familial, even with my mixed blood. And it's him. It matches the picture of him. Unless he's got a twin, it's him."

"Unreal," Sam murmured.

Sarah's eyes narrowed predatorily. I swallowed. Rachel wrapped her hands around my arm, staring Sarah down.

Dominic looked hard at me. "What are you thinking?"

Rachel wasn't going to like this.

****

"Kyp, I hate this," Rachel said late that afternoon once we were back at the house and I'd had a nap. Mom hated the plan as much as Rachel and was processing by taking a walk near Jonathan's house. Rachel paced the living room.

"I'm not wild about it either. But I think this is the best shot we have of getting the upper hand."

"I know. I just hate that it's you." Her jaw set. "What if it ends badly?" she whispered, glancing up at me through her lashes. I felt her fear and Wolf rose protectively. *Mate.*

"I'm going to be fine." I wasn't sure I was going to be fine, but I was hopeful. Victor was egotistical. He'd be flattered that I wanted to join his pack. At least I hoped so. I was an Alpha coming to him under the guise of reconciliation—submission. I knew very little about the man who fathered me, but I knew he lusted for power. And the submission of another Alpha, son or not, would be a significant stroke to his ego.

Rachel covered her mouth with her hand, her jaw still clenched.

"Come here," I whispered. "The hardest part of this is going to be keeping my distance from you."

She looked up at me, her heart in her eyes.

"If you don't come back, I'll kill you myself," she threatened.

I smiled at her. "Noted."

I dipped my head and caught her lips. She reached up on tiptoe, pressing against me. We'd kissed enough to know how we fit together. My hands came around her as her fingers snaked into my hair at the base of my neck. It sent goose bumps shivering over my shoulders and I think I groaned when I felt the tip of her tongue against my lips.

Confident enough at last, and tinged with desperation, I let myself kiss her the way I wanted to. My tongue slid into her mouth and my heart thundered in my chest as I let my hands trace where her waist met her hip in that delicious curve that made my blood race. I touched Rachel in a way I'd never touched a girl. It was all innocent enough, but it made the blood pound through my veins. Wolf was aware of every feather of feeling from his mate, responsive to every place her hands fell. Though innocent, it made me feel things—things that were infinitely more intimate. A taste of things to come once Victor was dealt with and Rachel was mine for keeps.

I kissed her jaw, her neck, let my hands tangle into her hair, listened as she sighed against my ear, and sent heat sizzling through every cell. Her chest rubbed against mine as she reached up to kiss my mouth again and I grunted. I was getting close to the point where I needed to stop. My hands were going to be all over her curvy bits where they shouldn't be just yet. Even as I thought it, my hand slid up her ribs, stopping millimeters away from off-limits territory. Wolf was nearly frothing.

"I hope your parents believe in short engagements," I growled as I locked my hands together behind her back and rested my forehead against hers. My chest heaved. It didn't help that hers did, too.

"I suppose we could always elope," she teased with a smile.

"I want to be married right now," I confessed. As if she couldn't tell already.

"I'm a willing party. Although I don't have a dress."

"I'd marry you in jeans and a t-shirt."

She smiled.

"There is one other thing I want to do before I leave tonight," I told her. She sobered.

"Anything," she whispered.

"I want to formally Claim you."

Chapter 43

Rachel

Sam and Megan, Jennifer and Jonathan, Sam's parents, Austin, Sarah, Cade, Raven, Rev, and George Carmichael were invited to our Claiming. It was a rushed affair, quickly making calls and getting everyone to the clearing just beyond Sam and Megan's cabin, but everyone was assembled just as the sun set the tops of the trees on fire as it slowly sank behind them.

Wolf was anxious—in a good way for the moment. This was the pinnacle of romance in the werewolf world. Megan nudged me from the side. We stood just inside the tree line, both in fur, waiting. I rubbed my head against her shoulder in a wolfy hug. We watched as the invited wolves filtered into the clearing and took seats on their haunches in a semi-circle. Jennifer helped Grandpa into the clearing and onto a stump where he settled himself with a smile on his weathered face, his hands clasped lightly on top of his cane.

Then Kyp came out of his side of the clearing. The last rays of the sun caught on his black fur and made the reddish ends fairly glow. My heart lurched. I was completely in love with him. He stood proudly, chest out, head erect, looking every inch the Alpha in the middle of the semi-circle of our friends. Then it was my turn.

I stepped out of the trees, Megan just behind me. I came to stand before Kyp as Megan melted into the semi-circle next to Sam.

Kyp found my eyes, his chocolatey ones smiling down. Gently he touched his nose to mine in a sweet sign of affection. Pulling back, his wolf eyes searched my face once more. My face was stretched into the wolf equivalent of a smile.

Slowly and carefully, he opened his mouth and gently bit down over my muzzle. Happiness zinged through me as Wolf's tail wagged furiously. We were Claimed. We were bound to Kyp now. As more than just a pack mate. As more than a girl he'd changed. We were his. He stepped back and I repeated the gesture, taking care that my canines didn't come down too hard on his sensitive snout. A shiver of pleasure ran down my limbs as I paced back. Claiming was the ultimate show of belonging together. We were married in the eyes of the packs. The only thing more we could do was complete our mate bond. And we'd do that as soon as Victor was dealt with and my parents came to terms with our getting properly and humanly married.

A chorus of howls rose around us from our friends and Jennifer and Grandpa clapped. I nudged his cheek with my nose and then we howled, too.

****

As darkness stole over the land, Kyp and I stood inside the copse of trees again, just the two of us. I clutched my robe tighter around me, dread mixing with my earlier euphoria. Kyp was leaving…to infiltrate the enemy. Wolf whined inside me.

"I don't know when I'll get to see you again." His

fingers tucked an errant curl behind my ear.

"Will it be safe to use our link?"

"I hope so. I hope it will still work. It should be stronger now, too, since we're Claimed." His hands framed my face. "I love you."

"I love you back."

He kissed me once more on the forehead and then he disappeared into the trees.

Chapter 44

Kyp

Adrenaline surged through me as I let Wolf out again. Giving a mighty shake, I let myself exult in the feeling of Claimship. It wasn't something I'd ever dared hope for in the Kentucky pack, and was scarcely something I'd allowed myself to wish for with Rachel. But in a wild turn of events, I was here. Completed. And now I was leaving my mate to go and meet my father—history's most hated werewolf—for the first time.

Leaving the grey robe on the forest floor behind me, knowing someone would pick it up on the next round of patrols, I looped the strap of my packed duffle around my neck and set off through the forest to the place I'd last scented Victor. It was irritating, going through the brush with a bag looped around my neck, but it was still quicker and more accurate than going on human feet. And I'd want some clothes once I got where I was going. Especially if things went according to plan.

If they didn't…well, I didn't want to think too hard about that.

****

An hour later, I scented what I was searching for. Shifting back to my skin, I shivered as the cold night air whistled over my skin as I dug out some clothes, boots, and my coat. Looping the bag back over my shoulder, I trudged on.

I smelled the wolves at the same time they sent up a warning howl. I knew I must smell foreign to them, but probably reminded them of Victor's scent. I held up my arms at my sides to show that I came as no threat and to show that I was aware of what the two snarling wolves that bounded out of the woods truly were.

"I want to speak with Victor." The words left me like cold, hard rocks that fell to the forest floor with finality. Alpha's words. One of the wolves gnashed his teeth at me but kept his distance. The other howled again and was answered with a howl that raised the hair on the back of my neck. Wolf paced inside me, terrified, horrified, but a small part of me still longed to meet my father.

The wolf to my left jumped up to grab my coat sleeve. Wolf jerked inside me and I brought my opposite fist smashing down onto the wolf's muzzle. Growling he let go and backed away, properly warned that I would not be cowed. I growled back, still in my skin. Gratified that I carried enough Alpha about me, I watched the wolf sink lower to the ground. The other wolf yipped and jerked its head toward the forest. I followed.

****

Tents and a few tiny mobile homes were set up in the clearing the wolves led me into. Wolf paced inside me and I swallowed, unsure what to expect, but knowing I was irrevocably immersed in enemy territory.

I waited while werewolves and people both came

from the shadows and surrounded me. Wolf's hackles rose as did the hair on the back of my human neck. There would be no escape if Victor gave the order to end me. I willed my heart to stop its wild careening and took a measured breath. My finger rubbed over my thumb. The rest of me stayed perfectly still.

A large black wolf with dark eyes and a patch of silver fur on his chest came from between a mobile home and a tent. His eyes were on me, looking me over, his lips curled back in a snarl. Wickedly sharp teeth glinted in the moonlight as a low growl slid from between those sharp incisors. The wind blew and I caught his scent. I couldn't stop my head from jerking as that same dark undertone met my nose.

His scent was familiar. It wasn't Victor, but it reminded me of him. I stared the wolf in the eyes. The wolf narrowed his at me but stopped growling.

I was pretty sure I'd just met my brother.

My gaze was ripped from him as a door banged open. Victor sauntered down the steps and my heart hammered in my throat.

My father.

Moonlight filtered down onto his strong features. He was heavily muscled, well groomed, and his face was arranged in annoyed nonchalance.

"And who are you?" he asked as he stopped at the edge of the ring of his pack. Wolf puffed up his chest. I was an Alpha. I was this man's equal, I reminded myself. He may be my father, but that didn't mean he had control over me. I hoped. I swallowed.

"I'm your son."

A twinkle shown in the man's eyes and he threw back his head and laughed. It was a hard, cold sound that filled the clearing. His pack shifted nearer to me, closing the circle around me.

"You're my son? Prove it. You don't smell wolf."

A dozen scenarios thrummed through my brain. Prove it? I had no idea how he expected me to do that short of a DNA test. Of course, I didn't smell right. *Shift*, Wolf told me. Without breaking eye contact I let my bag fall to the ground. My coat dropped after. Taking an inhale and realizing everything about this was going to be as public as possible, I steeled my resolve and let my face assume the blank look I'd carried so often in Kentucky. I jerked my shirt over my head and kicked off my boots while ignoring the yips and grunts starting to sound from the pack. I realized their goal was to embarrass me. To shame me. I briefly wondered if Victor was urging them on as I unzipped my jeans.

With my clothes in a pile beside me and the moon streaming down on all my skin, I locked my jaw in defiance, threw back my head, and let my arms swing wide so everyone looking could watch my shift.

Wolf shifted slowly, letting every pair of eyes in the clearing get a full view of the fur coming through my skin, the way my bones twisted and corded with muscle, of the way my humanness melted into the animal. It was graceful, and when I was fully wolf, I stood as tall as I could, chest out, ears forward, Alpha radiating.

I met Victor's eyes and was equally gratified and irritated when his only reaction was a raised eyebrow. He was surprised.

He sniffed and his other eyebrow rose to meet the first.

"You're an Alpha. That's interesting," was all he said. "Shift back. We'll speak." He turned his back to me and entered the nearest RV. The door snapped shut, making my ears twitch.

A low growl sounded from my right and a mottled wolf inched forward, lips pulled back in an ugly snarl.

I growled back, letting Wolf show our Alpha status. My muscles tensed. I could tell this wolf wasn't going to let things rest.

He yipped again, sharp and angry. I bared my teeth.

The door whipped back open. Victor looked hard at the mottled wolf and with a whimper he suddenly flashed belly up on the grass, writhing in pain.

"Get in here," Victor said to me.

I was already homesick.

Chapter 45

Rachel

I paced. I swear I was wearing a path in Megan's floor.

"Rachel. Come have some tea." Megan's voice was weary as she put two mugs on the table.

"Megan, I hate this. I hate it, I hate it, I hate it." Wolf was jumpy. We were agitated. We were anxious and unsettled.

"I know." She plopped down at the table. "I'm nervous for you. I know how I'd feel if it were Sam."

Sam glanced back at his wife, concern on his face, before staring back out the window. We were all on edge.

"Okay. Let's bake." Megan got back up from the table and started getting bowls out. Relief swept through me. Something constructive I could do.

"I hope you have a lot of flour stashed away," I commented dryly as I put the measuring cups on the counter.

"Maybe we can pretend to be focused on business and college stuff while we create." Megan gave me a wry smile. I returned it.

"For sure."

Cookies, a batch of biscotti, and rising bread dough later, I felt better. My stomach was still all tangled up in knots, but at least some of the tension riding in my shoulders had released.

"Better?" Meg asked.

"Some." I put the cover back on the bowl of bread dough and set it on the counter closer to the oven so it would rise nice and fluffy.

"So I wasn't entirely kidding when I was talking about college stuff. In between training and all, I have managed to do a little research."

"Seriously? This sounds like another good distraction. Haul out all your notes. Let's take a peek."

Sam chuckled. "Meg, is it okay if I eat a few of these oatmeal cookies? Are you saving them for anything?"

"Nope. Go right ahead." Megan smiled at him as she grabbed her laptop and sat down on the couch. She patted the seat next to her and I plopped accordingly.

"Did you make a spreadsheet?" My lips twisted up again as Megan pulled up a spreadsheet of business courses offered at the three closest community colleges.

"I did. Look. These here in blue are my favorite of the offerings. I think these are going to give us the best selection of what we want for the bakery business."

I perused the blue courses. They did appear inclusive. "How about the pink ones? Next favorite?"

"Yep. These all sounded pretty good, too, but they don't offer anything related to baking specifically. And the courses in green, that program doesn't have as strong a marketing course. The other perk about doing the blue route—that's at Tri-Falls College—is that they have an on-site culinary program. Sometimes they host demo nights for students. They do baking ones. I thought that might be helpful and make up for the fact that they're fifteen minutes farther away."

"I like the idea of the culinary demos. I bet we could befriend some students for some additional tips. Maybe even find someone to hire on part-time to help with stuff if Raven gets too busy with her graphics design stuff."

"So you like Tri-Falls?"

"Looking at these courses, I think this sounds great."

"Yes! Let's pull up application forms and get on it. Right now!"

We high-fived each other. One step closer to opening *Nutmeg & Crumbs*.

But still so far away from Kyp.

Chapter 46

Kyp

The inside of the RV was sparsely furnished. It looked like an office. I got the distinct impression that Victor didn't live here.

My father took a seat at the table and swept his arm toward another chair as if his letting me sit in his presence was a great honor. I swallowed as Wolf's hackles rose. I knew I'd be lying to myself if I said I didn't want this man's approval even as the thought turned my stomach.

"What makes you think you're my son?"

I searched his face. I saw it in his eyes. He already knew I was his. He could smell it on me.

"You already know I'm your son," I said boldly, refusing to let him see how scared I truly was. His eyebrows rose again.

"Is that the way you address your father?" There was a dark edge to his words.

"How would you like to be addressed?" I was bordering on disrespect. Partly because I needed to know what buttons were the right ones to push, and partly because I wanted him to know that I was still my own Alpha.

"Sir will be fine for now." I said nothing as he studied me.

"What's your name?"

"Kyp."

He smirked.

"Your mother named you that and nothing more?" The sarcasm was heavy.

"Alexander Daniel Kypson."

"Kypson is not a wolf name. Who is your mother?"

Something was bothering him, but I could tell he couldn't quite place it.

"Jennifer Kypson."

"Kypson. Kypson. Where did I meet her? I don't recall a Jennifer Kypson."

He was trying to get a rise out of me. I clenched my jaw to keep from verbally attacking him. I no longer wanted his approval. I wanted his apology.

"You met her in high school on an Academic Team trip to DC."

I watched his eyes widen.

"Your mother *isn't* wolf?" This time his face did register his shock.

"No. She's human."

Victor threw back his head and cackled.

He hadn't been trying to get a rise out of me. He honestly didn't have any idea who my mom was. I felt ill.

"She's human and yet you have still managed to become an Alpha. Very interesting indeed." He appeared pleased with himself. As if somehow his ego were boosted because of it. "So tell me. Why have you come to me?"

I took a breath. Time for all the acting lessons Rachel had crammed into me to go to work. "I hear we have a common enemy."

"Go on."

"The Wolfe pack." I let a growl come out as I said the words. "They have taken something of mine. I want it back."

"Wolfe pack, you say?" He leaned forward, putting his hands on the table in greedy interest.

I nodded. Victor assessed me. I could see the wheels turning as he warred against his desire to know more and not give anything away. Finally, he leaned back.

"You want something."

"I want your help," I ground out. It was surprisingly hard to say the words as I realized I wanted nothing to do with this man who had fathered me.

"Ah. Never was there a child who didn't want something from their parent." His lips twisted cruelly. "I don't do handouts. You're on your own." He waved a hand as if to dismiss me and fear churned in my belly. He couldn't tell me to go. He had to accept me to make this work.

"I can get you closer to the Wolfe pack. I know them."

He speared me with a look.

"I know you want their pack out of the way. I can help you."

"How do you know that?" His eyes slit.

"I hear things. I'm good at blending. Half-human, remember? I can walk in both worlds without either side knowing I'm there." Wolf shook inside me, teetering on the brink of the plan. Victor continued to watch me. My face remained impassable, my thoughts an avalanche of turmoil.

"What did they take from you?"

262

"The girl I want."

"Dirty thieving dogs. They have a long history of stealing what doesn't belong to them. Women especially." Victor's fist clenched against the grain of the table. I wondered what he could possibly mean but didn't dare ask.

"You want them out of the way. I'll help you do that. In return, I want your numbers at my side to take back the girl."

"What's her name?"

I barely kept my teeth from clenching. I didn't want anything about this man touching her. "Rachel."

Victor looked at me thoughtfully again. "When is your birthday?"

That brought me up short. Quickly, I schooled my face once more. "November 3rd." I'd turned eighteen at the beginning of the month.

"You're eighteen?"

I nodded. A devious smile crept over his features that chilled my blood. He glanced at the tabletop and grabbed a set of keys out of a dish at the far end.

"If you want my help, you have to join my pack."

Wolf growled. I wasn't surprised, but I wasn't pleased either.

"And if I refuse?"

"I'll kill you."

I believed him.

"I'd have to give up my status as Alpha to do that."

"That's the price you pay for my help. How bad do you want that girl?"

I stared at him, making him think I was mulling over his suggestion. In reality, I knew it would come to this. I'd already made peace with it, though the thought of joining this maniac's pack sent tremors rocking down to my core.

His eyes were chips of flint.

"Okay," I said at last when I could tell he was losing patience.

"Let's go back outside."

****

Victor's pack hadn't dispersed. More had joined. Wolves and people milled around. Some with blank or vacant expressions, some angry, some despondent. It was a disturbing assortment. And there were a lot of them. More than I'd expected. I prayed my link to Rachel would hold up. Dominic and Austin had to know about this.

"This boy here claims he's my son. He's going to join our pack."

He pulled his arm up high and dropped the keys he still held in his hand.

Pick them up.

The order tumbled around inside my head. Victor was trying his mind control on me. I could feel the order, could hear it clearer than anything I'd ever heard through a pack link. But I felt no compulsion to act on it. I looked at Victor and screwed up my courage. I let my eyes meet his, mine narrowing slightly as I bent down and picked up the keys.

"You do not need to control me. You only need to ask," I said softly as I met his eyes again and extended my hand with the keys.

"You are aware!" Victor crowed. "You shouldn't have known you were being controlled at all. Very interesting." Victor's black eyes glowed with a manic sort of light, probably buzzing scenarios through his brain of how he could use me. "I think I like you. Even though pack hierarchy follows bloodlines, I will not have a weakling. You must prove to me that you are able to take your rightful place as my Beta. You must fight my current Beta. Your brother, Bowen."

Become his Beta? That's why he asked about my birthday. I must be older than his current Beta—*my brother*.

Fear tripped down my spine and icy dread settled in my gut. Bowen—my brother—stared stonily at me from his human form, his face impassive, brown eyes dull, toned, muscled body significantly larger than mine. The breeze blew his scent to me and I recognized him as the black wolf with the silver patch on his chest. I refused to let myself swallow or show any emotion at all. I could do this. Wolf nudged me and puffed out his chest. I was an Alpha in my own right. At least for now, and I had years of fighting experience.

Bowen stepped toward me, moonlight drifting down on his white shirt and making it glow as he reached his arms back and took it off over his head. I knew it was a display of intimidation. If I hadn't grown up around strutting male werewolves, most of them bigger than me, I would certainly have quaked at the sight of chiseled abs and biceps that were defined well beyond what they should have been on a guy younger than me. Bowen was an athlete. Down to his toes.

Not willing to be outdone, Wolf growled low. I took off my shirt. My muscles were every bit as defined as Bowen's. Years of hard training and fights had seen to that. But I was slighter. I had less bulk. I prayed that would make me faster. Several grunts sounded as my scars became visible. Since I healed slower than a full-blooded werewolf, I bore scars from most of my fights. I was covered in them. Pale and slithery, some gnarled and raised that cast slight shadows in the cold moonlight. I briefly ran my fingers over the three scars Rachel had given me as I changed her. Those scars I treasured. Bowen's eyes widened only slightly, his only indication that he'd taken note of my marks and what they might mean.

In minutes, we'd shifted to our wolves. Bowen was bigger and darker than me and had one silver patch right on his chest.

"All right, boys. Last one to surrender will be Beta of the pack," Victor said.

And that was all the warning we got.

Bowen lunged at me, and if I hadn't already been tensed as a pulled bowstring, I would have been a sitting duck. As it was, Wolf jerked us out of the way. I had enough purchase with my back legs that I was able to leap onto his back. I didn't get a good grip, but my teeth grazed him. I tasted blood.

Bowen snarled and flipped his haunches in the air. I went tumbling, righting myself from the dirt just before Bowen pounced on top of me.

"Ha! Little fighter—we've got blood!" Victor's jubilant voice sounded in the background noises.

I raked my paw at Bowen, but he jerked back just out of reach.

Teeth flashed, and he was on me again. He tried to pin me with his bulk and would have if I hadn't caught one of his forelegs in my mouth. I bit down hard enough that he yelped as I yanked my head to the side so that his forearm covered my throat. He couldn't bite my neck unless he bit his own leg.

It was a stalemate. With a savage snarl, he shifted enough that I could wiggle. I clamped down harder and blood seeped into my mouth around my teeth. Bowen growled and lifted enough I shimmied out from under him.

But I wasn't quick enough this time. Before I could dance back out of the way, as I rolled to get to my feet, Bowen followed my momentum and bit my shoulder.

I barked in pain and surprise. He'd caught a full mouthful. Not only had he pierced my hide, I felt his teeth cutting into the muscle on my shoulder. He shook his head and I had no choice but to follow the movement unless I wanted him to tear a chunk of my shoulder off.

We were at an impasse again. I would not concede. I wasn't hurt *that* bad yet. But neither of us could do any further damage locked in the position we were in. I couldn't reach his neck—the one place that would take a wolf down the fastest. Wolf braced his legs.

If I had a few more inches to crane my neck around, I would have just a moment of full access to Bowen's throat. My brother growled in frustration, not willing to let go, but understanding that there was no way for us to continue the fight unless he released me. He shook me again. Ripples of pain radiated down my shoulder to my paw.

I took a breath.

This was going to hurt.

Gritting my teeth, tensing my body, and planting my feet, I jolted back and tried not to cry out when I heard my fur and flesh tearing. Tried not to howl as the pain nearly blinded me. Tried to ignore the hot, wet blood that soaked down my chest and my leg and spattered the ground.

Instead, I lunged with all the strength I had and caught Bowen in a solid hold around the front of his throat. My momentum took us both tumbling to the ground. I put all the weight I possessed on Bowen's chest. My teeth locked like a vice around his neck.

He thrashed below me, and I snapped my jaws tighter, cutting into his air supply. If I could hold on, I would win. My eyesight was getting fuzzy just at the edges, and I knew I needed to end this quickly, or I was going to pass out from pain and blood loss and Victor would probably literally feed me to his wolves.

Loathing that I needed to, I sank my teeth deeper still into Bowen's neck. He resisted. Blood filled my mouth and he gasped for air.

After what had to be an eternity, Bowen stilled and whimpered.

"Welcome to the pack, Kyp." Victor's voice was cold, hard, and amused. I shuddered as I backed up off Bowen. He wheezed and rolled to his belly.

He looked at me with the same dull brown eyes. But even as I felt his stare on me, I felt my Alpha recede. Terror gripped me with an iron vice. Mental cords stretched to Victor and I nearly recoiled when I felt the black void that was his mind. Bowen watched me closely, his wolf's eyes slowly gaining spark and losing their lifelessness.

With a giant shake and spatter of blood, he whipped his head back and howled. It was wild, broken, but as I listened closely and watched his wolf's expression, I realized there were undertones of joy.

My skin prickled with dread.

****

The next week was the longest of my life. Thanksgiving meant a few days off school and left me nothing to do but hang around the camp while my anxiety gnawed at me and Victor's wolves watched me. In silence, I waited for the next wave of my father's darkness to touch me. Victor's mind was a hideous tangle of dirty manipulation and pain. He gave me frequent commands to remind me who the boss was and rid me of any Alpha thoughts, or so he intoned using his Alpha link. The link was disturbingly clear. Sometimes I could hear the other wolves, though Victor gave me little cause to use my mental Beta connection. He liked to control everyone, all the time. I could also clearly hear Bowen. But he steered clear of me and watched me from the shadows, careful to avoid Victor as much as he could help it.

The one reassurance I had was that Victor didn't know his mind control didn't work on me. I merely acquiesced with the proper facial features he expected and completed whatever menial or humiliating task he set me to.

I couldn't always hear Rachel. Our Claimship had strengthened our bond but joining Victor's pack had weakened our link. As her Alpha, it had been clearer. Even as it was, I'd gotten it through to her how many Victor's pack held and as many other details as I could. And I told her every night how much I loved and missed her. I think she heard me most of the time. I bided my time, watching, waiting for the right time to rally the packs and take Victor down.

Chapter 47

Rachel

"Sweetheart, I don't think we're going to be able to make it home for Thanksgiving. But we want you to fly here. To be with Joanie. We miss you so much," Mom said. Longing squeezed my heart and Wolf whined inside me. I missed my family. Desperately. But if I left, so did the connection with Kyp. And I refused to abandon him to Victor Atwood.

I realized with a sudden weightiness that I was the one thing that stood in between Kyp and Victor, and also the one connection that could let Dominic and Austin know when to bring their forces to obliterate our common enemy. Cold sweat broke out on my forehead and my palms.

"Mom, I miss you guys so much, too! I want to come. I do. But—" how could I say this and not offend my mother? "I…I was hoping that maybe I could spend Thanksgiving with Jennifer and Kyp this year." It was true. I did want to spend Thanksgiving with Kyp, even though it was impossible.

"Oh." My mother's startled voice echoed on the phone line and I winced.

"Are you angry?" I whispered.

"Oh, Rachel, no. I'm not angry. Just surprised. And we *do* miss you. Things are going that well with Kyp?"

"It's very mutual. And yes. Kyp and I are doing *very* well. I think we're getting fairly serious." I swallowed and continued before Mom could pounce on that. "I'm not sure I'm ready to see Joanie yet either," I confessed. While I would have happily flown out to Colorado to be with my family, maybe even dragged Kyp with me, it was true that I wasn't sure I was ready to face Joanie. "Honestly, Mom, I'm still angry with her. I've forgiven her, but I'm still working through things."

Mom sighed.

"Mom?"

"I know." Mom was still angry, too. Knowing Mom was struggling with her emotions over Joanie somehow validated my own and sent a warm shiver down my spine. Wolf nudged me supportively.

"Are you and Daddy all right?"

"We'll make it. It's a daily struggle. And it probably will be for a while. I'm grateful we're here, but I also feel like I'm missing out on important parts of your life. This is your senior year. Do you feel we're being completely unfair?" I could hear the worry in Mom's voice.

"Of course I miss you and Dad, but I'm fine. Truly." Besides, it was much safer for them to be away from Rock Falls at the moment. "You haven't missed any huge milestones of my senior year yet." Aside from becoming a werewolf... "Will at least one of you be able to come home to see the play?"

"Absolutely." The finality of the word wrung a smile from my lips.

"It's only a week away. Why don't we save the plane ticket for you or Dad to come home to watch my directorial debut? I'd rather miss Thanksgiving with you than have you miss my first time directing."

"You're sure?" Mom pressed.

"I'm sure." Because if we hadn't taken Victor Atwood down by then, I'd go after him myself.

"All right then. Now tell me more about this boy of yours."

****

It was torture seeing Kyp at school on Monday and pretending to snub him and ignore his existence. Wolf and I both screamed inside to go fling myself in his arms. But if this was going to work, I had to play my part, too.

By Friday, I needed a few minutes to collect myself before play practice. Just another week and we'd have our five rounds of nightly fame as we performed. No one was in the hallway by the back door of the choir room, not far from the back exit of the school. I knew several wolves were staying late while I was still at school, and I knew I needed to check in with them. I leaned back against the cool cinderblock wall painted a garish puce and let my eyelids flutter closed for just a moment.

Kyp, if you can hear me, I love you. I miss you. I can't wait until this is over.

I was so intent on thinking at him that I didn't hear anyone approach until it was too late.

Rough hands clapped over my mouth and nose. Before I could scream, before I could shift, before I could struggle, a needle jabbed me in the neck and Wolf faded from my consciousness.

"Be still or I'll knock the rest of you out, too," a husky voice rank with the smell of rancid meat whispered next to my ear. My body went rigid. Thoughts of Lenny crashed into my brain and set my heart hammering against my breastbone.

"I know about your friend. The one Shelby wanted out of the way. Come with us now, and we won't hurt her. But cause us any trouble and things will get ugly."

The panic was crushing. The weight of it suffocated me. *Wolf!* She was gone. They knew who Megan was! They would go after her to hurt her—maybe even kill her—if I didn't go with them. Blood rushed in my ears and I fought to stay conscious.

But it was too much. I fainted dead away in the back hallway of the school.

****

Everything was murky, and my head pounded. I struggled silently, assessing myself for injury. Aside from the tympani section going full throttle in my brain, I didn't feel hurt. I searched for Wolf to have her do a check of us, too.

She wasn't there.

She was gone.

There was nothing but a black void. No link. No Wolf. My heart thundered in my chest.

I cracked my eyes and winced as nausea roiled through my middle. My hands were tied in front of me. Flashbacks of being chained to the wall of that outbuilding sent my pulse spiking and my breathing coming in shallow pants. Black dots spun in front of my open eyes. I could not pass out again!

Before I could process anything else, a door banged open and two men barged in. The scream died in my throat as one man grabbed my arm and the other held the door of what I only then processed as a camper trailer.

"You're going to be such a fun little plaything once the Beta is done with you."

"Let go of me." My voice croaked like it was caked in dust.

The man smirked.

Moonlight streamed down into an open clearing where wolves stood in a semi-circle, the forest flanking them behind. My teeth chattered as the cold November breeze went straight through my light pink hoodie.

A door slapped open and my head jerked painfully toward the noise.

A man who possessed so much authority and Alphaness that he could only be Victor Atwood pushed Kyp out the door and roughly shoved him down the steps in front. My chest stuttered with the pounding of my heart.

"Kyp," I whispered.

Kyp locked eyes with me, terror momentarily flashing through his eyes before he schooled his face into an unreadable mask. His finger flashed furiously over his thumb.

The plan was in ruins. It was over. We were both going to die here. I had no way to tell Dominic or Austin that the time to come was *now*. There could be no good outcome from this. Tears formed and I blinked them back as best I could while panic threatened to make me blackout again. I couldn't. I would meet my death with dignity. I'd be strong for Kyp. My insides quaked. I desperately missed my wolf.

"We have a special treat for our Beta tonight!" Victor spread his arms wide like a showman as he addressed his pack. His voice was cold, cruel. Fear rippled over my skin.

Every eye of the pack fixated on Victor and Kyp.

There was a sudden movement in my periphery. For one second I stared up into dark eyes astonishingly like Kyp's, and then they were gone.

But there was a weight in my hoodie pocket.

As carefully as I could, I wiggled my half-frozen fingers inside my hoodie pocket. It wasn't easy as my hands were tied together at the wrist.

It was a phone.

Sudden yelping sounded from the opposite end of the clearing and the movement drew the attention away from me.

My fingers flew over the keys to text a number I knew by heart.

I knew I'd only have one shot at this. I punched in Megan's number then the only text I could think of that would let her know it was me.

TTEOTE

To the ends of the earth.

The struggle stopped and all eyes returned to me as Victor pointed. My fingers stilled along with my heart. I hoped it was enough. It had to be enough. There was very little chance anyone would get here in time to save either of us.

Chapter 48

Kyp

He had Rachel. No other thought entered or exited my brain. I just looped over on that one fact. Wolf frothed and struggled against the restraints that tied me to Victor. *Rachel! Mate!* I blanked my face as Victor led me to the middle of the circle of the pack.

Dread cramped my gut.

"We've got a treat for our Beta!" Victor crowed. My stomach revolted and I swallowed down the bile, burning a trail of blistering fire down my throat to mix with the fear racing through my veins in place of blood.

Two wolves yelped and whimpered like they were in pain and my eyes ripped away from Rachel long enough to assess that they weren't a new threat.

Victor growled low in his throat and the scuffle stopped. He turned back to me, his eyes cold and calculating.

"We've stolen something back from the Wolfe pack for you. I trust you know what to do with ungrateful dogs who do not accept our leadership."

Kill her.

It was a strong suggestion, but not a command. My chest tightened. I could make my stand without revealing my greatest asset. But there was only one thing I could think to do to save Rachel.

"I'll fight you for Alpha instead. I challenge you for the right to lead this pack." The words dropped like lead, and for the first time, true surprise flashed across Victor's face.

The surprise quickly morphed into fury and black rage that crescendoed in a howl that ripped from his still-human throat. Every hair on the back of my neck stood straight and my flesh crawled with horror.

I could hardly believe the words had passed my lips. Wolf growled low and menacing inside me. As Victor's Beta, I was the only one who could challenge him. I guess Bowen could have since he was blood related, too, but he'd have had to fight me and Victor. I gulped. Alpha passed to the eldest offspring.

"Bring the stakes," my father growled while giving me a murderous glare. Wolf rose within me, Alpha power tingling. I was still Victor's Beta, but he did not hold the sway over me that he thought he did. I readied myself for the pain of what I knew would come. I couldn't break the mental ties to him, or the fight would be for nothing. If I didn't take his place as Alpha of the pack, his wolves would only turn on me next, wild and leaderless. And that still wouldn't save Rachel.

I had to take my place as Alpha. Of Victor's pack.

I'd have to kill my own father.

Anguish, fury, and fear curled into a piercing ball of emotion in my belly.

While half my brain grappled to come to terms with what I had to do next, the other part of my brain watched as pack members brought bundles of sharpened two-foot wooden stakes out from one of the trailers and drove one end into the dirt, leaving the other pointed end exposed and forming a fighting ring.

They didn't hurry. I knew the slow pace was deliberate on Victor's orders to make my dread of the coming fight even worse. Victor's favorite weapon in his extensive arsenal was fear.

Some of the pack sent me looks of pity, alarm, or sadness. It took a solid twenty minutes for the stakes to all be put into the ground, leaving me plenty of time to confront my raging terror. Victor stood immobile, arms crossed, black fury emanating from him. The last stake was pushed into the earth.

I stole one last look at Rachel's ashen face, nodded to her, and braced myself for the coming fight.

"To the death," Victor said, his voice already changing to a growl.

We stepped into the ring.

With everything to lose, I didn't wait. I shifted. My clothes fluttered to the ground around me. I gave Wolf his head and felt my muscles bunch and cord. My head lowered, my hackles raised, watching the man who fathered me—the man I'd have to kill to save my own skin and my mate—as his face darkened in rage and elongated.

Black hair that seemed to suck the moonlight right out of the sky pushed through his skin. Ears came through. Wicked canines curved and glinted in the night. He took his time, letting his shift stretch out so I could see every hardened muscle, every inch of him that towered above me.

I refused to be cowed. He was bigger than me. Bigger, meaner, nastier, and he knew it. But he didn't know that he couldn't control me.

He would have to win this fight on his fighting merits alone.

It was the one trump card I held. But I wouldn't be able to hold it forever. I had to end Victor. Before he ended me. Before he ended Rachel.

Saliva dripped menacingly from his canines as he lowered his head, his eyes red slits in the moonlight.

We circled. His voice echoed in my head.

Little boy. You cannot beat me. You cannot win. One word from me and you'll be a quivering mass on the ground, willingly offering me your neck.

I blocked it out. Until he started a new line that sent my blood pounding and bile rising.

I will wait to kill you. I will make you watch as I take that girl. Over and over. She's pretty. Nice curves. I'll show her what a real man feels like.

My jaws snapped as he went into more detail. Ironically, the link I'd spent my life desperately trying to find was the one thing I now wanted to tear out of my head.

With no warning, he lunged at me. His bulk gave him the ability to jump quick and jump high.

Wolf rolled us under his feet, missing his pounce by inches.

His wolf chuffed as we righted ourselves. My heart thundered. We circled.

Little snipes, little jabs, flashes of teeth, and occasional tufts of fur. Each of us boasted a few nicks. A few drops of blood spattered the ground. He was trying to wear me down with his mental tirade and show himself the supreme leader to the rest of the pack before he used his command. He had to make a show of it. I danced out of the way of his teeth as he gnashed at me again.

A familiar wolf howled in the perimeter of the

forest surrounding camp, and Victor jerked to attention.

"Dominic!" Rachel shrieked.

The others had come! This was my chance.

I leaped from the ground and launched myself at Victor's throat. I would have had a clean bite, but my foot caught on a protruding stone, sending the rock skidding from its resting place, and making my landing just off-center. I caught part of his shoulder and his ruff. Without hesitation, I bit down and tasted the bitter tang of his blood as it entered my mouth.

Victor howled in rage and nipped my flank, catching mostly fur before he shook me loose with another bite to my side. I had to let go or he'd disembowel me with a swipe of his claws.

I stepped back, ready for the next attack, Wolf surging with hope. Dominic was here. Risking a quick look at the tree line, I recognized wolves from both the Wolfe and Thornehill packs melting from the trees. They were here.

Lay down so I can kill you.

I threw back my head and howled my defiance to my father, signaling Dominic and Austin to move in at the same time.

Victor jumped a step backward, realization crashing into him the same instant that the packs came charging to swarm over Victor's, meeting with a clash of fur, flesh, and howls of rage. The scent of blood saturated the air within seconds as growling, cracking, and ripping flesh filled my ears.

Move! Attack them!

I could hear his commands. Victor's attention was divided, controlling, commanding his pack.

Careful to keep my footing, I sprung for a second

assault.

He met me, our teeth tangled, biting, nipping, making purchase. Pain seared down the shoulder I'd injured fighting Bowen. It wasn't fully healed. It was still tender. Victor gnashed at it, catching some of the unhealed skin.

With a yelp, I jumped back, readying my stance again.

Again, and again we went at each other. Victor grew more and more desperate to control the fighting around him and keep me off him. A wheezing noise sounded in his chest, and I realized he probably hadn't had to actively fight for some time, able to merely command his wolves to do it for him.

He turned and barked instructions and I used my skull like a battering ram. I caught him square in the side and he skidded back several steps.

The dirt below us was speckled with blood as the battle raged around us, steering clear of the ring of spikes, leaving us locked in our own fight.

Like a knife, Rachel's scream cut through the air. Immediately my head swung to her where a large wolf was approaching her.

Rachel! My brain screamed.

Teeth sunk into my back and agony ripped jagged lines of fire down my limbs. Victor heaved and my paws left the ground. He yanked his head around and I felt the raw power, and sensed his fear, as he threw me to the side of the ring. My back hit the ground and I skidded into the base of the ring of spikes, sending a fresh wave of torture whipping over me.

I lay there, exhausted, in pain, bleeding.

"Kyp!" Rachel's shout broke through the haze in

time for me to register Victor catapulting himself toward me.

Scrambling to get my feet under me, I rolled to gain enough purchase to keep Victor from landing on me and finishing me off.

Victor roared, rage coming off him in waves as he lunged through the air toward me. Desperately hauling myself out of the way, time slowed. This was the end. I could not move fast enough. He would land on me, and it would all end. I'd given it everything I had.

Moonlight glinted on teeth that reached for my neck. But then, just as his teeth should have closed over my flesh, I rallied the last of my strength and with my back paws, flipped his body backward over the top of me. A whining yelp tore through the air.

I rolled the rest of the way over, tugging my front legs trapped under the sudden weight of Victor's torso.

There.

On the spikes he'd set out, Victor's head lay impaled. Blood dripped down the spike, his tongue lolled out of his mouth as his body spasmed.

Even in wolf form, I heaved my head to the side and wretched.

Silence descended as I pulled my broken body out from underneath my dead father.

Tingling started at the base of my paws and worked its way up my shaky legs.

My Alpha senses returned, and my head filled with the sudden onslaught they brought. I tipped my head back and howled to the moon, my voice answering an aching primal call that trembled in my gut and sent power racing through my veins.

My eyes found Rachel. She nodded. She was safe.

Wolves limped toward me, as the fighting ceased.

I needed my voice.

I grunted, trying to hold back the second howl of pain that tried to escape my lips as I shifted back. I felt my body retracting to its human form, but growing, muscles cording, bones lengthening, shoulders widening, mind sharpening, torn places mending together.

Raw and throbbing all over, I stood, realizing I was inches taller than I had been as the full role of Alpha fell on my shoulders. I'd changed when I'd become my own Alpha, but now that I'd inherited a full pack, somehow, I'd inherited Victor's mantel as well.

I surveyed the stunned wolves around me. I was the only one in skin and I had to find the voice I so desperately needed.

"I am not your enemy. But I am your Alpha." The words reverberated around the clearing and I felt a quiver of wills from the wolves in front of me. "I will not hold anyone here who wishes to leave. But those of you who stay *will* obey me." Wolf puffed his chest inside me, and I stood straighter despite the lingering pain in my back.

A snarl ripped through the stillness and the dark brown wolf—Victor's right-hand man, Drew—lunged at me.

Before I could shift back, Bowen, bloodied and standing at the sidelines, dove in front of me and tackled Drew with a heavy bite to the brown wolf's throat. Bowen snarled menacingly through his teeth and Drew relented.

I'm with you, Bowen thought to me. I nodded solemnly. Bowen was Beta again. My Beta. My brother. My blood. Behind me, Dominic and Austin's packs closed ranks, moving in closer to stand behind me. Their numbers and their support swelled Wolf inside, humbled but elated with their confidence.

"Anyone else?" I called out. A clear challenge. A few wolves paced. I felt their tethers wiggling in my mind.

"You may go." I released the knot of seven wolves in my mind and I suddenly felt their absence. It was one thing to leave a pack of your own volition. It wasn't violent, I then understood, if it was mutual.

I stood as tall as I could, heedless of my naked state, and met the eyes of every single wolf in my pack. We were a motley crew of misfits and broken minds, but misfits I understood, and we'd find help for the broken ones. Lastly, I met Rachel's eyes.

Her hair made a wild halo of red around her head, and her eyes were shining.

I love you, she mouthed.

I love you back, I answered clearly in her head. Her smile nearly stretched off her face. Surveying my pack once more, Wolf sighed in satisfaction.

Shifting back to my wolf form, I allowed myself to feel a moment of embarrassment at standing stark naked in front of three packs of werewolves. I pushed it aside though and paced up to Bowen, still with his paw on Drew's chest.

Looking down at Drew, I let him see every bit of dominance Wolf possessed. My lips curled back from my teeth in a wicked growl.

He had not been released but I would not have him in my pack.

Get out. I thrust his will back at him. He howled

and shook his head back and forth. I nudged Bowen's shoulder and with one more snarl at Drew, Bowen backed up.

With a yip, Drew was up and streaking for the trees, tail tucked between his legs.

Bowen leaned over, tipped his neck up in a show of vulnerability, then scented me. I scented him back. Seconds later, the rest of my pack was queuing up to exchange scents. To reacquaint themselves with each other after such a massive shift in power.

When at last it was Rachel's turn, blessedly back in her wolf form, she rubbed her head against me, and heat filled my chest. Wanting to show my pack exactly who Rachel was and where she was in the hierarchy, I nudged her back, barked for everyone's attention, and then gently closed my mouth over her nose. There was a rumble from my pack as they acknowledged her as my mate.

Rachel licked my cheek and stood close enough to me that our shoulders touched—although she was a few inches shorter than me now. That would take some getting used to.

Chapter 49

Rachel

Kyp's arm tightened around my shoulders as I curled up on Mary and Dominic's couch, a mug of Megan's hot chocolate clutched in my hands.

It was after midnight, but my blood was still thrumming.

"Rachel, how did you get ahold of a phone? Your text was brilliant, by the way," Megan said, her eyes still bright with excitement that Victor's threat was done. She settled next to Sam who hadn't let her out of his sight since we'd all—Dominic, Mary, Sam, Megan, Austin, Sarah, Kyp, Jennifer, and me—piled into the Wolfe's living room at the big house. Although, judging by the way he was looking at her, I was pretty sure he wanted to take her back to their place.

I grinned. "I didn't know who it was at first—just some guy who had eyes like Kyp's that shoved a phone into my hand and disappeared." My heart warmed knowing that Bowen had risked extensively to end his father's tyranny and set Kyp up as Alpha.

"We were close on your scent trail, but having that text narrowed things down. Gordon Rockwell was able to ping it, is that how he said it?" Austin asked with an arched brow and a glance at his daughter. "Anyway, it got us there quicker.

Bowen had elected not to come back with us. He was staying at the camp with the fractured pack Kyp had inherited. Kyp and I would need to go back in the morning, but we desperately needed some time to process and some time to be together.

"Kyp, where do you plan to locate your pack?" Dominic asked. His tone was laced with curiosity, no animosity. Kyp's shoulders tensed slightly and mine did, too. Would we have to move?

"Obviously, I haven't had much time to think over it, but I was wondering, and I'll need to speak to Bowen about this, but would it be possible for us to stay here for the time being? I don't want to intrude onto your pack and your lands, but honestly? I need help. I need an example other than the ones I've had. I'd like to stay and learn how to be a good Alpha."

The room was silent at Kyp's words, a swell of emotion filling the silent spaces.

I could have sworn the barest hint of a sheen came over Dominic's eyes before he blinked. The big man cleared his throat.

"We'd be honored to have you."

Sam grinned wide at Kyp, then at me, while Megan beamed. Relief flooded through me again, and I knew that Rock Falls would be home for a good while yet.

An hour later and we were all dispersing, exhausted, most of us still needing to shower away the stench and blood of battle.

"Kyp, is it all right to come back with you? I've called off work tomorrow and could use the extra sleep, if you don't think you'll be needing the space?" Jennifer asked as we headed toward Kyp's truck. My face flushed. Did she mean if Kyp and I needed the space—together? Like *together-together*? My heart kicked up a notch.

"No, it's fine, Mom. Victor owned several properties in the area. If any other pack members need a place, Bowen and I will look into putting them there. Since we're going to be here a while, we should consider a place not on Wolfe lands." Kyp smiled, pride in his voice and heat curled in my belly as my embarrassment eased down a fraction. The heat spread into satisfied responsibility. Our pack. We would need a place for them.

****

Back at the house, Jennifer hugged us both tight, then said her goodnights. She'd had to wait out the fight with Rev, Megan, and some of the youngest members of the pack at the cabin, getting a play-by-play and worrying herself to death. I didn't blame her.

The house was quiet and dark, with only a few lights on. Kyp held my hand.

"Are you going to shower or go straight to bed?" he asked quietly.

"First, I'm going to hug my *fiancé*, then I'm going to go wash off the filth of everything that happened. Then I might need another hug. And probably a few kisses. If I can stay awake that long."

Kyp's chest rumbled softly under my cheek and his hands looped around me. His lips met the top of my head and I smiled. His increased height had fit us together even better than before.

"Go shower upstairs. I'll wash down here. Meet you after when I smell better."

****

Twenty minutes later I came into the living room,

freshly scrubbed from scalp to toe to find Kyp sitting on the couch in the dark. I didn't need any further invitation when he opened his arms.

His lips found mine before I was even fully seated, and he pulled me down next to him. His lips danced over mine, tired, wanting, but content.

"I love you," he whispered.

"I love you back."

"Should I ask if you want to go ring shopping, or should I surprise you?"

"I like surprises. We should probably ease my parents into this. They may not like the surprise as much as me."

"Agreed. Sorry, I need to move. My back is still pretty sore."

I practically leaped off the couch.

"Does it hurt a lot still? Do you need me to get you something for it?"

Kyp chuckled. "It's not that bad. It's all cleaned and patched. Just sore. Come back here." He stretched out on the couch and patted the space beside him. I crawled up and he wrapped an arm around me.

"Can we just stay here tonight?"

I snuggled in deeper and his cheek rested against my forehead as my eyes drifted shut.

Chapter 50

Kyp

The buzzing of Rachel's phone woke me as early streams of sunlight drifted through the crack between the curtains. We'd only been asleep a few hours, but I had an impressive crick in my neck.

It was a small price to pay to wake with Rachel pressed up against me.

"Mom?" she sleepily answered her phone. I yawned and my ears popped, keeping me from hearing the immediate conversation.

Rachel's face sprouted a grin that radiated like sunshine.

"Mom, that's wonderful. Really wonderful!"

I let my hand stroke over my favorite curve.

"I love you, too. Okay. Talk to you in a few hours."

"Good news?" I already knew it was from the light shining in her eyes.

"Mom and Dad are bringing Joanie home. They're going to move her to a facility closer to home where they can visit frequently, but where they'll be *home*. Mom said they decided they couldn't help one daughter and neglect the other."

"And it's safe for them now."

"What do I tell them about being a wolf? Can I tell them anything?" Her forehead creased.

I shook my head sadly. "You can't. Maybe someday we'll figure out a way to tell them. But, since we're dating, assuming they have no great objections, we'll go out every night. Make sure your wolf has all the attention she needs. We'll make it work. And hopefully, your parents will be on board with an early summer wedding. I don't want to wait forever." I smiled down at her, but it was the truth. She was killing me, and we hadn't even kissed.

She smiled up at me and leaned in to kiss me when my phone rang from the kitchen where I'd plugged it in hours earlier. I sighed.

"I want to ignore that, but I'm afraid it might be something important, given what happened last night."

"And you are the Alpha now," Rachel smiled as she squeezed my arm. I slugged off the couch and grabbed my phone. It was Bowen.

"Kyp. I'm sorry to wake you this early, but I think you should come back. Things are under control, but some are getting restless. They need their Alpha. And we need to figure out some stuff. I'm not sure we've heard the last of Drew. He left his calling card on the stump next to the edge of camp."

I sighed, a sense of pride, trepidation, and a hunger for my own pack filling me. It was a strange combination, but one I embraced. I was theirs and they were mine.

"I'll be there in half an hour."

I was the Alpha.

A word about the author...

AJ Skelly is an author, blogger, and lover of all things fantasy, medieval, and fairy-tale-romance. As a former high school English teacher with a master's in Creative Writing, she's always been fascinated with the written word and has spent many years working with teenagers. She lives with her husband, children, and many imaginary friends who often find their way into her stories.

http://www.ajskelly.com